THE PERFECT CATCH

SAMANTHA VÉRANT

Storm

PUBLISHING

To request permissions, contact the publisher at rights@stormpublishing.co

Ebook ISBN: 978-1-83700-014-2
Paperback ISBN: 978-1-83700-015-9

Cover design: Blacksheep
Cover images: Depositphotos, Shutterstock

Published by Storm Publishing.
For further information, visit:
www.stormpublishing.co

ALSO BY SAMANTHA VÉRANT

The Lucky Widow
The Private Chef
The Writers' Retreat

*To Tracey, code name Trixie, my best friend for over forty years.
You are a part of this story, and you know the true inspiration
behind this one.*

PROLOGUE

"Always dress like you're going to see your worst enemy."

~ Kimora Lee

I'm kicking through the junk he's left behind. Trashy paperbacks with broken spines, some of which are mine. Empty hangers sway in the closet. Some designer T-shirts I'm thinking about cleaning the toilet with. Useless things, fragments, the litter of a man who tore through my life and left a mess in his wake.

A room that looks just as empty as I feel.

My apartment has an echo to it, a hollowness, and an aftertaste like a sweet deal gone sour. I can still taste the betrayal.

What an idiot. What an ass. What a sucker.

I'm talking to myself. That's what it's come to.

I'm furious. I'll admit that much. Angry at him, for sure, but I'm even angrier at myself for my naiveté. For my stupidity. I'd ignored all the warning signs—even when they flashed brighter than the lights on the Vegas strip.

He probably thinks I'm too soft to track him down. But he didn't know me at all. Never did. Never will. He'd told me a lot of things. Some of them true, some of them downright pretty. Pretty enough to wrap me around his damn finger. The rest of his fabricated life is threaded with lies. Cheap lies. Slick lies. Lies he thinks I'll just quietly accept.

But I've seen enough of his work to know just how to finish him off. His past is going to catch up with him. Mine won't. He won't get away with anything. Just wait.

ACT ONE

"Over the years, I have learned that what is important in a dress is the woman who is wearing it."

~ Yves Saint Laurent

ONE

LEXI

I'm so out of my element it's almost a joke.

The poolside party at The Regent in Santa Monica, celebrating the close of LA Fashion Week, sparkles. The flashes from all the cameras are dizzying. I'd rather be wearing comfortable gym shoes and my athleisure brand over the heels and bodycon dress I'm currently squeezed into. I'm finding it hard to breathe and, embarrassingly, to walk. Tricia, code name Trixie—my best friend and business partner—raises her champagne glass, clinking it with mine.

"We're on our way, Lexi," she says with a wide grin.

We're standing on the sidelines, by the exit. I swallow, eyeing the well-heeled crowd. I'm thinking of running. But not in these shoes. "To where?"

"The big time." She pinches the index finger and thumb of her free hand together, and then she winks. "We're this close."

"To what? Bankruptcy?"

"To achieving our dreams." She nudges my side and scoffs. "Stop being such a pessimist."

Tricia never does subtlety—not in her look, her salesmanship, or her faith in me. I find her optimism maddening, but having her at my side counts for everything. And it's true that our brand, LexI-

CON, is finally hitting its stride. We're getting tons of press and selling to all the major boutiques on the West Coast, but I'm constantly wondering if we're expanding too fast, over-leveraging our bottom line.

I take a sip of champagne. Shoot her a tight smile. "This is good."

"Haha. On a serious note, the Style Sphere convention is going to put LexICON on the map," she continues. "I still can't believe we've been approved for the emerging brands expo. We have one month to prepare."

My heart rate accelerates. I hope I'm not about to have another panic attack—a recent phenomenon brought on by sleepless nights and stress, financial instability the catalyst. I've been borrowing from Peter to pay Paul and then pay back Peter, the cycle endless. I exhale a deep breath. "Brands can't emerge if their bank account is running on paint fumes. We have to be careful."

Tricia glares at me. "Pessimist."

"Realist."

"We're just experiencing growing pains," she says with a beleaguered sigh. "Because we're *growing*."

I'm expecting her to continue with her soliloquy about growth and how we're going to take the athleisure market by storm, so I'm surprised when she says, "Holy shit, look at him."

"Who?"

Tricia fans herself with one hand and then playfully tucks a stray strand of hair behind my ear. Her eyes widen, flicking to the left, as if unveiling a revelation. "Why are you looking at me when you should be looking at him?"

I follow her gaze to a man across the floor: tanned, sleek and too perfect for words.

"I think he's with Vescari," she whispers.

Vescari is that inescapable brand where street style meets high fashion, and half of the fashion world is trying to emulate its cool. Hell, maybe half the planet is trying to be Vescari.

"He's looking over here," she says, eyes wide. "Who do you think he's checking out?"

"Whoever is standing directly behind us," I reply. A quick assessment of the crowd, nothing more. He'd paused on Tricia and me before moving on, likely to some hotshot designer or model with mile-long legs. "And does it matter? You're married."

"I can look. I just can't touch," she replies, feigning a swoon.

For a moment, I'm completely fixated on the handsome stranger, the way he moves through the crowd, the way he commands attention. His smile lights up the terrace. He seems to know everybody in the fashion world. Yes, there is an impossibly hot guy—even by LA standards—striding through the room as if he owns it. Perhaps he does. And he probably has six-pack abs. And I don't know why my mind is going there. I shake my head as if to clear it. He's unmistakably with Vescari, his sheer presence creating waves of admiration across the terrace.

Tricia turns to me, her jaw dropping in silent awe. "Can you even imagine?" she manages to mutter, almost speechless for the first time.

I hold up a hand. "Just stop."

He glances in our direction again, a slow, confident gaze that has both of us holding our breaths before he moves on, smooth as glass.

Tricia lets out a long, exaggerated sigh. "My body is ready."

"Your body," I tease, "has no shame."

"And your body..."

"Needs to focus on building up our brand."

She chortles out a laugh. "You haven't dated anybody in over three years..."

"I'm focusing on other things." I shoot her the stink eye. "Like our business."

Before she can respond, he—the walking sex dream on wheels —makes his approach.

Tricia whispers, "Go for it," and then sashays over toward the bar. "You can thank me later. I'm getting us a refill."

He regards me with calculated nonchalance and then meets my eyes. "I heard you're making waves in the fashion world. Re-inventing athleisure?"

"S-something like that," I say, noting his beautiful French accent. "Are you in fashion?"

He shakes his head. "The beauty industry—skincare."

I stand there in a stunned stupor, looking at his perfect suit, staring at his chiseled jaw line, his inky-black hair. I have to say something. Anything. "I saw you with Vescari. You must have a lot of connections."

"You could say that." His hazel eyes sparkle with mischief. "But not like yours, I'd guess. Your name is Alexis Marlowe, *oui*?"

"*Oui*," I say, clearing my throat. How does he know my name? "Most people call me Lexi."

"Christophe," he replies with a smile, revealing perfect white teeth lined up in perfect rows. "Christophe Montclair."

Montclair. The name sings like the title of a bestseller. I've read about this family in the same articles that taught me what caviar looks like. Old money, French aristocrats, the people who put beauty on the map with their multi-billion-dollar conglomerate. Skincare. Hair care. Make-up.

"Health, beauty and fashion," I say, the words slipping out of my mouth before I can stop them, my mind in overdrive.

He watches me with obvious interest, a gleam in his eye. "Exactly what I was thinking. I know this might come across as forward, considering we've just met, but I think our companies have synergy. You and your line are the talk of the town." He pauses. "May I have the honor of taking you to dinner tomorrow night?"

As his invitation reverberates in my ears, a blush prickles my cheeks and Tricia's voice urges me from within: *Do it. Do it. Do it.*

"That would be lovely," I say, shifting my weight from side to side.

He grins and lifts a brow. "Then we should probably exchange information."

I stutter out my phone number.

"I'll need your address," he says, and my face goes blank. "I have meetings all day for my company and I'll send a car to pick you up. Is eight good for you?"

His lips curve into a curious smile and I'm just standing there, blinking. This is all so surreal. He raises an eyebrow.

A drop of perspiration rolls down my back. "Is this for a business meeting? Or a date?"

Damn it. Why did I say that? *Way to play it cool, Lexi.*

He grins again and my heart stutters. "We'll find out tomorrow night." He winks and then squeezes my hand, holding it a moment longer than necessary, rubbing the top with his thumb. "I have to get back to Vescari." He leans over and whispers in my ear, "If you meet him, don't let his over-the-top Italian accent fool you. He's from the Bronx."

"Right," I say.

"It was nice meeting you, Lexi. I'll see you tomorrow night."

As he walks away, my heart flutters, trapped between disbelief and the thrill of possibility.

TWO

CHRISTOPHE

The party hums like an expensive beehive, spread out in manicured hives of ambition. They've made themselves at home here, thriving in artificial light, feeding on the currency of attention. I catch words as they float in my ears—plush, bespoke, covetable. I'm nodding along, feigning interest in Vescari.

He leads me through the crowd like a show pony, pulling out all his usual stops, introducing me like I'm a god. This is *the* Christophe Montclair! Vescari's wares this season are impressive if you find metallic neoprene sports coats innovative, which I'm thankfully not wearing. My tastes are more sophisticated, tailored.

"My new collection," Vescari says. "Very pop futurism, *n'est-ce pas*, Christophe?"

"Very something," I agree. As I listen to Vescari ramble on about his collection, I can't tear my gaze from Lexi. There's something fearless about her, the way she moves. Something real. I like that.

A photographer and his assistant snaps pictures of us, the flash nearly blinding me. Vescari swings his arm around my shoulders, tells me to smile, but I frown. "My family is private. I don't really like the limelight."

"Get used to it," he grumbles, shooting me a look.

"I know who you are, Mr Vescari," says the photographer's assistant, holding up a pad of paper and a pen. She eyes me. "And you are?"

A beat of awkward silence.

"Christophe Montclair," blurts out Vescari when I don't answer. "The founder of Miracule, from the famed Montclair Industries family."

A photograph of me with my name. This is a risk and, in my head, I'm praying none of the news outlets pluck any of the photos of me for publication. It could be a death sentence.

I scan the party, half listening for any snippets of conversation that might lead to a lucrative opening. That's when she finally comes into focus again. Vescari stops short, grabbing my arm in mock shock. His wide eyes settle into a reverent stare.

"I saw you speaking with Alexis Marlowe." He chuckles and then lowers his voice. "The new heiress to the throne."

She's like a mirage on the far side of the room, vibrant but not quite focused, talking to her animated friend. From this vantage point, Lexi is even more enticing, her long brown ponytail flicking against her back as she moves. I'd been ready to pass her off as another cute, struggling startup clinging to the coattails of the fake Europeans—but not anymore. I'm looking forward to tomorrow night.

"So, she's one of them," I muse. "A Marlowe."

"Rumor is she's the granddaughter. But she's running this new brand herself. Like you. How do you say—incognito?"

"She seems to be doing a good job of hiding," I reply.

"Not for long," Vescari predicts, but my attention has already drifted beyond him. I watch her more closely. Her athletic form moves with quiet assurance. Her stance alone is in a different league, commanding but effortless. A heavy hitter in a lightweight ring.

She's fresh, in a way. At least, fresh enough to make me curious about what she's peddling. I'm already building the story in my head, seeing the angles unfold. Heir to an empire, a line for the people. The press will eat her up. They'll all come knocking, the vultures. The market is due a new darling. And so am I.

I've seen all I need to see tonight, done what I've needed to do. I leave the terrace, about to head up to my room, when I turn to see two thug-like men making a beeline toward me. My jaw goes slack. Although they've aged since I last saw them, I'd recognize these two anywhere—their straggly unkempt hair, skinny bodies, and shifty eyes. Although they are dressed to impress in fashionable clothes, I can't be seen with them.

"Remy. Gilles," I say, ushering them into a dark corner, speaking low and in French. "You don't belong here."

Remy smiles, flashing yellow teeth. He gives me a friendly punch on my arm. "Christophe, is that how you greet two old friends?"

We were never friends.

"You're a tough man to track down," says Gilles.

"Maybe I don't want to be tracked down." I straighten my posture. "How did you find me?"

"We followed the money and it led us here—the closing party for Fashion Week." Remy flashes a wicked grin. "You should be more careful. Your photos are all over the place—the ones with you and your new best friend Vescari."

I bristle, knowing I should have been more careful. "What do you want?"

"Your talent and your connections." Remy shrugs and then blows out the air between his lips. "You seem to be living the good life, *non*?"

I startle. Their arrival could ruin everything.

THREE

LEXI

When I step inside The Regent, I head straight for the dining room, as instructed. I take in the room with one single sweep—the linen napkins, the crystal glasses. In the far corner, Christophe waves me over. His suit is navy, his jaw shaded by a twenty-four-hour shadow. Perfect looks aside, I tell myself that I'm not here for romance; I'm here to talk business.

He stands when I reach the table, and he's taller than I remember. He offers a handshake with a confident grip.

"Lexi," he says, as if greeting an old friend. "I'm glad you found me."

His French accent is fainter than I remember.

"I just told them I had a meeting with Christophe Montclair. The maître d' nearly kissed my feet," I say.

He grins and nods, a dimple folding into his left cheek. "As he should. Please, sit." He pulls the chair out for me.

"*Merci*," I say, smoothing the skirt of my dress beneath me.

"Would you allow me to order for us?" Christophe asks. He holds the wine list with two fingertips, inviting but not insistent.

I smile. "I trust your taste."

He pauses, reading my face, then flags the waiter. "A bottle of the pinot noir, please. The Ojai." He glances at me, eyebrow arched. "It's not French, but it's the best California offers. And I like to support local."

When the waiter leaves, Christophe leans forward.

"*Alors*, Lexi. What do you want to know about me, my business? Or are you just hungry?"

I smile as I pick up the menu, skimming it, even though I already read the online version before leaving home. I know the prices. "Depends on what you're serving," I say. "Aren't we here to talk about the synergy with our companies? Fashion and beauty?" I clear my throat. "I hear your company is doing interesting things in skincare."

He doesn't blink. "More than skincare, actually. The fountain of youth. The next ten years will see a revolution in how we treat aging."

The waiter pours the wine—rich and nearly purple—and Christophe gestures for my glass first, letting the aroma rise between us.

"To new ventures," he says, lifting his glass. His eyes are even more hypnotic up close, almost green. I toast him, careful not to let my hand shake.

"To new ventures," I echo, and sip. It's smooth, jammy. I like it more than I intended to.

He asks about LexICON, and I tell an abridged version of my story. When I'm finished, he says, "I have to confess, I googled you. Impressive. I particularly liked your interview with *Fashion Fix Daily*."

"I got lucky," I say, which is partly true. "She was charming."

He winks. "Not like me, of course."

The food arrives—two plates of seared sea bass, crisp and golden on a rectangle of porcelain. He waits for me to taste before he lifts his cutlery. I oblige, and the fish is perfect, flaky and mild, the sauce an electric green.

"So," he says, after a few minutes of companionable silence, "do you want to know why I started my company?" He laughs when I nod wide-eyed, sips his wine, then traces the rim with a finger. "Prior to taking over Montclair Industries, my mother was a model. She was beautiful, but in the way glass is beautiful—fragile." He glances away, the smile gone. "When she turned thirty-five, the industry declared her obsolete. She spent the next ten years trying to undo the clock. Diets, creams, surgeries, whatever they could sell her."

"And it didn't work," I say.

"Of course not." He laughs softly. "But she believed in it. I watched her pour herself into this myth of preservation." He stops. "I suppose I wanted to build something that was real. Or at least"—his eyes cut to mine—"less fake than the rest."

I wonder if he thinks I'm a poser, if I'm after his money, and my question is answered a couple of beats later.

"I want you to know," he says, lowering his voice, "that I am not trying to sell you anything."

"Not even a miracle serum?" I tease.

He shakes his head. "No miracles."

He signals the waiter for dessert menus.

I let out a breath I've been holding since the fish course. "You're very convincing," I say. "I bet you could sell ice to an Eskimo."

He lets out a short laugh, meets my eyes. "So, Lexi, can I see you again tomorrow night?"

Our second meeting is nothing like the first. This time there's no doubt it's a date. He's dressed in casual clothes, and we're both more relaxed. We walk the length of the Santa Monica pier together, eating hot dogs. Afterwards, he wins a bear for me in the arcade, then the passionate kiss we share on the Ferris wheel is so hot it practically melts my insides. But at the end of the evening, he seems on edge, constantly looking over his shoulder. My gaze follows his. "Is something wrong?"

He runs a hand through his hair and sighs. "You're going to

think this is crazy. Sometimes my family has me followed. They like to keep tabs on me."

I get it. He's a Montclair. I survey our surroundings, my head whipping in every direction. "Are we being followed now?"

"I'm probably just being paranoid." He pulls me close, hands on my hips, eyes meeting mine. "But I won't blame you if you never want to see me again."

I smile and raise a brow. "Might as well give them something to watch."

He returns my grin, and our second kiss is even better and more electric than the first.

Back at home that night, I collapse onto the couch. Clutching the bear, my lips tingle as I replay the date in my head.

My phone chimes with a text.

> I can't stop thinking about you. What are you doing Friday night?

I smile to myself. Love. Infatuation? Whatever I'm feeling, I know he's exactly the kind of man I've been looking for.

FOUR

CHRISTOPHE

I'd told a little white lie to Lexi tonight, but it's for her own good. Remy and Gilles are lurking in the shadows like rats, up to something, and they'd been the ones following us. When I'd come back from our date they'd been waiting for me in the lobby of The Regent, waving me over to their table.

I cringe internally. The Regent is polished, with clean lines. Remy and Gilles—creased jackets, skinny necks, eyes that never blink enough—are a different kind of animal. Predators in a glass cage.

"Strange thing," Remy says as I approach. "Reception doesn't have you listed. No record of your room."

That is by design, of course. I'd told the front desk to keep my details private, no exceptions. Privacy is one of the few luxuries money can actually buy. But with men like them, it is never enough. They always want more.

"I asked for discretion," I say lightly. "Some of us value our sleep."

"Or they're hiding something," Gilles rumbles. His eyes flick toward the elevators, maybe imagining Lexi's laugh echoing from behind a door. The thought of them dragging her into this makes my stomach knot. I don't sit. I stand, arms folded.

They want something. They always do.

"We've got something good going on," Remy says, lowering his voice. "Perfect for you. Like old times."

I shake my head. "There are no 'old times.' Not anymore."

"You think you're respectable now?" Gilles snorts. "Heard the rumors last night. A skincare company?" He says the word like it is filth. "What, little jars and pretty labels? You can't wash off what you owe."

My voice comes out steady. "I don't owe you a thing."

Remy leans in and I catch the scent of stale cigarettes and whiskey on his breath. "Then consider this: you don't play, maybe we pay a visit to your pretty date. Tell her what kind of man you really are."

The smile I give them doesn't reach my eyes. "How much to make you go away?"

They blink, caught off guard, exchanging a look. Remy nods.

Gilles holds up two fingers. "One hundred. Each. Cash."

"Two hundred thousand," I repeat, as if tasting the number. "Give me a week. I have to move things around. That's a lot of money."

"It is," says Gilles, running his tongue over his lips.

Remy's grin comes back, slow and satisfied. "Don't keep us waiting. Or there will be—"

"I'll call you for the rendezvous," I say, cutting him off.

"You don't have our numbers," says Remy. "And we don't have yours."

"That's easily rectified," I say, holding up my phone.

We exchange information and they nod to their table, a bottle of expensive whiskey set on it. "I'll take care of that," I say, wanting them to go before anybody sees me associating with them.

Gilles's mouth twists into a smirk and I know they'd been planning on having me take care of the bill, either that or they'd cause some kind of embarrassing scene. They are both so very predictable. "Don't come around here again."

"Don't give us reason to," says Remy, beady eyes narrowing.

I wave a dismissive hand and they down their drinks, standing up. Gilles raises his glass. "Until next time, Christophe."

They leave it at that, sauntering out into the night like they own it. I watch them go, pulse drumming in my ears. A week. Seven days to figure out how to make them disappear from my world without paying a cent.

Because I'm not giving them money. Not one euro. And they really shouldn't have threatened me or my relationship with Lexi.

FIVE
LEXI

It's not long before we're officially a couple. The morning after we first spend the night together, Christophe takes me to his candlelit hotel suite, two stone tables side by side. There is soft music, something with bells. I climb onto the table, face down, and feel the memory foam mold around my hips.

The heat from the hot stones seeps into my muscles, makes me weightless. When the therapists finish, they leave us with glasses of cucumber water and a tray of honeyed figs. I find myself drifting, floating, and then I'm sound asleep.

When I wake up, I find Christophe on the balcony, phone pressed to his ear, pacing tight loops. Even through the glass I can hear the hard edge to his voice. The call goes on for five minutes, maybe more. At last, he stabs the phone off and leans against the balcony rail, head bowed. He comes back in, eyes wild, chest rising and falling as if he's run a marathon.

"Is everything okay?" I ask, keeping my tone light.

He wipes a hand over his mouth, then offers a smile. "Just some issues with Miracule."

I feel like he's deflecting, but I won't push. "What inspired the name?"

From a drawer across the room he pulls out a beveled bottle.

"This is only the prototype packaging. I'm in the process of getting FDA approval and patenting the formula—snail mucin..."

"Come again?"

"Have you ever seen a snail with wrinkles?" He grins. "The other ingredients are hyaluronic acid, spilanthes, which is nature's Botox, niacinamide, copper peptides, and zinc." He raises the bottle, his eyes lighting up, his voice rising with excitement. "This is the new fountain of youth. A miracle. *Alors*, you're the first non-investor to hear about it. And, on the subject, you don't need it." His hand grazes my cheek. "You have beautiful skin."

I'm confused. He's a Montclair, from a family worth billions. "Why would you need investors?"

His eyes darken for a brief moment. "I thought you of all people would understand. I want to do this on my own—build something on my own merits, not my family's name."

I do understand his reasoning and it's nice to slow down with him, to talk about dreams, and we're finally talking about his.

"I get it," I finally say.

He leans over to kiss my forehead. "That's why we're such a good match."

Are we, though? We're from different sides of the pond of life. I'm pretty sure his family would push me off the curb and into the water if they met me, knew about my upbringing. Or perhaps they like go-getters.

"You might reconsider," I say, realizing something. "You haven't been over to my place yet."

"How about tonight?"

"Aren't you getting sick of me?"

"*Jamais*," he says, pulling me closer.

I feel myself relax, the knots loosening. He pulls me tighter, breathes me in, holds me until I think he might never let go. I surprise myself with how easy it is to open up your heart to somebody, how effortless. Save for Tricia, I've blocked everyone from my entire life. I find myself wanting to let him in.

SIX

LEXI

Letting Christophe into my world, my home, is like taking the next step and I'm almost ready for it. Almost. I fluff a pillow and arrange it more artfully, with its button and zipper facing the edges of the wall. I listen to the ticking clock and hear the sound of every second, louder, closer. I look out the huge picture window and see the blur of traffic, bright and impatient. I'm trying not to be either of those things.

I sit down. I get up again. It's the fifth time I've been to the bathroom in the last half hour.

A silver Maserati glides to a stop in front of my building. I watch the sleek vehicle gleaming under the streetlights with a mix of curiosity, anticipation, and dread. Christophe steps out with an air of casual confidence, his presence commanding.

He doesn't see me from the street, but I can see the expression on his face. He knocks and I open the front door.

"You live *here?*" Christophe asks, not bothering to contain his surprise, his eyebrows arching slightly.

"I do."

He sighs. "I hope this neighborhood is safe."

He bounds up the steps, kisses me on the cheek, and then saunters inside the place I've chosen to call home. It's not large by any means, especially compared to what he must be accustomed to.

"You expected chandeliers and gold leaf?" I ask, leaning back against the concrete wall.

He chuckles, a practiced sound. "I expected something different." His gaze sweeps the room, taking in the lack of ornamentation, the spartan but intentional décor. Everything in its right place. Everything saying, this is who I am, not who you think I should be.

"I'm not the kind of person to hoard things I don't need. Two bedrooms, one I use as a studio to design my line."

He gives an almost imperceptible nod, acknowledging the undercurrent of meaning. "Very efficient," he says, as though he's just reviewed my financials.

"Efficient. That's me."

He sets a bottle of wine on the coffee table, and his gaze sweeps across the open living area again, this time more thorough. He notices the prints, the arrangements, the labels on the jars. He admires the view from the window, the sweeping panorama of the city that looks so pristine from a distance. It's a view I paid extra for, a reminder of how close success is and how it could slip away when the lights flicker out.

When Christophe turns back to me his expression is unreadable. He strolls across the room, pausing when he reaches my desk. He picks up a photo. "This is you?"

"Yes, my mother and me. I think I was ten."

"She's beautiful. Like you," he says, placing the frame back down. "I can't wait to meet her."

I swallow, squeezing my eyes shut for a moment. I haven't spoken to my mom in seventeen years, but I can't tell him that. He'd go running out of the Hollywood Hills if he knew the reason. "Let's take things one day at a time."

We settle on the couch, drinks in hand, and he studies me with those sharp eyes, the ones that make you feel like he's peeling away all of your layers. Or your clothes. I've caught these looks before, looks that measure what's beneath the surface.

He lets out a soft groan. "We need to talk."

I gulp. Here it comes. "About what?"

"Us." He meets my stunned eyes and squeezes my hand. "I think our relationship is going somewhere. And I'd like to invest in your future."

I'm not sure I'm hearing him correctly. My eyes go wide. My heart races. "You want to invest in LexICON?"

"No, I want to invest in us." His lips twist into a sly smile. "I have something for you. I wanted to give it to you before your big event in Vegas. A gift to celebrate your success."

If Christophe is love-bombing me, I like it. I sit in a stunned stupor as he pulls something shiny out of the pocket of his jeans. I can't stop blinking as he clasps a sparkling diamond tennis bracelet around my wrist. Regardless of the gift, it's the look in his eyes, the intense passion, the way he believes in me. I find myself wondering about the future—what it would be like to be Alexis Montclair.

On Tuesday morning, I meet Tricia at our makeshift office—her house. "You're late," she says, huffing. "And you blew me off yesterday."

"Sorry, *mom*, I was with Christophe."

"You know you're losing focus at the worst possible time."

"You're the one who said go for it..." I shoot her a smirk.

"Aside from his name and the mind-blowing sex you're probably having, what do you have in common?"

"We have a connection. We talk about our dreams, our goals. We want the same things—to travel, to grow our brands, to succeed..."

"For LexICON to succeed you have to get your head out of the clouds." She shoots me a tight grin. "We've got to plan for the Style Sphere show. We need a lot less Christophe. More LexICON."

I sigh and mumble, "Fine," knowing I'll see him tomorrow night and probably the night after. "Christophe will be in Vegas."

"And you'll be with *me*, focusing on the success of LexICON." She glowers at me. "Remember? Your dream? Our dream?"

She doesn't need to remind me. LexICON represents everything I've worked for.

Tricia's lips pinch together. "I may have tried to do some research on him. Find his digital footprints..."

"Why?"

"Because I want to be sure he is who he says he is," she says, clucking her tongue. "Only his mother, Florence, comes up in the searches." She pauses. "You may want to ask him why his Instagram is private."

I shake my head and then glare at her. "Christophe is the real deal. He's a Montclair."

I need to believe this. Have to.

"What if he isn't? And what if he is?"

"All that matters is we share a connection." I lift my chin. "We have synergy."

Our tense Mexican stand-off is shattered when she sees the intensity in my eyes.

"You're a lost cause." Tricia throws her hands into the air, resigned. "By the way, I've booked us a suite at Mandalay Bay."

My fingers fly to my temples. "We've discussed this. There are cheaper places off the strip."

"If we're going to Vegas, we're doing it right. I'm not an off-the-strip kind of woman. No arguments," she says with a shrug and an over-the-top shudder. "It's a business expense. The company will reimburse me when it can."

I look down at my shoes, shaking my head. "That might take a while."

She gives me a sly grin. "Not if you keep your head in the game and focus on the company."

Oh, believe me, I am.

SEVEN

CHRISTOPHE

Pressure doesn't come in waves—it slams all at once. Remy? He's relentless. I stopped picking up after his last call, especially since Lexi was in earshot, so now he's pivoted to sending an onslaught of texts.

> The clock is ticking. Expecting $ in a week.
>
> A deal is a deal. Hold your end of the bargain.
>
> Or else.

I have to roll my eyes at the last one. I text him back.

> Somebody needs to work on their patience. Stop calling. Stop texting. I'll be in touch when everything is set. Got it?

I'm tracing a crystal of condensation down the side of my Pellegrino, thinking about Lexi, when the manager descends, shoes reflecting The Regent's marbled lobby floor, with a tight bun and tighter mouth.

"Mr. Montclair," she says. "Do you have a moment?"

I meet her stare with a slow, unhurried smile. "Always. To what do I owe"—I tip my head to the side—"the pleasure?"

With a quick flick of her pen, she points at my account summary, which is thickly marked with highlighter and exclamation points. "There's been an issue with your—well, several issues, but primarily the matter of payment." She lowers her voice to a hushed whisper. "Your credit card has been declined, and the desk has left you several messages this past week. You haven't called them back."

"I can assure you," I begin, "this is a temporary situation. A wire transfer is en route as we speak. I apologize for any—what's the word—friction."

She takes a small breath, as if calibrating my words.

"We value discretion at The Regent, Mr. Montclair. But you must understand, we have procedures. I'll need to see proof the wire has been sent."

I force a smile. "Listen..." I lower my voice, leaning just far enough to bring her into my confidence. "I'm having breakfast with Franco Vescari in a few minutes. I'll get everything sorted out after. I promise."

She hovers a second too long. Then a nod—curt, but with the faintest shimmer of respect. "Of course, Mr. Montclair. After your breakfast." And then she's gone, clicking away in a tempo that means I'm on the clock and the bill must be astronomical.

For the past month, I've been spoiling Lexi and myself with room service, ordering lobster and champagne, spa services, and my dry cleaning. I check my phone. Nothing from Lexi, but a new message from Franco:

I'm on my way down.

I scan the lobby for him.

A couple of moments later, there, walking with deliberate grandeur, is Vescari and I internally cringe. Jacket the color of midnight, a pocket square. I think he wants to be Karl Lagerfeld's long-lost twin. Same hair color: white. Same large black sunglasses covering his face.

"Christophe!" he calls, loud enough to project across the lobby but not so loud as to embarrass himself. I rise and walk over, every step a calculation.

"So," Franco says, sitting in the chair opposite mine. "You wanted to talk about the great Miracule. Let's hear it."

After ordering from a server who instantly appears, I paint the urgency in broad strokes he will understand: "Our biggest problem, Franco, is demand. We have Sephora, we have Goop, we have that K-beauty subscription box ready to sign—there's more, but you get the idea. I just need capital. Or a bridge loan, until the FDA approval goes through and I get my American accounts in order."

Franco listens, the corners of his mouth tight with skepticism. I notice his fingers tracing the rim of his espresso cup, as if he's counting down the seconds until I stop talking.

He waits for me to finish, then sets the cup down. "You know, Christophe, when I was your age, I lied to everybody. Built my first million on stories I knew I'd never be able to deliver. The trick is to deliver anyway." He smiles, warm and vicious. "I know you can deliver. How much do you need?"

"Two hundred." Not one to beat about the bush, I hand him a piece of paper. "Wired to this account this morning. You'll double your investment in a couple of months."

A beat of silent tension.

"What's the rush?" he asks.

"Production costs with my manufacturers in France and shipping logistics," I say and he nods with understanding.

"They're holding your product ransom. Happened to me when I was launching my label. Don't make me regret this." He stands with a small grunt. "What time are we leaving for Vegas?"

I eye my watch. "Tomorrow afternoon."

"You better drum up more interest."

Oh, I will. I already have a plan. I watch him walk away, pulling out his phone. I'm hoping he's calling his banker. The moment he's gone, the manager reappears at a tactical distance, holding a thin folder. She catches my eye, raises one eyebrow, and sashays over to my table.

"I'll be paying the full balance in a couple of hours. I just had to sort out some banking issues." I shrug. "French banks—they don't work as quickly as American banks do. But it's handled."

"Thank you."

"No, thank you," I say, and mean it. "You're the best in the city."

She blinks once, unsure of the compliment, then nods. The transaction is complete. Although I won't be coming back to The Regent after Vegas, I can't burn any bridges. Not yet.

EIGHT

LEXI

Glamour. Glitter. Chaos. After a five-hour drive in a rented U-haul, we're in Vegas, baby. On the way, Christophe has been texting me.

> I wish you'd change your mind, stay with me.

> Trixie and I have to work.

> You don't need to stay with Trixie.

> But I do. Trix and I will be working non-stop.

> :(

I don't like being put in this position, feeling guilty. He knows how much this show means to me. How much pressure I'm under. How hard I've worked for this specific moment. How everything could blow up.

Style Sphere has been pitched as the Holy Grail of fashion expos, and Las Vegas intends to make it a spectacle. Luxury brands dazzle, and our booth seems almost intimate by comparison. I remind myself that I'm aiming for intimacy, not audacity. But this is Vegas: all or nothing, with rich buyers, vast ballrooms, champagne, and plastic smiles; meanwhile, I'm one infinitesimal booth away from being completely overlooked.

I'm glad Tricia talked her husband, Jeff, into loaning us a couple of men from his construction crew, the guys happy for a little time in Vegas, me happy to have the help even though we can barely afford it. I hand them each two hundred dollars after they've unloaded the U-haul, bringing our goods to our little corner of the world. They grin and take off, heading to the casino or a strip club, probably both.

"Ready to wow them, Lex?" Tricia asks as she carefully arranges a neat row of sports bras. I love her more than ever in that moment. We are being dwarfed and outsparkled by industry titans, but she is too driven to care. We are there. We are doing it. My heart booms inside my ribcage to the tune playing through the speakers. Before a panic attack sets in, I remind myself: I'm an optimist. I've worked hard for this moment.

I breathe in, absorbing the competition—all lace, leather, and glittering fixtures—and breathe out, trying not to drown in it all.

"Alexis," says Tricia, her hands flying as she folds our inventory into neat stacks, "we are going to nail this." The glitter on her fingernails catches every stray beam of light. Maybe that's what I need to feel more comfortable—more glitter.

"If by 'nailing this' you mean putting Ikea furniture together, then yes," I reply.

"Exactly! The Swedish look is huge. Modern and minimalist. We're getting *hygge* with it."

I swallow back my laughter. "Okay, Fresh Princess of Bel-Air, I think you meant cheap and tiny."

"Authenticity," she corrects me. "Charm. That's what people want. Tonight we're having drinks. We have to celebrate every tiny step, every little victory."

I see Christophe through the crowds with Franco Vescari. As they approach, Vescari calls, "Alexis Marlowe, you're the talk of the town. Everybody wants to know who you are, what you've got. Are you ready?" He waves a dramatic hand. "For all of this?"

I shift my weight from side to side. "I-I am."

"Knock 'em dead, kiddo. And come to my closing party, bring your friend." He grins and then nudges Christophe. "Time to go. There are some people I want you to meet."

Christophe shoots me an apologetic smile, his lips twitching.

As Christophe and Vescari walk away, a strange feeling overtakes me. Even with support and praise, I still feel that I'm in way over my head. With Christophe. With this show. With everything. And then I notice two figures in the far corner of the room—tall, skinny, dressed head to toe in black and wearing dark glasses. When one of them motions toward me and grins, a shiver runs down my spine. If my memory serves me well, I've seen them before—at the Santa Monica pier. They must be here for Christophe, but they don't look like they're watching him; they're watching me.

NINE
CHRISTOPHE

I've always enjoyed circling the periphery, watching people. The trick is to make it seem like I'm nowhere, and yet somehow everywhere at once. It doesn't take long before Lexi's eyes meet mine. Even from this distance, I can sense the attention they attract, drawing the rest of her face into position.

Her booth is refreshingly quaint, the complete opposite of the designer madness that saturates the floor. She stands out without trying, a diamond in a bin of synthetics. Her audience is meagre, a few clueless sycophants lapping at her heels—gym shoes—while she remains nonchalant, talking to them as if they were equals. It's cute.

Franco may be right; I could be falling in love. Anything is possible, especially in Vegas. She doesn't seem to want anything from me. But I do want something from her.

I move in closer, savoring the perspective. Her profile is pure accessibility, every part of her saying trust me without really trying. And, God, she's young. At least, young enough to wear ambition like a fresh coat of paint. Her easy posture suggests she doesn't even need to play the game, though she probably knows she's only just begun.

American royal starting from the ground up, born to fortune

but striving, making her own mark. Or pretending to. I'm suddenly not sure which, but it doesn't matter. The lack of polish only makes her more appealing.

I wait for the telltale spark of recognition, the moment she realizes the caliber of company she's in. She doesn't have it yet, but I have no doubt it'll come. Maybe tonight. Maybe tomorrow. Maybe right now.

Vescari nudges my side. "You're supposed to be focusing on Miracule."

"I am."

"No, you're looking at Alexis like a lovesick puppy," he says, turning on his heel and walking away. Over his shoulder, he says, "There are people from Neiman Marcus I want you to meet. Follow me and get your head together."

My head *is* together. I have dreams, a vision. And that vision has nothing to do with Miracule right now.

Before I leave the exhibit floor, I look at her one last time. Lexi's breath catches as she meets my gaze. There is a charge, a silent negotiation. I wouldn't have guessed how thrilling this could be. I love the immediacy of a new adventure. The way things unfold so beautifully when they're unplanned, spontaneous.

By the way her eyes meet mine, then look away, I know the deal will be done.

TEN

LEXI

Aside from messaging one another, our paths have barely crossed, a wink here, a stolen kiss there. I miss Christophe, miss his touch, miss his smile, but I have to stay focused on my business, not his pretty face. So far, the show is going well and we're getting orders from boutique stores across the country. Chicago. New York. Atlanta. We'll break even, covering the costs of the show, maybe with enough left over to buy a mascot—one of those tiny dogs in tutus we've seen hanging out of purses.

I haven't warned Christophe about the men I saw lurking on the showroom floor, mostly because I haven't seen them again and I don't want him to think I'm nuts. I think stress has spun my imagination into overdrive. And, 'by the way, I think two men are following you' is not the type of thing you write in a text after 'I miss your lips on mine.'

At night, Tricia and I order in room service while soaking our tired feet in salt baths, passing out and snoring shortly after. Adrenaline keeps me moving. Hope keeps my dreams alive. I'm surprised when Franco Vescari approaches our booth with a swagger. He kisses me on the cheek, also a surprise.

"Ms. Marlowe," he says with a grin. He waves a hand and then brings his fingers into a chef's kiss. "Your offerings are lovely. I always look out for my friends. And I'd like to introduce you to a friend of mine."

Okay. Christophe must be selling this guy something. I didn't realize that I'm friends with Vescari.

A woman steps forward, takes off her shades, and she smiles. "Interesting line," she says, with one of those vaguely European accents that always sound high end. Her eyes are shrewd, and I'm not sure how to read her yet.

Tricia clutches my arm like she might never let go. "Oh. My. God," she whispers. "It's Trendline, isn't it? You're Trendline!"

We both turn to the woman, waiting for her to confirm our suspicions. As if we need her to say it out loud, because we can't believe it's true. She takes a second, savoring our anticipation, then delivers.

"Yes," she says, lifting up her chin slightly. "I'm Margaux Duval, the founder."

Tricia tries to play it cool, but there's no way. Unlike me, Tricia has unlimited funds and she's addicted to the shopping channel. "Huge fan," she says, breathless. "Such a huge fan."

"I am, too," says Vescari with a wink. "It's how I got my start."

This is real. This is happening. It's all I can do to keep from bouncing like a lunatic. I take a deep breath, steadying myself for the biggest moment of LexICON's very short life.

Margaux nods again, this time more decisively. Her attention flickers toward Tricia, and I realize she's actually listening. Considering. "Our audience does like good value."

"They'll like this," Tricia says, nodding along with her. "They'll love it."

"Some buyers take a chance on what we call 'emerging brands', especially when they've got the stamp of approval from Vescari," Margaux continues, glancing back to me.

I'm sure she can see the hope on my face. It must be obvious. It must be embarrassing. I have to say something smart, reel her in. "We're reinventing things with bamboo—it's breathable, better than cotton. Sustainable."

"We love sustainable."

She's playing with me. Playing with my emotions. Playing me, full stop. But I'm in too deep to care. Tricia is ready to leap over the display table and hug the woman.

She hands me a card. Not her own, of course. I doubt people at this level even have their own. The letters shimmer in platinum and possibility. I think I might die from excitement.

"You'll need to negotiate with our buying team," Margaux says. "And there is one condition you should be aware of. It's standard for all new vendors."

"Standard," I say with force, a little high on adrenaline, "is fine. Standard is good. Standard is what we live for."

"If the line doesn't sell, we have a fifty percent return-to-vendor policy. And we order a lot."

My heart drops to the pit of my stomach, where it twists into a giant knot. A fifty percent return rate? That's massive. That's terrifying. But Trendline. Trendline. I have to struggle to keep my grin from collapsing into something more serious. More desperate. I have to keep myself from collapsing with all the stress. I place my hands on the display to steady myself.

Tricia stares at me, caught somewhere between pure thrill and utter disbelief. I stare at the card in my hand, weighing everything that one small piece of paper might mean.

"We'll be in touch," Margaux says. "We'll set up a meeting at your showroom."

Vescari shoots me a wink and whispers in my ear, "I'll see you tomorrow night at my party. And don't let Christophe take this opportunity away from you. He should be focusing on Miracule, not your business."

With that, the power duo glides into the sea of luxury brands, leaving us clinging to the possibility they've left in their wake. I'm also feeling the pull of Vescari's words; it's as if he's warning me about Christophe.

"This is the big time." Tricia clasps my hand. "We need to find a showroom and quick."

My eyes sweep the hall, my attention drawn toward a woman talking with Christophe. He leans against the wall with casual arrogance, his shirt perfectly untucked, as if he has trademarked the look. He shrugs, smirks, and points to our booth.

The woman he's talking to turns.

Sabrina Vale. The actress. Nominated for three Academy Awards—never a win. Her black, glossy hair and patent leather boots are both sharpened to points. She looks like she could eat lesser people for breakfast and then send them thank-you notes. Sabrina spots me watching them, locks onto my eyes, and saunters over.

She points to the workout pants, the bangles on her wrists jangling. "I'll take the blue, the purple, and the black with matching tops." She surveys a rack of shirts, eyes the tag. "Throw in a couple of these T-shirts. Bamboo. Love, love them. And I love the cashmere ballerina wraps. I'll take one in each color."

I startle. "This isn't a store. We're not selling to consumers."

She lets out a short laugh. "I'm not buying anything. You're giving the swag to me. Think of me as your brand ambassador. An influencer. I go running with my dogs in Coldwater Canyon every weekend, the paparazzi following me around in packs. Christophe Montclair gave me the idea."

Tricia coughs into her hand.

"I, uh…" I don't know how to respond.

Tricia nods, deliberating. Her eyes brighten. "We'll send you the goods after the show. Where should we ship?"

Sabrina grins and hands over a business card and saunters back toward Christophe. I watch their interaction with an eagle eye. Her hand runs down his arm. Her smile. His smile. There's something intimate about the exchange. I watch them leave the floor together. And I don't like it. This whole scene feels like a minefield or a paved road to disaster.

"Trix, this is all too surreal," I whisper. "Something feels off. First Vescari, then Trendline, and then Sabrina..."

"All Christophe's connections," she says, tapping her lips with a pensive finger. "He's after something. He might not be here working his skincare line; he may be working *you*. I feel it in my gut."

"So do I," I say to myself, my eyes flicking to the side.

Across the room the two men I'd thought were figments of my imagination are staring me down again. I nudge Tricia's rib with my elbow and whisper, "Don't be obvious when you look, but do you see those two men wearing black? The ones watching us?"

She tucks her chin into her shoulder. "I do. Scary. Definitely not in fashion or press."

"Exactly," I say, taking a deep breath. "And I'm going to find out what they want."

Tricia tries to grab my arm, but I'm a woman on a mission and I wriggle out of her grip. Clenching my teeth, I stride right up to them, folding my arms. "Can I help you with something?" I ask.

Twins, save for a slight height difference; the shorter one grins and replies, "You must be Alexis Marlowe. We're friends of Christophe's. Can you tell him Remy and Gilles are looking for him?"

He speaks English with a heavy French accent, yet it's not as refined as Christophe's. "You're from Paris?"

They both give soft laughs. "*Oui*, Paris."

I can't see their eyes, hidden under dark sunglasses. I can smell the alcohol on their breaths, the cigarettes on their clothes. Their greasy hair is tied back in stringy ponytails. These are not the kind of people Christophe associates with.

"Christophe left the floor a couple of minutes ago. You just missed him," I say, tilting my head to the side. "If you were friends you'd have his number. Tell his family to stop tracking him. And you can also stop watching me."

"Just tell Christophe you met us," the taller one says with a grin, eyeing me up and down. "And he's one lucky man."

"If his luck doesn't run out," says the other.

With that, they both turn and walk away, leaving me stunned. I'm thinking I'll send Christophe a text, but decide against it as I'm seeing him tonight. Right now, I can't be concerned with two thugs; this is my life, my world, and my dream.

Tricia taps me on the shoulder, grimacing. "What was that all about?"

"Nothing," I lie. "They stumbled into the wrong center, looking for the sex convention. They thought I looked like one of their favorite porn stars. You, too."

"Gross." She grimaces and then smiles. "I guess it is a little bit flattering."

"Is it?" I link my arm in hers and she blurts out a laugh. "Now let's go kill it. Last day of sales."

ELEVEN

LEXI

After one more day of wheeling and dealing, peddling our wares, Tricia and I step into the scene of the high-luxe hotel-suite party hosted by Vescari at the Bellagio—a hurricane of glitz and gold where mirrors reflect thousands of glimmering pinpoints of light. The room is immense, the guests, impossibly glamorous, resembling living statues. My first instinct is to flee, but I force myself to stand my ground, gripped by an irresistible pull toward something extraordinary.

"Lexi, come on!" Tricia urges as she plunges into the crowd, tugging me along. She fits right in, as if she belongs in this world, while I feel like a misplaced alien. I'm taking in every absurd detail—champagne towers, trays of gourmet food that look more like art than sustenance, and delicacies like caviar and truffles that I've only ever seen on high-end TV. This is the stuff of legends, not at all like the simplicity I'm accustomed to.

I'm fidgeting with the bracelet Christophe bestowed on me. Tricia notices. "Where did you get that fancy-shmancy bling-bling?"

"Christophe."

"Is it a payment for something?" she asks with a laugh.

I growl. "You are not funny."

She laughs. "But I am. I'm going to get us some drinks."

"And I'm coming with you," I say, following her.

While Tricia charms a pair of sharp-suited men in the corner of the bar, I linger awkwardly nearby, hoping someone might spark a conversation—a lifeline. Leaning against the counter, I order a sparkling water instead of something stronger, determined to keep my wits about me. A bored bartender quips, "More celebrities than you expected, huh?" and I lie, "Exactly as many as I expected," although my wide eyes give me away.

Even the bartender knows I'm out of my league. An imposter.

An hour later, Tricia yawns. "I'm spent. Let's hit it. We have to pack up tomorrow and get on the road."

"I'll meet you at the room," I reply. "I haven't spoken with Christophe yet."

"Which is weird? Don't you think?"

"He's been busy. Like us."

"I'm never too busy for you." She kisses me on the cheek. "Don't wake me up when you come in. I need my beauty sleep."

After Tricia leaves, I order a margarita, then another, trying my best to remain level-headed despite the liquid courage. My eyes leap to Christophe, arguing with Sabrina Vale in the far corner of the room. This time, Christophe does not see me watching. Sabrina's face twists into a scowl. A tear slides down her cheek. Her dress fans out like a peacock's plume as she turns and stomps toward the door. Christophe lowers his head, running a hand through his hair. I'm setting my glass down, about to turn to run like Cinderella out of the ball, when Vescari approaches me.

"Now is not the time"—he leans forward—"but I'd like to speak with you about Christophe."

I swallow. "What about him?"

He holds a finger to his lips, his eyes darting to the side. It's at that moment Christophe makes a swift approach. He places a protective hand on the small of my back. "What are the two of you talking about?"

You. We're talking about you. Or we were about to.

Vescari pipes up first. "Alexis's first successful trade show."

"It went well?" asks Christophe.

"Well enough, I suppose." I want to ask him what had ruffled Sabrina's feathers, why she'd stormed out, but I don't. I also want to know what Vescari was going to talk to me about. Again, it feels like he's warning me. "I'm exhausted."

"I hope you're not leaving," he says, clasping my hand.

I muster what I hope is a mysterious smile and reply, "Depends on who's asking."

"Your future husband."

"You're funny."

"I'm not joking."

Vescari lets out a harsh laugh. "Maybe he'll give you a life of glamour with his snails—if he gets his company up and running."

As Vescari walks away into the crowd, I watch Christophe's eyes. He seems unfazed by the obvious cutting remark. He just pulls me toward him, nuzzles into my neck. "Don't mind him. He's mad that I've been talking about you non-stop. He wants me to focus more on Miracule." He kisses my cheek. "Right now, I think we should celebrate your success."

A bit buzzed, I take a step back, wobbling slightly. He's constantly putting the focus back on me. "What about yours?"

"There were a few bumps. Sabrina and Vescari are expecting a quicker launch, but everything is going as planned. I had some really lucrative meetings." His eyes meet mine. "But this is the one rendezvous I've been most excited about."

Now is the time to tell him. "I met two of your friends today."

His forehead crinkles. "Who?"

"Remy and Gilles," I say. "They were staring me down."

I meet his gaze, see his jaw clench. "They spoke to you?"

"So, you know them," I say, my tone flat.

"I do." His eyes darken. "And they are not friends. They are the people my family hired."

"That's what I figured. I told them to stop."

"They didn't say anything else?"

"No," I reply, wondering why he'd flinched ever so slightly.

"Good. Don't worry. Ignore them. I'll call my family. This is getting out of control."

I let out a sigh of relief. Everything is as I'd thought, and Christophe will deal with them. His hand brushes my lips. "What have you been eating?" He licks his fingertips. "Salt."

"I haven't been eating. I've been drinking margaritas," I say, realizing I should get something in my stomach.

He grins. "Let's order a couple more."

"And then what?" My stomach growls. "Grab some dinner, with sustenance?"

He shakes his head and whispers, "We'll see where the night takes us."

TWELVE

LEXI

The sun slices through the curtains, blinding me. My brain feels like it is about to explode, pulsing and throbbing. Club music still plays and spins around in my head. Thwack. Boom. Boom. Thwack. Beyond hungover, I can only remember flashes from the previous evening—mostly drinking my fair share of margaritas. And, ugh, the champagne. How many glasses did I have?

I don't normally imbibe—so all of this pain is new to me.

I struggle to open my eyes, but unforgiving, sticky clumps of mascara have sealed my eyelashes together. So far, I've broken two of my steadfast rules—I drank too much, and I didn't wash my face. But I figure I can cut myself some slack, considering I've been celebrating the success of LexICON's first fashion trade show, and, well, I'm falling head over heels in love with a gorgeous Frenchman.

Christophe's finger traces my back, starting at the nape of my neck and traveling down my spine. "You are so beautiful, my wife. *Très, très, très belle,*" he murmurs.

I jolt upright. "Did you just call me your wife?"

"We got married last night," he says, blowing out the air in between his lips.

I turn to face him, my jaw dropped open. "Please tell me you're joking. I thought it was a dream."

He lets out a short laugh. "I'm not joking. And you are my dream."

My tongue feels as though it has doubled in size inside my mouth, so thick and meaty I can't speak. Every muscle in my body tightens as I peer at my left hand, letting out a gasp. A shiny gold wedding band adorns my ring finger.

I swing my legs over the side of the bed, my back turned to him. With my contacts glued to my eyes, I try to focus through a haze of champagne and tequila mirages. A drag queen and Elvis? Why won't my legs move? It's as if I'm paralyzed, although my trembling lips find a life of their own.

"*Mais*, what's wrong?" he asks. "You were happy last night. But you don't seem 'appy now."

I shrug his hand off my back. Before Christophe can utter another word in French or English, I race toward the bathroom, careering into the wall and nearly falling down.

"Are you okay, my beautiful wife?" he asks with a snicker. "That looked like it might have 'urt."

Nothing about this situation is funny.

"I'm fine. And please, for the love of God, stop calling me your wife."

"But you are my wife," he says and I freeze again, my spine rigid.

My eyes dart away when he catches my shocked gaze. Finally, I manage to get inside the bathroom, slam the door shut. To keep my legs from giving out from under me, I brace myself against the sink. As I face my reflection in the mirror, I try my best to replay last night in my head.

Glitter. Chaos. Loads of champagne. Margaritas. Repeat.

I turn the shower on and sink to the floor, letting the water rush over my body as my back presses against the cool tiles. I can't even call marrying Christophe a mistake; it is something far more calculated, and way too difficult to unravel before coffee.

I have to breathe, to think. I have to get out of this shower before I turn into a prune.

Hesitantly, after putting on a bathrobe, I open the door. Cool, calm, and collected, Christophe sits at a desk like a man expecting room service. I stop, mid-panic, caught off guard by the casual authority he wears like a bespoke suit. There is something unsettling in the way he's looking at me.

"About last night," I begin, my voice shaky. "Whose idea was it to get married?"

"Both of ours."

"This is a m-mistake," I stutter.

"It isn't. Look at the photos on your phone."

I scramble to pull my phone out of my purse, click the gallery open. There is a photo of me smiling like a fool, wedged in between a drag queen with towering, glittering hair and an Elvis impersonator in a rhinestone-studded jumpsuit.

"We were *actually* married by Elvis?" I ask, bewildered.

"No," Christophe replies with a chuckle. "He was the witness."

"Why aren't there any photos of you?" I question, flipping through the gallery.

Christophe grins. "I was the one who took the pictures."

"Where is the marriage certificate?" I press further.

"I'm getting it framed." Christophe merely shrugs. "For posterity."

There is a pause, a charged expectancy in the air. And now, seeing the pictures, I remember everything. Damn those margaritas. My fingers fly to my temples. "We need to get an annulment. Immediately."

His eyes flicker with something that might be amusement or pity or, worse, affection. I can't quite decide which unnerves me more. "You can trust me," he says, and I'm left questioning everything, especially why I should trust him when, save for my business, I can barely trust my own decisions, until he continues, "I, for one, don't want to get an annulment. Why not see where this goes? Give it a little time."

There is no trace of panic in his words. He makes this predicament sound so simple, like disentangling an earbud cord or leaving an uncomfortably long party. The contrast between us is stark. He is calm water while I am crashing in waves.

"We have potential," he says, gripping my hands. "Big potential."

I want to scoff, to tell him he's insane and that I am not the reckless idiot my wedding pictures suggest. But I don't. Because even through my wariness, there is a strange magnetism to the idea, a current of possibility I can't dismiss. "Potential for what, exactly?"

My question lacks the edge I'd aimed for because I'm seriously considering this arrangement. There is always a truth hidden between the lies. And I have fallen for him. This could be good.

"Us," he sighs.

I need to know more. If he is so important, a Montclair, he'd be all over social media. Believe me, I've looked. Apparently, so has Tricia. I scroll on my phone, intrigued. "Why is your Instagram private?"

"Because my family is very private," he offers.

I get it. He's a Montclair, but something isn't adding up.

"I want you to friend me now," I demand.

"Done," he says with a nod, picking up his phone.

Silently I flip through his photos, not at all surprised to see him alongside numerous celebrities and images of him with his mother, Florence Montclair—on yachts, in Cannes, in Saint-Tropez. "Why are your comments blocked?"

He purses his lips, blows out a breath. "I don't want or need to know what other people think about me and my life. Any other questions?"

I do have one. "Why did you marry me?"

A long stretch of silence punctuates my breath.

"Because when you find a good thing, you don't want to lose

it," he says, gripping my hand. "I'm in love with you, Lexi. And I believe you're in love with me. Let's give us a chance."

For all his smoothness, I notice a flicker of uncertainty in Christophe's expression. It seems he's laid his cards on the table, but there is more to it than strategy. A glimpse of vulnerability, the knowledge that this could all fall apart at the seams, which makes his invitation more compelling than any line he's rehearsed.

"I must be out of my mind," I finally say, unable to hold back a nervous laugh. "I think I've been blinded by the lights of Las Vegas."

But if I'm being honest with myself, he's blinded me with his charm, and I have nothing to lose and everything to gain.

THIRTEEN
LEXI

I have half an hour to get back to my hotel and get ready, or face the wrath of Tricia. Due to some very unforeseen circumstances, I'm running late. I practically leap into the elevator, breathing heavily. A couple takes a step backward, clinging onto their little girl.

"I can't believe a hotel of this caliber allows prostitutes," the man whispers to his wife.

"Mommy, what's a prostitute?" the little girl asks.

"Ssh, ssh," says the mother.

Not a *Pretty Woman* moment; I keep my eyes averted. The doors open and I walk hastily toward the exit, my over-the-knee boots clacking on the floor. Raised eyebrows and wicked stares follow my every move as I exit the hotel, leaving frigid air conditioning and immediately hit by the desert heat. Already sweating bullets, I hail a cab to take me back to my hotel—Mandalay Bay, thanks to Tricia.

Finally, I make it back to our room to find Tricia smacking cherry-red lips in the bathroom mirror. "Look what the cat dragged back in," she says, shooting me a smirk over her shoulder and wiggling her brows. "So, what did you do last night?"

A very good question, one I'm not sure I have an answer to.

I slump onto the bed, rolling over and pushing my face into a pillow. "Apparently, I got married to Christophe," I mumble.

Her footsteps resound on the floor. She taps my shoulder. Hard. "Sorry, I don't think I heard you correctly. Did you just say you got married?"

I hold out my left hand, waggle my ring finger. She grabs my wrist, flipping me onto my back. "This isn't good, Lexi. This is so outside of your wheelhouse. I was all for a fling, but seriously, you've only known him for a month. You can't just marry somebody on a whim. What do you have in common?"

I shoot a glare in her direction. "I already told you. He's launching his own line of skincare—Miracule, removed from the Montclair name. He wants to make his own mark. Snail mucin is the basis for what he's calling the fountain of youth..."

She coughs. "What in the flying fuck is snail mucin?"

"Snail drool."

"Gross," she says, crossing her arms over her chest. "You better get this marriage annulled. Like, today. Well, today after the convention."

I swallow. "What if I give it one month?"

She cringes. "Nope, nope. And hell no. We'll talk about this boiling hot mess you've put yourself in later. Right now, we have to focus on our business. Or are you forgetting about LexICON and what we've accomplished together?"

"I'm not." My mind is miles away, debating the wisdom of my marriage. Maybe she's right. But I'm also thinking about him, how I'm Mrs. Montclair, and I grin.

"Wipe that crazy smile off your face," Tricia barks in a voice that jangles me like alarm bells. She's already dressed, eyes on the prize. "Last day. We're packing up. This is not a solo mission."

"I know, I know," I say, wanting to throw the word "mom" in, like she's a parental figure. She cocks her head, eyeing my half-assed outfit. I'm still holding my top, fabric pooled in my hands. "I'm not feeling so hot today, but I'll get right to it. Give me five minutes."

"You're feeling hungover, and you have to snap out of it," Tricia says with force. She smiles with enough wattage to illuminate a small city. "Take off that cheap-ass ring. And, after we leave Vegas, we'll get you out of this marriage." She pauses. "I'll give you ten minutes. Jeff's guys have already started breaking down the booth." She shoots me a grin, narrowing her eyes. "You're welcome."

"Thank you," I mumble, the nagging feeling of guilt setting in.

As we're packing up our goods, Christophe saunters over, and he's so close that I can see a small scar near his left eye, a hint of the past he hasn't told me about yet.

"Do you need help?" he offers.

Tricia eyes her husband's crew and then Christophe in his suit, probably Prada. "We're good. And you don't look like the kind of guy who enjoys manual labor."

"Appearances can be deceiving," he quips, an eyebrow raised.

"I hear congratulations are in order," says Tricia.

He grins. "*Merci*. I'm the luckiest man alive."

Tricia forces a smile, turns her back on him, and mumbles, "For fuck's sake."

Christophe's eyes shoot invisible daggers into her back.

"So," I say, trying to change the gears, the subject, and to sound like this hasn't been the most bizarre week of my life, "how do you know Sabrina Vale?"

Christophe looks over at me, measuring the question. "She's an investor in Miracule," he says, not offering anything more. "Aren't you happy I sent her over to your booth?"

Besides shellshocked, I don't know what I am. "And what about Remy and Gilles?"

"It's taken care of," he says. "They won't be bothering us again."

I have so many questions, but he continues before I can ask them.

"When are you headed back to LA?"

"After Trixie and I pack up. Tonight."

"I'll see you in a couple of days," he says and my face twists with confusion. "I have some things I need to take care of for Miracule and then we'll get our lives started. Together."

I gulp. "Where are you going to live?"

"With you," he says with a sly grin. "We're married. And, while we're on the subject, I'm going to have a realtor look at some new places, ones with a two-car garage."

His statement brings me back to reality.

FOURTEEN
CHRISTOPHE

Lexi has headed back to Los Angeles, and a strange feeling sets in. A trace of her perfume lingers behind on the sheets and I inhale her scent—citrus and spice. This really isn't like me to get emotionally attached. Two more nights here, and I might be gambling to stay in this game. But what she doesn't know won't kill her.

My window overlooks the bright sin of the strip. We are not so different, Vegas and I. Our lavish promises, our seductive fronts. Each roll of the dice one more risk. I'm staring at myself in the mirror, buttoning up my shirt with that trademark smirk that says I always win. I like winning. Through the curtains, the early evening light barely filters in, but I don't need it to shine—I'm my own spotlight. I sip my martini—shaken not stirred—when my cell buzzes. Sabrina. Instead of ignoring her call, I pick up.

Her words come out in a huff. "Why do you keep blowing me off? We haven't been together in over a month. One whole month. And don't you dare tell me it's business."

"It is business," I say, rolling my eyes. "Don't you want a return on your investment?"

"I do," she whines. "I also want to see you."

"And you will. Tomorrow."

"Promise?"

She's so easy to appease. "Have I ever broken one to you yet?"

"Fine. I'll see you tomorrow." She sighs. "You better not blow me off."

The line clicks to a close.

Before leaving my room, I glance back at my reflection, a man who thrives on risk and revels in his meticulously executed plays. Sure, sometimes doubts and whispers spin around in my brain, but they're just background noise to my brilliance. I know who I am and what I'm capable of.

The poker game I've been invited to is deep underground, where Vegas's glitter is lost in shadows. A cocktail of adrenaline and cigarettes infuses the air, the heady signature of those with more money than caution. Cufflinks and connections wink in the dim light. I claim my place at the table, slipping twenty-five thousand across the felt with a practiced indifference. I am here to win, but in this company, the game is about much more than cards.

The buy-in vanishes beneath the dealer's expert hand, transformed into a promising stack of chips. They feel solid in my grasp, and I can't help the smile that flickers across my lips. Among the players are a hedge-fund whisperer with an unfortunate nose, a Russian with a reputation as strong as his cologne, and a real-estate mogul who's rumored to have bought up most of Brooklyn. My eyes meet theirs. With a perfunctory nod, I take a sip of cognac, relishing the burn that follows.

The first hand is dealt, and I let my thoughts drift over strategy, over chance. They settle on my mentor, as they so often do, and I wonder what she would think of this display. "Trust, my dear," she might say, "should be dispensed as judiciously as the finest perfume." Her wry smile, always knowing, is something I can almost see on the faces around me.

Cards change hands with dizzying speed. I place bets with calculated coolness, but the tide is unkind. Losses begin to stack, each one chipping away at my façade. It's merely the game, I tell myself. One hand turns to two, and then too many to count. There's an art in how my opponents corner me, a predatory elegance. Chips slip from my grasp with alarming grace. It should unsettle me, yet a perverse thrill courses through my veins. This, after all, is why I'm here.

I lean back, surveying the players, feeling the weight of their gazes and the pulse of the room. These men can smell desperation, the same way I can smell their cologne and ambition. The stakes double. Another hand, another loss. A silence I hadn't noticed shatters as the dealer calls my attention to the dwindling stack before me. The heat in the room seems to intensify, along with my determination. I'm sweating, my shirt sticking to my neck, my armpits.

With an elegant flourish, the Russian pockets his winnings, casting me a look that's half amusement, half warning. The table's air grows sharper. Shadows creep closer as my options narrow.

As if on cue, a man steps forward. Unassuming yet formidable, he's been watching the whole time. I've heard of him—a man who runs games and gun collections with equal efficiency. "You're a Montclair," he says, his voice smooth as Italian leather. "I know you're good for it." He nods to the empty space that once held my chips, his meaning clear.

I hesitate, pride and necessity warring within me. A Montclair doesn't flinch. A Montclair wins. And so, I nod back, sealing the unspoken deal, ignoring the shiver that runs down my spine and what it might cost me.

"I'm in," I say, and the bookie nods to the dealer, in seconds a pile of new chips sitting in front of me.

I nod again, and the game resumes like a nightmare. The fresh stack vanishes, and my prospects with it. I remain poised even as my cards betray me. The men at the table are wolves with bloody grins. A final round. I leave the table with nothing but my name. The bookie is on me with the certainty of a reaper. "Christophe," he says, with slow and infinite satisfaction. "I want my money back in a week." He doesn't raise his voice. He doesn't need to. The other men pretend not to listen, but I see their ears twitch in my direction, hungry for the spectacle.

I keep my face neutral, my posture relaxed. "You will have it," I say, hearing how hollow it sounds, how rehearsed. But I'm not discouraged. I have one last card up my sleeve and the winner, me, will take all. My wife, whether she knows it or not, will get me out of this predicament. Soon I'll be out there again, chasing the next big mark, savoring every moment of the game. And once my time with Lexi is up, I'll throw her back in the water, knowing the real thrill is always in the catch—and in knowing that I'm the best damn fisherman out there.

FIFTEEN

LEXI

We're not even close to Los Angeles, but my mind's too fuzzy to continue driving, a cocktail of shock and disbelief swirling through me. "Time to switch duties," I say, pulling off the exit ramp, heading toward a ghost of a gas station, its lone pump looking about as reliable as my crazy marriage.

"Good," says Tricia, already unbuckling her seatbelt. "I need to pee." Her nose wrinkles. "Do you think it's safe here?"

I scan the rundown building, my gaze landing on a broken window patched up with cardboard. "As long as you don't sit on the seat."

"What about clown killers?"

"Clown killers?"

"I really hate clowns."

She gives me a grimace, but she's out the door and headed toward the facilities, walking as gingerly as a person can. The desert light, the way it shimmers with heat, makes my vision waver. That's how my life feels right now, like nothing is solid or sure. Just doubts and questions multiplying. I figure I might as well fill the U-Haul up. I slide the business credit card into the slot, praying it won't be declined, considering everything we've paid for the show. It isn't and I let out a sigh of relief. While the gas pump chugs and grumbles, my phone pings with a text. I pull it out of my pocket.

> You don't know who Christophe Montclair really is.
> You need to get away from him.

A cold spike of dread shoots through me. I glance over my shoulder, paranoia creeping up my spine, when another text chimes in.

> We also know who you are and what you've done.

My breath catches. Every hair on my arms stands on end. The world tilts. The words leap off the screen. I shudder, an uneasy chill settling over me. Somebody is taunting me, threatening the very identity I've tried so hard to reshape. My pulse pounds against my ears.

I've spent years building a new identity, brick by brick, convincing everyone—myself—I've left my past behind me. Now the past is sending me a digital harpoon.

Peering into the shadows, I try to imagine who could be behind the messages. Did I leave loose ends, things I assumed were long buried? Or is this someone closer, an enemy I don't yet see? My heart races as I run through the possibilities, each scenario more troubling than the last. Did the Montclairs have Remy and Gilles dig up dirt on me? I swallow. Whatever the case, somebody is doing their best to mess with my head.

My palms feel clammy. The cold glass of my phone presses into my fingers, grounding me in the moment. I consider replying with a bluff—claiming I know who they are—but even that seems too risky.

Tricia bounds toward me, a bottle of water in one hand and a look of alarm on her face. She tosses the bottle in my direction, but I'm too out of it to react fast enough. It thuds onto the ground right in front of my feet.

"Are you okay?" she asks. "You're looking kind of pale."

I take a deep breath, forcing my shoulders to relax. I slip the phone into my purse, zipping it shut with a deceptively calm click. I really need to figure out how Christophe plays into this. A man from his swanky background must have his reasons for marrying me. And those reasons can't be good.

"I'm fine," I say, but it's a shaky reassurance, one I'm telling myself; even I can hear my tone. "It's just so hot here." I pick up the bottle of water, dusting it off. "Thanks. You read my mind."

Tricia's eyebrows knit together as she looks at the gas pump, the nozzle still inserted into the reservoir, the numbers on the screen showing the full amount.

"Let's hit it, Mrs. Montclair," she says with a smirk.

I nod and throw her the keys, place the pump back in its place, and screw the gas cap back on. We hop into the cab, Tricia now in the driver's seat.

"Two more hours and we're home," she chirps.

I swallow. "If we're lucky."

"It's Sunday. Traffic won't be too bad." She nods and starts the engine. "You can call Christophe on the way. Demand an annulment."

I pivot to stare out the window, pretending to be absorbed by the passing scenery. Technicolor signs for palm-readers and pizza joints whiz by. A couple of tumbleweeds. I bristle, although in my heart, I know she's right. If things look too good to be true, they usually are. "Tricia, I told you I wanted to see where this goes."

"Nowhere good," she says, lifting up her chin.

"Just stop." I pull out my phone and call Christophe. He doesn't pick up, so I leave a message. "Hi. It's me. Lexi," I begin, letting out a shaky breath. "Call me back when you get a chance."

"At least you have his phone number," says Tricia.

I swallow. "We're married."

Tricia lets out one of those dramatic sighs of hers, the kind that says she thinks this whole thing is as absurd as her husband Jeff's alien conspiracy theories. She starts to mutter something under her breath, but I don't catch it. Or I pretend not to. Either way, I know she thinks I should bury Christophe in the Nevada desert, wedding ring and all.

Shaking her head like I'm a lost cause, Tricia fiddles with the radio, flipping through stations until she hits on something she likes, when a loud voice startles both of us:

"Breaking news. This just in. The entire fashion world is in shock. Famed designer, Franco Vescari, was found dead earlier this morning by a hotel maid. At this time, authorities are not ruling out foul play…"

My bottom lip trembles as I tune out the words. He'd wanted to warn me about Christophe. That's no longer an option. I hang my head and bite down on my inner lip. Am I in a marriage of convenience? Perhaps.

"Christophe…" Tricia begins.

My grip tightens around my phone. "Has nothing to do with this."

"And you know this how?"

"Because I was with him all night."

We drive in silence for a few minutes, the tension in the cab as stifling as the air outside. She's waiting to see if I'll call him again, to break down and admit she's right.

The blare of a horn snaps me awake and I'm completely disoriented. My mind reels as I try to piece together the last few days, the text messages. The hangover pounding behind my eyes feels like a hammer. I force myself to take a slow, steady breath. Blinking rapidly, I find myself staring out of the window at a desolate building. We are not in front of the storage unit, but in a dark and deserted strip mall with flickering lights. Rubbing my eyes, I turn to Tricia, confusion etched on my face.

"Where are we?" I ask, my voice hoarse.

"Brentwood." Tricia grins, mischief dancing in her eyes. She points to what looks like an abandoned restaurant. "Surprise! Jeff pulled through for us. This is our new showroom! I know what you're thinking, and it isn't a problem," she says like it's no big deal. "Jeff can't sell the space. It's been on the market for over a year and he's loaning it to us for four months. And, if we get Trendline on board, we can lease it for a good price. Could be our first retail space." She winks. "I might have an in with the owner."

"It's an abandoned restaurant," I manage to gurgle.

The word "abandoned" echoes in my mind, conjuring up images of decay and neglect. Like my mother. Like my adoptive family. Like everything I don't want to be.

"And it could go through a transformation to make it what we need it to be." Tricia laughs, holding out her arm, pretending she has a magic wand. "Bippity. Boppity. Boo."

Panic floods my entire system. Tricia knows we're struggling, barely getting by with what little cash flow we have. Did she really think this through? Did I? Do I even know how to think anymore?

A cold sweat beads on my forehead. My chest tightens as memories of mounting bills and half-paid invoices flash in my mind. Late nights hunched over spreadsheets, trying to eke out one more sale. Waiting for payments, some of them often late. I swallow hard. The expansion dreams we've discussed feel suddenly reckless, and uncertainty gnaws at my resolve.

I think I lost all of my brain cells in Vegas.

SIXTEEN

CHRISTOPHE

After a sleepless night, I'm still trying to figure out how to get out of the predicament I've put myself in when I turn on the television, finding reporters and paparazzi swarming the Paris Vegas. One reporter, Melissa Barnes, a cute blonde in a short skirt, is front and center, her face serious.

"We're following up with the breaking news we shared last night regarding Franco Vescari's surprising demise. The police have confirmed that the illustrious designer's death was not a suicide, as first speculated, but murder, and they will be questioning all of Vescari's known associates."

A drop of perspiration rolls down my back. Everybody who is anybody saw me with Vescari. The past twenty-four hours have turned into a bona fide nightmare. My fingers shoot to my temples. I'd appreciated Vescari. We were friends. And now we're not. In my head, I say a little prayer: may you rest in peace, wherever you are. You will be missed.

But this is Vegas, and the show must go on.

I'm getting out of the shower when a hard knock rattles the door. "*Oui?*" I say.

An officer's voice, clipped, not an invitation: "Mr. Montclair, we'd like for you to come down to the station."

"Give me a minute. I'm getting dressed."

I hastily throw on a pair of jeans and a black Vince T-shirt and open the door. A gruff officer eyes me up and down. "You don't seem surprised."

"I just saw the news," I explain, lowering my gaze and shaking my head. "Franco was a dear friend of mine." I meet his skeptical gaze. "Is it true what they're saying? He was murdered?"

"According to the coroner's report, that's what we've deduced."

"Can I meet you at the station?" I ask, hopeful.

"No, we'll take you there."

And now I know I'm definitely a person of interest.

"Look," I say, "I'd like to help you out, but can we go out the back? There are so many reporters outside. I'm—"

"We know who you are, Mr. Montclair," he says, his tone terse. "Follow me to the cruiser. It's not out front. It's in the garage."

A half hour later, I'm sweating in a folding metal chair. The interrogation room is an interior-design nightmare—threadbare carpet, flickering fluorescent lights that buzz like dying flies. The heat is oppressive, but I'm doing my best to stay cool, calm, and collected. I sit tall, shoulders back, as an officer slides a lukewarm cup of water toward me, then leaves, slamming the door behind him. A theatrical touch, exit stage left.

Detective Banks arrives—off-the-rack suit two sizes too big, tie askew. He collapses into the opposite chair, leans forward. The smell of cheap cologne and desperation surrounds him. He clears his throat, soft as an accusation. "Mr. Montclair, we understand that you knew the victim, Franco Vescari."

I arch an eyebrow. "Victim?"

"We believe he was murdered," Banks says, as though that solves everything. "Strangled with a neoprene tie, left on the bathroom floor of his hotel room. His body found yesterday afternoon by housekeeping."

I lift my hand to cover a gasp. "I can't believe it," I murmur, each word calibrated. My voice trembles and I give Banks a slow, sorry smile. "I drove him to Vegas, and I was with him the other night—big closing party in his suite at the Bellagio."

"Yes, we know." He taps his pen. "Why didn't he stay at Paris?"

I shrug. "He likes the fountain show and that Italian restaurant."

I'm met with a steely gaze and a grunt.

"He is..." I clear my throat, "was... a great friend of mine. I don't know why you're questioning me."

"I'm questioning everybody." Banks scribbles something down on his notepad. "We have witnesses who saw you arguing with Vescari about money."

A flicker of surprise—just a flicker. We didn't argue about money. We argued about Lexi and what he'd found out about me. I take in a deep breath, let it out slowly.

"He's an investor in my new company. Miracule Skin Care. He was pushing for an early payday. I asked him to wait. He agreed." I shrug, loose and confident. "We parted amicably. But—"

"But what?"

I flex my fingers, choose my strategy of what to say, what not to say. I keep my tone low, conjuring scandal. "Franco had eccentric tastes—particularly with male models."

Banks jots notes, pen tapping like a drum. "And you know this how?"

"He bragged. Ask his circle—they'll confirm."

He eyes me up and down. "You resemble a model. All polished. Stylish clothes. Styled hair. Did you have a relationship with him?"

My upper lip curls. How crass, how insulting. "I did, but it was strictly platonic."

He shifts, eyes flicking to the clock. "What time did you leave the Bellagio?"

"Around one," I say, offhand. "I got married."

His pen freezes mid-tap. "Married?"

I let the confession roll out. "Yes, I was exchanging vows with a wonderful woman."

Banks pinches the bridge of his nose. "Her name?"

"Alexis Marlowe."

I let her name sink in. He's impressed. I am, too. His expression shifts: interest, curiosity, disbelief. "And she was with you all night?"

"She was," I confirm. "We took a limo to the chapel."

His tone cools. "Can she corroborate your timeline?"

I lean in, silhouette framed by that flickering light. "She can."

"I'll need her contact info." Banks leans back in his chair. "Marlowe? That family?"

"The very one. And she'll vouch for my timeline." I let out a soft laugh. "Good luck, detective. If Vescari was murdered, I really hope you find out who did it." I swallow. "He was a good man."

"You can go. Thank you for your time." He rubs his chin. "And until we find out who's responsible you are not to leave the country. Capeesh?"

"Understood."

I stand, pick up my empty cup, and stroll toward the door.

Fuck my life. Vescari's death could mess up all of my plans.

SEVENTEEN

LEXI

Tricia and I have to do our best to turn an abandoned deli that smells like greasy ham and spoiled cheese into a showroom for athletic wear. The buyers from Trendline are set to arrive next week. Regardless of Jeff's crew offering their help, we're getting our hands dirty—literally—and I'm doing my best to push the threatening texts out of my head.

My marriage, if I can even call it that, has gotten off to a very rocky start. I haven't heard from Christophe in over twenty-four hours. He hasn't responded to any of my messages, including the one where I expressed my condolences regarding Vescari. Finally, a text notification chimes in and I almost drop the phone in a can of paint in my rush to grab it.

> Yes, the fashion world is pretty shaken up. I am too. BTW, a detective may call you. They're checking into everybody. Nothing to worry about. I'll see you in a few days, my beautiful wife. Will call when I can. I've been dealing with Vescari's death. Je t'aime.

I reread the words twice, my eyes narrowing in focused disbelief. *Je t'aime?* My fingers grip the phone so tightly I'm afraid I might crack the screen. Tight-lipped, I tuck my phone into my purse. If Tricia adds another question mark against my new husband, his text would turn it into the biggest exclamation point she's ever seen.

And here it comes. She shoots me a disappointed side look. "This whole situation screams disaster. You had your fun," she says. "Kick him to the curb."

"No. Not yet," I reply.

"When?"

"He's connected to the fashion and beauty world. H-he—"

"Lex, you're not the kind of person to marry somebody for their connections." Tricia snorts. "I'm going to run out and grab some Brillo pads." She wrinkles her nose. "We need to scrub the dirt out of our lives."

I pick up on her innuendo. And I don't respond. She throws a sponge into a bucket. "I've had enough for one day. I'm out. You coming?"

"No," I say, scrubbing. "I'm channeling my inner Lady Macbeth."

"At least it's ketchup, not blood." Tricia laughs and pats my back. "I'll see you in the morning."

"I'll probably be here on the floor." I look up at her and grin. "I'm stubborn."

Right after she leaves, my phone vibrates in my pocket, a new call from an unknown number with a Vegas area code flashing on the screen. My heart leaps with cautious optimism, hoping for another interested buyer, someone to take the mountain of inventory off our hands. Perhaps word from Christophe. I wipe my forehead, a bead of sweat threatening to fall into my eye, and answer.

"Hello?"

"Alexis Marlowe?" a gruff voice demands.

Not a buyer. Not Christophe.

"That's me," I reply, trying to keep my voice steady.

"Detective Banks, Las Vegas PD," the voice says. "I'm investigating the murder of Franco Vescari. Christophe Montclair gave me your number. I was hoping you could answer a few questions."

A chill races through me, head to toe. This can't be good. I'd married Christophe in haste and he's connected to a murder investigation, one I'm now a part of. It wasn't supposed to be like this. We're supposed to be synergistic, building our lives, building our brands.

"I-I barely know Vescari," I stammer. "Only met him a few times..."

"Yes, I realize that." He pauses. "I'd just like for you to confirm that you were with Mr. Montclair on Sunday night—between the hours of one and three in the morning."

The question hits like a punch. I draw a breath, trying to sound confident even as doubt eats away at my insides, my brain. "I was with him."

Did I just lie? I don't think I did.

"Did you notice anything unusual? Anybody acting suspiciously at Vescari's party or at the convention?"

I should tell him about Remy and Gilles, how they looked completely scummy and dangerous, how they'd been following Christophe, maybe even me, around, but the words won't form. And they won't until I figure everything out. I don't want to incriminate Christophe.

"Everybody was having a good time," I say. "The usual pomp and circumstance. And, well, I got married."

A long, deliberate pause.

"I understand congratulations are in order." The detective's voice turns smug. "To the happy couple. Thank you for your time. I'll be in touch if I have any more questions. Please don't leave town until we conclude our investigation."

"I live in Los Angeles," I say. "Not Vegas."

"I realize that." He lets out a breath. "Everybody at Vescari's party is being questioned and if we have any more for you or Mr. Montclair, we're expecting complete cooperation. Understand?"

"I do."

The line goes dead, leaving me reeling. Christophe's words—*Je t'aime*—linger in my brain. Love? Or camouflage? I can't tell anymore.

EIGHTEEN
DETECTIVE SAMSON

Six cases sit on my desk, each with their own flavor of misery. A string of garage break-ins in Pacific Palisades; a missing-person file that's almost certainly a runaway; an attempted home invasion where the homeowner shot the perp in the thigh but insists he "aimed to kill, like a real American."

I close my eyes for a moment. I count to ten and exhale, slow and even, the way the department shrink recommended after the last IA interview. It helps, a little, but the irritation is still there—gnawing, low-grade, something like hunger and something like anger.

I'm about to stand and dump my coffee when my personal cell phone vibrates on my desk in angry little spasms, like it's about to have a heart attack. It might. It's old and I should probably get a new one. The screen flashes with a number I don't recognize, but the area code is familiar—702. Vegas. That gets my attention.

I pick up the receiver and press it to my ear, thumb ready to hang up if it's a telemarketer or one of those chain-smoking PIs trying to sell me gossip.

"Samson," I say, voice flat.

"Jesus, Joe, took you long enough to answer," Detective Eddie Banks says, and right away I can hear he's in the bullpen—slot machines in the background. "I figure you old guys are always glued to your phones." He shifts, and now the tone is pure business. Banks is never subtle about the pivot. "You got a minute? I just wrapped Vescari, but you're about to get the gift that keeps on giving."

I sit up, set my feet flat on the floor. "You're handing me a body?"

"Not exactly. More like a couple of walking liabilities. Your jurisdiction, though, so heads up."

He gives me the quick version: He brought Christophe Montclair down to the station for questioning. "I'll say this for him, Montclair—he's a cocky son of a bitch, but smooth. Even with the blood still on his sleeve, he's talking like a guy at a wine tasting." Eddie pauses, probably picturing it, or maybe just reaching for his own mug. "If I ever get clipped, make sure it's by a guy with that much panache."

"Duly noted. So he's your suspect?"

Banks lets that hang a second, then: "Hell if I know. He's got an alibi, but it's Vegas, and the only thing more full of holes than his story is Swiss cheese. I'm not convinced, but it's what I got. Married a woman named Alexis Marlowe that night, said she's from *the* Marlowe family."

I write a note: MONTCLAIR/ MARLOWE—CHECK ALIBIS.

"So what does the girl have to do with this?" I ask.

Banks snorts again. "I did a little digging and there's no way she's related to the Marlowe retail conglomerate. The real name is Alexis Cooper, bounced around from foster home to foster home from the age of thirteen until she was adopted at the age of sixteen by the Marlowes in Miami. Her biological mom, Candace, is doing time in Florida, some ugly business—manslaughter. Shot a guy in cold blood. Plus, the mom has a previous record. Small stuff at first, shoplifting, pickpocketing, but she got creative fast. Bunco, forgery, credit card scams."

"That's your idea of trouble?"

He laughs. "Hell, my idea of trouble is my ex-wife with a credit card. But this is a different animal. Alexis's adoptive parents, the Marlowes, died in a fire, daughters, too. She's not afraid to get her hands dirty. My hunch? She's responsible and they're working together. A perfect match."

I glance at the cold coffee, decide to pass. "So why am I receiving the honor of this call?"

"They're headed your way. She lives in the Hollywood Hills. I flagged your captain. Figured you'd want to greet them personally, given the break-ins and the smiley-face bandit bullshit."

He's not wrong. There's something about the pattern that's been gnawing at me, and the fact that Banks is putting his chips on these two makes it that much more interesting. "You got a case file on them?"

"I'll send over the interviews and security footage we've captured."

"Evidence?"

"None. The rest is mostly speculation and my gut, which, as you know, is substantial." He belches, as if to illustrate the point.

"Motive?"

"Fuck if I know."

"Got it," I say. "Thanks for the tip, Eddie. I owe you."

"Damn right you do. You ever want to win back that hundred, you know where to find me."

I click the call to a close, open a new document, and start typing up my notes: Montclair, Christophe. Marlowe, Alexis (Cooper). Check travel records. Cross with recent 459s. Watch for next move.

New case. New game. I'm already looking forward to the first hand.

NINETEEN
CHRISTOPHE

After dealing with the dick of all detectives, I call an Uber to take me back to the hotel. We pull up into the driveway and the driver's eyes lock onto the fake Eiffel Tower. "Remind you of home?" he asks before I step out of his dusty Ford Fiesta.

"Not really," I reply, and that's the truth.

"Nothing like the real thing. The wife has always wanted to visit Paris." The driver's eyes meet mine. "There are so many reporters. A big celebrity must be arriving. Maybe Beyoncé? My wife loves her."

Apparently, the news of Vescari's death has spread, and I've been doing my best to stay out of photographs unless they are curated by me. This time, however, I face a conundrum. There is no way I can get to the front door without passing the reporters and the paparazzi. It's a real shit show.

"I don't think they're here for Beyoncé," I mumble and then sigh. "Can I buy your hat, sunglasses, and T-shirt?"

His baseball cap is ratty, with the slogan "same shit, different day." The sunglasses are wire framed and could have belonged to Jeffrey Dahmer. And the T-shirt is from one of the strip clubs, The Devil's Lap, and features an image of a stripper performing a lap dance, horns peeking out from behind a round ass.

He pivots to face me. "Are you famous?"

"More like infamous," I reply with a slight laugh. I can't believe what I'm about to do. "Look, I don't want to attract any attention." I pause. The sunglasses I'm wearing are Tom Ford, the T-shirt Vince. "I'll give you my glasses, the shirt off my back, and an excellent tip."

The driver smiles, his eyes lighting up. "Deal."

We swap goods in the back of the Ford. I hand the driver forty dollars and he lets out a small yelp. "Thank you!"

With dread, cringing in what I'm wearing, I step out of the car, slamming the door behind me. Somehow I make it past the throng of cameras, straight to the front door. I'm in desperate need of another shower and then I text Sabrina. She knows the rules because she made them. Apart from public events, we can never be seen together, which works for me.

What are you doing?

Nothing.

Come to my suite?

Give me a half hour.

Freshly showered and changed, I throw my disguise into the garbage bin, wanting to burn it. I'm glancing at the time on my phone when I hear a knock on my door: less than ten minutes late, fashionable even by Sabrina's standards. I brush an imagined speck from my collar, straighten my jacket. I blink and force a smile, pushing the door open.

Sabrina's outfit reeks of privilege, more money than taste. Her garish red lipstick matches her nail polish. Her dark hair is pulled back into an efficient ponytail. She doesn't look at me. I couldn't care less, mostly because she reminds me of my mother and that isn't a good thing.

"I thought we agreed on eight," she says with a dramatic pout. "It's only three in the afternoon."

"Which gives us more time together," I say. "Come on in. I'll order something. Whatever your heart desires."

"I'm in the mood for champagne... and a shrimp cocktail. Maybe some oysters."

I turn and pick up the phone. "Consider it done."

While we wait for room service, Sabrina sits on the sofa, picking up the latest issue of *Fashion Fix Daily*, one of mademoiselle's favorite publications, and strategically placed. She thumbs through the pages, looks up. "Your friend Alexis seems to be getting a lot of press. How do you know her?"

Because we're married. But Sabrina definitely does not need to know this. It would ruin everything. It's time to change the subject. I turn, setting a large bag on the coffee table. She shoots me a suspicious look. "What's this?"

"A little gift, *mon amour*. I feel horrible for putting business before you."

She pulls an enormous leather Celine purse out of the bag and narrows her eyes. "This is gorgeous, but I thought I was part of the business—the face of Miracule."

"You are," I say with a shrug. "Consider it a small token of my appreciation."

"Speaking of tokens," she says, throwing the bag to one side. "When do I get something back on my fifty thousand investment? It's been over a month, and I've heard nothing about it from you."

I hear another knock at the door and raise a finger. "Hold that thought."

After room service leaves, I plop down next to her and pour us glasses of champagne, watching her over the rim. "Sabrina, Sabrina," I say, shaking my head with feigned hurt. "Do you think I'm not going to honor our agreement?"

"You could call me back once in a while. And what were you doing these past few nights that was so important?" Her tone turns from sweet and hurt to accusatory. "And don't tell me it was business."

I consider the question. How much does she suspect? How much does she know?

"I was very tied up," I say.

She slams the magazine down on the table. So predictable.

"What is that supposed to mean?"

It means that I lost my shirt last night. And it means I'm here to redress. I shoot her a grin. "I'm working on a few different angles. Miracule is positioned to blow up. Don't worry. Everything is on track."

"But it isn't. What if Calvin finds out about the money I've invested?" she asks. "You don't know how he gets. This is serious."

"He's having his own fun," I reply. "Besides, he loves your fame too much to care. Wasn't he the one you slept with to get where you are?"

Her eyes flash with indignation. Her mouth, with its alarming crimson, opens and closes as if she's not quite sure how to respond. Like a fish. I want to throw her back into the water and return to Lexi, but I need something from her.

"As for your investment," I say, rescuing her from having to put together a reply. "Testing is in the final stages."

She doesn't look convinced.

"And I need a little more capital," I add.

Sabrina lets out an exasperated breath. She's not used to being asked for anything but favors, and even those are usually requested through publicists and stylists.

"If you could invest another fifty thousand, I can make sure you get your return even quicker. Think of it as making sure the ship doesn't sink."

I watch her calculate. She is good at it—her career, her life— though she would never admit to as much.

"Double down," I say. "You're in Vegas."

"This is crazy," she mutters.

Her hesitation surprises me. She is more anxious than usual, less certain of my intentions. Or, more likely, more aware of her husband's suspicions.

"It will only be a few more months," I say, lifting an eyebrow. "And your husband can just produce another movie if he starts running out of money."

"Christophe..." she begins.

"Sabrina..." I answer, putting the same mix of indulgence and accusation into my voice.

"This is too much," she says. "I don't think I can do this."

"Suit yourself," I say, shrugging like I don't care if she pulls out now. "But it would be unfortunate for you to walk away just as Miracule is on the verge. Everything I've told you is on track. Why do you think I've been so busy?"

She looks out the window, her slender arms crossed in defiance. I can see her fighting the temptation, not wanting to cave so easily this time. But I also see the curiosity there, the way she can't help but be intrigued by my apparent nonchalance.

"Christophe, I—"

"Yes?"

I wait, knowing she will give in. And she does. The sigh escapes her, part exasperation, part submission. Sabrina makes a show of getting up and rummaging through her Birkin bag and then pulls out the money, bound in tight stacks with rubber bands. She thumbs through one of them. "I'm only giving you twenty-five," she finally says, pouting again. "Calvin is going to think I have a serious gambling problem."

"Maybe you do," I say and she smiles. "Come here. Let me thank you properly."

I let her maneuver my shirt over my shoulders. Sabrina gets so caught up in the intrigue of it all that she forgets how frustrated she was only a moment before. She loses herself in the supposed scandal, blind to how easy she makes it for me.

And I don't mind. A great con is a great love affair, and I am skilled at both. I indulge her in this, let her play the vixen and convince herself it's dangerous. My job is to sell the illusion, her job to buy it.

Her history makes it too easy to string her along. She needs my attention more than she needs a return on her investment. As long as Calvin is suspected of his own infidelities, she'll keep coming back. She won't leave him for me, and I wouldn't want her to. I could have gotten the money from him, if I were so inclined. But where would the satisfaction be in that?

"I hate you," she says, leading me to the bedroom.

As Sabrina dozes off, I remember past cons: like when I swindled that shadowy jewelry dealer in Montreal, a name so whispered about in the underground that most wouldn't dare cross me. Getting him was a masterpiece, another feather in my cap. I was only thirteen.

As for Lexi, she's a cut above. Something in that defiant glance and her effortless allure ignites a challenge in me that I can't resist. It's not just a conquest; it's proof of my genius, another notch in what's practically a legend of a career. Funny, the more I think about Lexi, the more I think about turning legit. I chuckle at the thought. Never going to happen.

TWENTY

LEXI

In the morning, the news on *Fashion Fix Daily* definitely catches my attention. Headline: LexICON poised to take over the athleisure market. Which is great. But the text following this blurb has me breaking out in hives: Alexis Marlowe, rumored granddaughter of the Marlowe Co. retail giants, is striding into the apparel market and making a mark on her own.

I can already hear Tricia's response. Telling me not to sweat it, to make the most of it, that all the publicity in the world can't make my ass look any bigger. And she might be right. But there's this other part of me that wants to call up the editor, pin him against the showroom walls, and scream into his eardrums until he prints a retraction.

I race into our temporary space toward Tricia, my mouth dropped open. I'm in the throes of a mild panic attack, breathing heavily. "Have you seen it? The article in *FFD*?"

"So?" Her voice is as calm as ever. "The wrong idea might be the right idea."

"It's not what I've worked for. It's not what they need to know." I don't sound convinced, and she doesn't sound like she cares.

"You are LexICON," she says. "You've got a hot new line. Hotter than my workout trainer in Miami."

"You don't live in Miami. And you don't work out. Stop trying to make me feel better."

"Never."

I know she wants me to laugh. I'd like to laugh, too. But it's hard. Harder than the floors we polished on our hands and knees last night. "What if Trendline thinks this is the way it is? That I'm the granddaughter of *the* Phillip Marlowe?"

Tricia blurts out a harsh laugh. "So what if they do?"

My face pales. What if Christophe thinks I'm one of those people? That would explain why he married me—two dynasties merging. I can't think straight.

"It's not true. They'll think I'm faking everything." It's the same fear I had when I started, when I decided to take this on by myself until Tricia came along. "What if they dig into my past?"

Tricia knows about my upbringing, at least a version of it, and now it's slamming my brain. How my mom taught me everything she knew, including how to sew. How my mom ended up in prison for manslaughter for shooting a man in the head. How, after her arrest, my mom cut off all correspondence with me. How I was shoved from one foster home to the other, how the foster homes blurred together, a series of sterile bedrooms and shared spaces where no one cared about me, but everyone cared about the rules.

Don't talk back. Don't eat too much. Don't expect more than this.

The windows were locked tight, just like my future, just like the past they tried to beat out of me.

The Marlowes—no relation to the retail giants—were supposed to be my big chance when they adopted me. They had what I didn't, what I thought I wanted. The things that would fill the hole she left behind. Their home was big, their bank account bigger, but their hearts were small. They called me their daughter, but I knew better. They treated me like an unpaid servant, like a shiny new toy that lost its luster after the first play. I learned quickly that love was a luxury they didn't offer.

My stitches kept their clothes mended, their other daughters dressed in the latest fashions. I worked hard, worked like I knew how, and they watched with satisfaction. A real Cinderella without the fairy godmother. I sewed the way my mother taught me, turning their castoffs into masterpieces. They never knew what they had. Not in me, not in anything. They scoffed when I told them I wanted to be a fashion designer.

The old familiar feelings wrapped around me like a second skin, tight and unforgiving. The sewing, the stealing, the survival. It was all I knew. All I could do. The Marlowes didn't break me. Not like they thought. Not like I almost let them.

I still remember the moldy scent of the dank basement I'd been "lucky" to live in, sometimes locked in it for days at a time, the panic of missing school; how, like my mother, I'd been imprisoned. How I'd never amount to anything more.

Such a shame the house burnt down with all of them in it. Being the sole survivor, this was how I put myself through school. As for the rest, let's just say there are some secrets that simply aren't meant to come out.

I tug at my hair. "I can't deal with this. Not now."

Tricia, my rock, has no patience for this version of me. "Sweetie," she says, "you built LexICON. What's one silly article going to do? I mean, your past would give the brand more of a story. Think about it. People like underdogs who make it. And the story fits."

I want to believe her. I think I almost do.

I clench my teeth. "I don't want anybody to know what I've been through. I want people to appreciate the products, not me."

"Does Christophe know?"

"He doesn't and I'm not telling him."

"Then that's on you. The truth always has a way of bubbling to the surface."

Every time my phone buzzes, my heart skips. I picture the ominous words "ALEXIS MARLOWE IS A FRAUD" scrawled in neon on a brick wall. I force myself to inhale deeply, reminding myself that I've survived worse battles. I can do this.

Tricia has taken to wearing a protective mask, but the scent of moldy bread hangs in the air and clings to everything like a bad reputation. For the past two days we've been attacking this dump with all the resolve of a cleaning commercial—using very aggressive chemicals. That's why we're both wearing two pairs of gloves and surgical masks, our eyes watering like we've just sliced a thousand onions. My scalp itches under the disposable cap I've tied over my ponytail; I wonder if it's sweat or shame clawing at my skin.

"I swear," Tricia says, scrubbing a patch of tile that refuses to turn white, "if I die from toxic chemical poisoning, you'll feel real bad."

She jabs the grout with an orange-bristled brush, her tone both accusatory and half-joking.

"If we don't get this done, I'll die of shame." I press a smudge with my thumb; it splits into three smaller smudges as if mocking me. I swallow the urge to curse. "And this was your idea."

"Let me just hire a crew to help us," she pleads, voice softening.

It's true she'd rather be home, sipping cocktails by the pool. Or anywhere with air-conditioning, cleanliness, and pool boys. But she's here—day two—and staying longer than any best friend or business partner should. Guilt nags at me: maybe I'm too harsh, maybe I'm driving her away. But I need her grit, her optimism. I can't do this alone.

"With whose money?"

"Mine."

"No," I say, lifting my chin. "You know how I feel about that."

In the back of my mind, I tally last month's credit-card bills: marketing; our manufacturers in Thailand, Turkey, Cambodia; and shipping. The numbers swim in my head like disapproving accountants. I can't let Tricia bleed out her savings.

"Fine. Beggars can't be choosers. Are you going to continue

working or just let buyers think yellow is the new white?" she says, shooting me a grin that usually turns me to jelly.

"This will get done," I promise, though my shoulders are sore from scrubbing. I feel the ache in my forearms as a reminder: I'm in over my head.

Tricia paces across the uneven floor and nods, not convinced. I'm not sure I am either. A bead of sweat drips into my eye. I blink it away with my sleeve—mask meet mold.

She spins a bottle of expensive cleaner, then rolls her eyes. "I've been with you since the beginning. And I believe in LexI-CON." She eyes the glass deli counter. "I know you're marketing, but I have an idea."

I brace for a sales pitch. She grins and points. "We use that counter as a display case. Roll up the sports bras and T-shirts in neat little rows." She taps her chin. "An old deli really doesn't give off health vibes, but a juice bar would. All we need is some fresh fruit in baskets and bursts of green with wheatgrass plants. What do you think?"

Her idea gives me a hit of adrenaline. I love the way she's thinking. I smile, surprising myself. Here she is—dust in her usually coiffed hair—staying as long as I am. And longer if I let her. I wrap her in a tight hug, masking my relief. "I love you, Trix."

She winks. "I know you do."

We take a break, opening another round of sanitized gel and a couple of waters. My throat is sore from talking over the hum of the extractor fan, and my lungs feel coated in chemical residue. My mind drifts: our first trunk show—the one that nearly sank us. The investor who ghosted. A voice telling me I'd never last in retail. I shut them all out. Not now.

Tricia wipes her forehead with the back of her hand, peering skyward as if planning an escape to the Bahamas. She shrugs, looks around the room, and sizes it up. I tap my foot impatiently. So much to do, so little time.

She hangs our banner from Style Sphere behind the counter. It still looks sad, sagging in one corner. "It looks good! Doesn't it?"

"It looks fabulous," I lie, picturing the banner tearing in my subconscious, the letters sliding off like shaky confidence.

"Look at you, always thinking like a million bucks," Tricia says, nodding. Her faith in me is both comforting and terrifying.

"Shouldn't I?" I force a smile. "I've got Tricia Hoffman as my partner."

I run through the list in my head: paint tomorrow—bright, clean, vibrant. Floor the next day—light wood, easy to sweep out dust and doubt. Mannequins, racks, inventory, lighting, signage, press kits, mood playlists. Enough neon to outshine the *FFD* article and those threatening texts. I sip my water, clamp down on the dread, and get back to work.

TWENTY-ONE
CHRISTOPHE

Moonlight is sneaking through the hotel's drapes when I pull on my pants and ease my shirt over my shoulders. I feel the fabric slide across my skin, and a cold thrill races through me—part satisfaction, part disgust. Sabrina was still sleeping when I slipped out of bed, her narrow form curled beneath the comforter, leaving my side as empty as she is. Her face, peaceful in slumber, makes me wince. I'm disgusted by how little she knows—by how easily I've used her. My thoughts aren't on her as I dress, fastening each button with calm precision. No, they're on the vanity, where a stack of jewelry waits like unpaid rent: careless, gleaming, familiar.

I half smile at my own audacity. Pride swells in my chest—an arrogant balloon rising behind my ribs. Everything about this morning reeks of cheap theatrics: the gaudy suite, the piled-on gifts, her oblivion. Yet in that stink I find fuel. I pad to the vanity and pause, looking at the ring again. It's as ostentatious as the room, a vulgar rock set off by platinum and Sabrina's delusions. Calvin spent a quarter-million on that diamond. He probably spent more on his conscience—if he has one. My lips curl. What else do you buy the woman who has everything and suspects just as much?

I can't help a pulse of smug pride at how simple this has been. I could sell it here in Vegas, pocket the cash before I hit LA. Or I could save it, let it simmer—have it for later leverage. The power of choice reminds me how superior I feel, how carefully I've orchestrated every step.

I slide the ring into my pocket. Too easy. My pulse flutters with a thrill that still feels dangerously close to joy. I should almost feel guilty about the satisfaction this brings me, but guilt smells like weakness. Disgust would be more accurate: disgust at her vanity, at myself for enjoying it so much. But pride drowns out even that. I leave Sabrina a note and check out. Everything is going according to plan.

Before I leave Vegas, I have one last issue to take care of. I send Remy a message.

> The Moulin Rouge Hotel. Abandoned lot. 900 W Bonanza Road 4 am. Have your $.

I pocket the phone and finish my drink, the ice long since melted. By four a.m. the strip will be sleeping off its sins, but I won't. I'll be there, watching the dark corners, wondering if Remy and Gilles will show... and what I'm going to do when they do.

I'm barely ten miles out of Vegas when the phone lights up, ringing insistently from my pocket. The road hums beneath the tires, a steady rhythm that drowns out the urgent trill. I have Vescari's money to thank for the Maserati. Perhaps it was an exorbitant expense, and one I could have held off on, but I love this car. I let the call go to voicemail, watching the strip's garish lights fade in the rearview mirror. I don't need to check the caller ID to know who it is. She's noticed. Faster than I expected, but still too late for her. I'm already halfway to the interstate.

When the second call comes, then a third, I feel that familiar purr of triumph. The screen pulses, insistent. My smugness surges, as if I've won a ridiculous prize at the carnival I call life. Something enormous and pointless—like the stuffed bear I won for Lexi on the pier. My only regret is that I wasn't there to see the exact moment when Sabrina realized her little treasure had gone missing. I wait a while before listening to the messages, half to stretch out the cruelty, half because I'm savoring the distance growing between us. At a gas station thirty miles out, I finally check in. Her panicked breaths crackle through the speaker. They amuse me more than they should.

The first one is measured, still controlled: "Christophe," she says, flat and brittle. "My ring is missing! Call me."

By the second, her composure is crumbling: "Christophe. This is not funny. I swear to God if you don't call me back…"

A fourth voicemail pops up as I merge onto the highway. I pull over at a hot, anonymous parking lot on the outskirts of nowhere. I don't care that it's far from shade. I'm too busy basking in my own cleverness. I hit play.

"For fuck's sake, Christophe. Calvin is going to notice my ring is not on my finger. I already lost my tennis bracelet. You have to help me!"

She's frantic now, and that makes it all the more satisfying. The messages grow more absurd, more melodramatic by the mile. I laugh, a low chuckle that surprises me—am I really this amused by her misery? I catch my reflection in the windshield: my mouth stretched into a smirk I almost don't recognize.

The phone rings again. I watch it, knowing she's counting on me to stay tethered. Waiting for the inevitable click as she hangs up and tries again. If it wasn't so pathetic, it might even be endearing. But I'm observing her persistence with cold fascination.

Finally, I answer, letting my voice carry a note of irritation: "Hello, Sabrina."

Her explosion of rage is as sweet as I anticipated. "You bastard!" she screams. "What have you done? You took my ring!"

"Relax," I say, my tone silky. I'm reveling in the sound of her panic. "I'm sure it just fell off somewhere. Or maybe the cleaning lady took it. I sure as hell didn't. Look around."

"We didn't have maid service."

"We did have room service."

"Calvin will kill me," she wails.

I wish I had earplugs.

"Calvin will not even notice," I reply, already scrolling to block her number. "I'm pulling into LA now. By the way, I gave you a late check-out. You can thank me later."

I click the line to a close.

I know I'll get a dozen texts by the time I reach Lexi's in the Hollywood Hills. A true drama queen, Sabrina will only see the thrill and none of the danger. She'll believe what she wants until the world crumbles beneath her heels. She'll talk herself back into this, I'm sure of it. My new wife, though—she may not be so willing. I've got to get my story straight.

On the outskirts of Los Angeles, I pull the Maserati over at a deserted gas station. I close my eyes and see my past. Weak. Pitiful. I open my eyes. Christophe now wrapped in silk sheets and expensive cologne. Confidence with a French accent. I laugh at the difference.

I am Christophe. I am something. I am light years away from the past, from being a scrawny boy with too many expectations and not enough nerve. But I can still see everything in the back of my mind. I hear it in my mother's sighs. I was never who she wanted. I was a failure. I was a ghost. But I am not him anymore.

I change my shirt, pulling on a rich white cotton that feels like Christophe. A luxury. The kind I never had back then. I know who I am, who I want to be. The boy I was in my past never did. The kid who wanted it all, who got nothing. I'm so much more than he ever was, more than he dreamed he could be. More than anyone dreamed I could be.

My past keeps me sharp. Keeps me going. Keeps me above them all.

TWENTY-TWO

CHRISTOPHE

Then

It is the cold I remember first, my breath a traitor in the alley, puffing clouds of fear, of weakness, of resolve. I only have this one moment to prove myself to the crew.

"He'll never do it," one of them laughs.

"It's a big job," says another. "Too big for him."

I don't look at them, don't listen to their taunts. I look at the lock. I take out the picks, take out the doubt, take out the fear I can't let them see. I remember the training. The technique. The lock clicks open.

The crew takes the jewels, and I take my place among them. I am in.

"Not bad, kid," Remy says, his voice gruff with approval. His hand on my shoulder is like the wind, thrilling me, claiming me.

I am in. I am thirteen. I am already more than they know.

I still hear them. Their laughter. Their oblivion. The acrid smoke that drowns me in stale dreams. A basement apartment with walls like old yellow teeth. My mind moves quickly. Quicker than the drugs they shoot into their arms. The other boys nod off, and I nod to myself. Counting the jewels. Counting my options.

"Where'd you get that eye?" Gilles asks. I don't answer. I don't know. It came from fear, from need, from wanting to be more than them. "You're not like the rest," he says. I almost believe him.

I look at the diamonds, the rubies, the precious objects, focused. That's why I'm better. That's why I don't lose myself in drugs. I am never as high as them. But I am. I am high on being better, being smarter, being what no one expected.

The dim bulb flickers above. The jewels flash below, a brighter reminder of our nights. I count the spoils, my mind quick and calculating. The cuts, the clarity, the worth. They sing to me, call to me, tell me I am not like them. I don't mind.

They think they have the life. Needles in their arms. The room spins. Not me. I watch it all, and it excites me, it bores me.

"Did you find the fake?" Gilles asks. He's smarter, sharper, older.

"Not yet," I say. But I will.

The other boys sink into the yellowed couch. I sink into myself, into the numbers, into my own desire. I see things they don't, the shine, the beauty, the danger. I see it all. They see what they want.

Gilles comes close, so close I smell the cigarettes on his breath. "You've got a talent," he says.

I do. I know I do. It's a talent they never saw coming. It's a talent they'll never take from me.

I am learning fast, faster than I thought I could. Faster than they thought I could. I feel the thrill of being good at this, of being better, of being the best.

"The blue one," I say. "It's a perfect fake."

They stare at me, stare at the diamond. It is a good feeling, their eyes on me.

Gilles laughs, a sound more real than anything else I've heard.

"This is going to pay off." He sounds surprised. But not me.

The stones don't lie. The cuts are clear, sharp, brilliant. I see them for what they are. I always do.

· · ·

My mind races. My body doesn't. I am locked in, locked away. I didn't think they'd catch us. I didn't think I'd be caught. Juvenile detention. The name feels like failure. Stark white walls. Clanging metal doors. The routine. It grates on my nerves, but it won't break me. I'm not hopeless. I am sharp, clever. I have to be. I have to find a way. I will find a way. I've played it before. I'm the best at it.

"New kid thinks he's something," they say.

I am. I know I am. But I say nothing.

I am biding my time. Waiting for the moment I see it. The strict routine doesn't crush me. It teaches me. I am learning. I am smart, smarter than they think.

A kid with no future, they say, but one guard doesn't see that and he takes me under his wing. He teaches me, doesn't know I'm teaching myself. Doesn't know I'm playing him, the way I play the system, the way I will play them all.

"Keep this up," he says, "and you might turn out okay."

I am Christophe. I am something. And I will be more.

TWENTY-THREE

LEXI

In the morning, my phone buzzes with an onslaught of alerts, comments, and emails. I glance at a few before I close the app. I clear a space on the cluttered conference table—a large circular booth in the back—pull out a pencil, and start writing plans, arrows, circles, anything that will remind me of how far I've come. How much I've done. I work until I hear that voice in my head I keep expecting from Tricia. But it's not her. It's from the past. It's my mom.

People will believe what they want to believe. Don't let anybody break you.

I swallow. My mom refuses to see me or even take my calls. Her actions have left me broken and, over the years, I've been trying to put the pieces of my life back together. Put my heart back together.

With all the work I've been doing for LexICON—and although we text and talk—Christophe has been on the periphery of my thoughts. Out of sight, out of mind. I'm in the middle of making final adjustments to our makeshift showroom when I receive a text.

Can't wait to see you, mon amour. Should be at
your place in a couple of hours.

My teeth clench together and my stomach turns. I've been putting off the inevitable, part of me hoping he may not show up.

I tap Tricia's shoulder. "Christophe's on his way. I've got to go."

A mind reader, Tricia gives me a tight grin. "Lock the door. Batten down the hatches. Don't let him in."

"You're not funny." I shoot her a mock glare. "I told you that I want to see where this goes."

"And I told you. You're on a road to nowhere." She crosses her arms over her chest. "You haven't even mentioned his name in two days."

"We've been busy. I have priorities."

She clucks her tongue. "Go. Just keep me updated—constantly. I don't want to read about your murder in the morning."

I startle, thinking about the cryptic texts I've been receiving. "Again. Not funny."

"Just keeping it real." She lifts up her chin. "And you should, too. I want to run a background check on him. Get me his social security number."

"He doesn't have one. He's French."

"Right." She shoots me a tight grin. "Maybe he married you so he could get a green card."

Or maybe like *Fashion Fix Daily*, he thinks I'm somebody that I'm not.

Back at my apartment, I'm waiting for Christophe's imminent arrival, nervous. What's it going to be like when I see him again? After setting out some light snacks—an apéro of charcuterie, cheeses, veggies, and olives, the French version of an appetizer course, the word for which I've looked up—and drinks, I'm sitting on the couch, wringing my hands, tempted to tell him about my past, but I need to hear more about his first. He knocks on the door. I let him in. He wraps his arms around me, his hands moving down my back to my ass. "I've missed you so much, *ma chérie*. Shall we pick up where we left off?"

I place a hand on his chest, pushing him away, and force a smile. "I put a lot of time and energy into this." I'm lying. I picked up everything at Trader Joe's on the way home from the showroom. I wave my hand to the coffee table and then narrow my eyes. "Where are your things?"

"In the car." He moves in for a kiss. "I'll get them later."

"Later," I say and he blinks. "We have plenty of time for that. Let's talk. Take a seat."

And so we do, sitting on the couch, knees almost touching. I survey his face—cool, calm, and collected as always. "How did Vegas turn out for you?"

He sighs and pours us wine. "*Formidable*, but I'm still a bit shaken up over Vescari's death."

I nod, even though he doesn't look upset at all. His hands don't even shake as he offers me a glass. "*Santé*," he says. "Everybody is talking about LexICON and you—making the American dream come true."

We clink our glasses together. I now have my opening.

"So you're really connected to the Montclair dynasty," I prod, wondering if he'll be candid. "And you're doing everything on your own? Like I am? Building from the ground up. Blood. Sweat. And tears?"

He shrugs with calculated elegance. "Yes, I wanted to see if I could build a company on my own merits. And that part of my life is complicated."

He's not wrong about that. The Montclair empire is both storied and shrouded, with rumors as varied as their product lines. They are a media-savvy dynasty with a ruthless business strategy and tend to stay out of the limelight regardless of all the scandals chasing them down.

"You mean there isn't a guidebook for being born into privi-lege?" I tease, even though a part of me really is curious about what he's after. About how deep his charm runs, whether it's skin or artery deep.

"Ah, but each chapter is a revelation," he counters, the twinkle in his eyes like he's letting me in on some grand inside joke. Or trying to.

I like to think I'm a good judge of character. So far, he fits the profile of men I've avoided in the past. But something about him is different. He wants something, and I'm not sure if that's a good thing or if it could be catastrophic.

I need more information. "I googled you. Found nothing."

He laughs. "The press are obsessed with my mother, not the black sheep."

"Let me guess," I say, "you're here to make me an offer I can't refuse? Do you need a green card?"

"So, that's where this attitude is coming from. I received my citizenship years ago. And I know you're thinking we should get an annulment."

I take a sip of my wine. "That would be the sanest thing to do."

His smile returns, cooler this time. "I was having my doubts as much as you," he says, pulling me closer. "But now that I see you, I know for certain that I—we—didn't make a mistake. We're a great match, *n'est-ce pas?*"

He's too smooth. "Are we?"

Without missing a beat, he pulls out a Cartier box from his jacket pocket. He opens the box with practiced precision, with the same confidence he opens car doors or conversations or champagne bottles.

"When I saw it, I thought of you," he says, and before I can say another word, before I can take another breath, the jewelry slips onto my finger, as extravagant and unreasonable as anything I've ever seen. It's the kind of ring you only see in magazines, where it's just a story, just a fantasy.

"Wait…" I say, but he doesn't.

I want to say that he shouldn't have. I want to tell him about the menacing texts I've received. I want to tell him what I really think. That this is too much. But I don't. All I say is, "Thank you. It's beautiful."

"We should probably plan our honeymoon," he says, stroking my back. "Anywhere you'd like to go."

This can't be real. He can't be real. My eyes light up. "Paris. I've never been there. And I could meet your family."

"You'd take back that wish if you ever meet them." He grimaces and his eyes dart to the side. "I was thinking more along the lines of someplace tropical, a vacation of dreams. Like the Maldives."

The warning bells inside my head are ringing. Something is off. "Okay. First Paris and then the Maldives. Sounds like a dream to me."

"Sounds perfect," he says, frowning. "I'll book the tickets once I settle in."

I don't know if I'm going to push him away with my next idea, but it's a risk I'm willing to take. I'm going to find out if he's truly into me or just spinning a yarn. Plus, sex has been a distraction, clouding my judgment. I need to keep my wits about me.

"I moved my office—the sewing machine, the art desk, the fabric swatches—to the showroom." I raise my shoulders into a shrug. "The trundle bed-couch is full-sized. Comfy mattress. Fit for a king. I'll show you to your room."

He blinks. "You mean our room."

"No, I mean *your* room. Until we figure out where things are headed with us, we're rewinding time."

We leave the drinks behind, half-finished, on the coffee table.

It's late. Or it's early. I get up and wander, thinking Christophe's in it for the long haul. Thinking maybe I'm wrong. I watch him while he sleeps. He is artfully relaxed. Practiced and polished. He is out of this world beautiful.

I don't know what has come over me. Maybe I just want to know he's real, that this is real and not something I've conjured up in my imagination. I lie down and press against him, my hand on his shoulder. It is the most grounded I've felt for years, the most settled. I finally drift off. When I wake up, I'm holding his pillow.

Not him.

I grab my phone, taking it off silent mode and a volley of texts comes in.

> Didn't want to wake you. Had an early meeting.
> Will call later, mon amour.

> Need address for your showroom. Have a
> package being delivered for Miracule.

> Taking you out on the town tonight. Wear
> something sexy. A dress. Heels. There are people I
> want you to meet.

These texts would be normal if they weren't sent one after the other—and if he wasn't telling me how to dress or assuming he could use my showroom for his business. Using me. I've always relied on my gut instincts. I've seen a flicker of something darker in Christophe and I know something about him is off—way off.

I'll see if I can learn what he's up to, find out what he really wants. What his plans are for me. I'll see how much he thinks he's ahead. See how much I can stay ahead of him.

TWENTY-FOUR
DETECTIVE SAMSON

I've always loved the view from the Hollywood Hills. Morning, the city still squinting into itself, nobody at their best. I'm two hours into my stakeout on a residential street that smells like fake lemons and grass clippings, my coffee cooling against my thigh.

My eyes are on unit one hundred and six, lower floor, blinds askew and curtains drawn. I'm here for Alexis Marlowe—née Cooper—who has a thing for athleisure, sugar-free Monster, and, if the department's informant can be trusted, building her brand, LexICON.

Christophe Montclair—they say he's a big deal in Paris, or at least he wants people to think so—steps out of her apartment at quarter past seven, heading to a silver Maserati. He's just another ghost in a luxury wrapper, floating from fake meeting to fake meeting, selling a dream nobody asked for. I watch him glide from the unit with a smoothness you can't fake—Italian shoes, wrist flashing some dubious platinum. He gets in and pulls off with zero urgency. Whatever he's into, it doesn't require speed.

Banks is right. He's an asshole. I let him go. My hunch is on Alexis, and right now, Christophe is just background noise. A pretty piece of furniture who doesn't know he's about to be repo'd. I sip my coffee, thinking about the case notes. Alexis is a person of interest because she's the last person to be seen with Vescari. And her biological mother is a piece of work.

At twenty past eight, Alexis emerges. No make-up, hair tied up, gym bag over her shoulder, her jaw set. There's a restlessness in the way she adjusts her leggings—like even her own skin isn't fitting today. She locks the door without looking back. Her hands shake when she drops the keys into her tote.

I log her steps: six paces to the curb, two to the white Jeep, a pause to scan the street. She spots the Impala and squints, but I'm behind the paper, classic as hell. She slides into her Jeep and waits a full minute before firing it up. That's smart; make the tail think you're not leaving, or you are, but only after you've made sure you're not being followed. I'm almost impressed.

The Jeep rumbles to life and idles. I keep my head low, pretending to read the comics. She checks her mirrors twice, then pulls out slow. I give her a full car length and merge into the stream. We crawl through the school zone, past desperate nannies and retirees with small dogs, then pick up speed on San Vicente. I let her get ahead, just enough to lose me if she tries. She doesn't. She drives like someone who's used to being watched, or at least like someone who knows the rules of this particular game.

The route makes sense: left on Bundy, a right at Wilshire, another left at Barrington. Apartment blocks and homes rise and fall in monotonous rhythm. She turns into the parking lot of a strip mall in Brentwood—yoga studio, overpriced juice bar, an independent coffee shop (tempting), and a nail salon with a sign that hasn't been changed since 2008. The Jeep parks, engine off, and she sits there for a good five minutes, hands on the wheel, not moving. I wait. Eventually, she gets out, shouldering her bag like it weighs her down, and heads for the unit at the far end.

I stay in the car, let her get inside, and count down from fifty. I'm not going to burst in. Not yet. I want to see who shows up, who else comes and goes. But I'm not expecting a crowd. In this part of town, these are the hours where everyone is supposed to be doing something productive, or at least posting about it.

The question is, does she know I'm onto her?

I finish the coffee. It's bitter, but the city's gotten warm and I can almost taste the morning's possibilities. In my line of work, it's always about the next move. But sometimes, you just have to wait and watch—see if the girl from unit one hundred and six is the apple or the tree—the product of her mother.

The way the morning sun hits the strip-mall glass, you can see every careless handprint, every dried spit of rain. She's scrubbing away at a breakfast bar—her MacBook's open, but she's not looking at it. When she sees me, her face is a clean white sheet. Not scared, but not ready. "Can I help you?" she asks, voice hoarse, like she's already been up for hours. "This isn't a store. It's a showroom."

I give her the smile that's gotten me punched twice and promoted once. "Detective Samson. I'm here to talk about Franco Vescari."

She blinks, slow. "Of course." She gestures to one of the tables. "Take a seat," she says. "Sorry if the chairs are a bit wobbly. This isn't a restaurant either. It's our temporary showroom." She gestures toward the back of the room. "We can sit in a booth if you like?"

"It's fine here."

I sit and she nods, taking a seat across from me. "I already told the other detective in Vegas, Banks, I didn't know Vescari well. I only met him a few times. But I liked him."

I wait, but she doesn't elaborate. "You don't seem upset about his murder," I say.

She looks away, toward a row of rolled yoga mats stacked like rifles. "I haven't cried in years."

"Since your mother got arrested."

She lifts her chin, something fierce in her gaze. "You know about that?"

"I do."

"My records are sealed."

"Law enforcement can unseal them with cause."

She runs her fingers around the rim of her water bottle, not drinking. "When you see your mother taken away when you're only thirteen years old, and you bounce from foster home to foster home, your tear ducts kind of dry up."

I let that hang and don't press on. From the way her jaw is set the questions would be futile, and I'm not here to talk about her mother. "You spoke to Vescari at the Style Sphere show last week." I flip my phone and show her the security still—her and Vescari, mid-conversation. She's looking up at him, something urgent in her eyes.

"Yeah," she says, "I remember that."

"You look upset."

She nods, then—very carefully—shakes her head. "I don't know. I think he was warning me."

"Warning you about what?"

She looks at the floor, then at me, her gaze meeting mine. "Christophe. My husband."

"Montclair?"

"That's right."

I drum the table with my pen. "How long have you been married?" I ask, even though I already know.

"Two days. Maybe three. I've been so busy"—she waves a hand at the space—"trying to get this set up. I've lost track of time."

"And how long have you known him?"

"One month. I know it's quick." She closes her eyes, collecting the pieces. "I was drunk. Buzzed on margaritas. I hadn't eaten. There was a wedding chapel, and, well, shit happens in Vegas."

"Romantic."

She laughs, for real this time. "Not really. We were married by a drag queen, and our witness was Elvis."

I shift forward in my chair. "What was Montclair's relationship to Vescari?"

"They were friends. Business, mostly. Vescari invested in Christophe's company."

"What's the company?"

Alexis pulls her knees up to her chest, hugging them. "It's a skincare line called Miracule. Not my thing. I'm more into performance wear." She looks right at me, not blinking. "I don't know what you want me to say."

"I want you to say you didn't kill Vescari."

She rolls her eyes. "I didn't. From what I knew of him, I really liked him. He offered to be my mentor, introduced me to people."

I nod. "You ever see Christophe angry?"

She hugs her knees tighter. "He yells a lot. At people on the phone, but never at me."

"Who else invested in his company?"

Alexis shrugs. "The only person I know of for sure is Sabrina Vale."

"The actress?"

"She wants to be the brand ambassador for LexICON, told me Christophe gave her the idea."

"Takes her acting very seriously." My brain tingles. "You know she has a black belt in Krav Maga?"

She almost smiles. "I didn't. Funny, so do I."

Interesting. I jot that down and close the notebook, gently. "I think we're done here."

Alexis stands, shaky. "Is that it?"

"For now."

She follows me to the door, standing in the threshold. The sun hits her face and she squints hard.

I pause on the way out, handing her my card. "If you think of anything else, call me."

I get back in the Impala. I look through the glass at her. She just stands, frozen, staring at the horizon like she's waiting for it to blink first. Even though she's implicated two other people—a sign of guilt—I know I've started this investigation with the wrong person. She looked me in the eyes, leaned forward instead of leaning back, and only looked startled when I brought up her mother. And I understand that. Banks is wrong with his hunch. I'm going to trust mine. I should be taking a closer look at Christophe Montclair and Sabrina Vale.

ACT TWO

"The most courageous act is still to think for yourself. Aloud."

~ Coco Chanel

TWENTY-FIVE
CHRISTOPHE

Lexi is not acting like the woman I've spent over one month with, the woman I'd married. And, honestly, I think I'm truly falling for this version of her. In a way, she reminds me of myself, turning the tables. Catching me off guard. It's a new feeling, a different kind of thrill.

I woke up this morning, surprised to find her next to me. I'd also woken up to at least fifty texts on one of my phones. No surprise as to whom they're from. Sabrina. They wait for me, these little missives, urgent and furious in their digital repose. I make my way to the kitchen, open up the cabinets looking for coffee capsules for the Nespresso machine. Everything is so organized it's kind of alarming. Part of me wants to rearrange everything, but I don't because I like order, too, and I see how much Lexi and I have in common. Instead, I finally look at my phone.

> The bastard found my bank statements, scared he'll ruin me, ruin you. Meet ASAP.

With each message, the pulse of the phone is regular, a calculated heartbeat that demands attention—more than my recent bride.

> Our cottage at Château Marmont. Please,
> Christophe. I need my money. He'll come
> after you.

Dozens of messages, and only now a real threat.

Her absurdity only adds to the entertainment. I ignore the latest round, debating my own options, trying to see where my game leaves me if I don't answer her call. Does Sabrina have enough at stake to out me? Would she go that far? I suspect not, but even so, I would be a fool not to consider the possibility.

Coffee will have to wait. I get dressed, kiss Lexi on the forehead before leaving. She doesn't stir, just lets out a small groan. I write her a quick note, leaving it by her side, and then I make my way to my beautiful car. Sleek and smooth, I run my hand over the hood, thinking Vescari's investment, among others, definitely paid off. He'd served his purpose, giving me credibility and, well, money; now he's gone. Lost in a world of glitter and chaos, nobody even noticed until it was too late.

Lexi and I should move to a place with a parking garage and security. I hold back a laugh. With the way things are going, I don't know how long Lexi and I are going to last. I'll have to start small with her and then see what the future brings. Part of me thinks I can be happy with her—happy enough.

The phone buzzes again. She's like a wasp, an annoying one I'd really like to swat. I do not slow down. Not yet. By the time I make it onto Sunset Boulevard, my phone has vibrated onto the floor.

I pull the Maserati in front of Château Marmont, jump out, throwing my keys to the valet. Sabrina's notifications hound me to the lobby. Perhaps I have underestimated her, or underestimated myself. The thought pleases me, makes me bold enough to imagine all the other things I might be wrong about.

A slight smirk creeps onto my lips as I read the latest volley:

> He's furious, Christophe. He'll kill me if he finds
> out about the investments. And he'll kill you.

Her flair for drama is rivaled only by her husband's for directing it. Her pride must be more damaged than she is letting on. Or maybe less, but with Sabrina it is always a contest of superficialities. Like the fact nobody can tell she has eyelash and hair extensions.

It is a brilliant piece of theatrics, but over-acted, if I say so myself.

I walk toward the cottage with measured confidence, with the kind of calm that tells even the greenest receptionist that my business here must remain private. Estranged lover. Important guest. All the same in a place like this, really. What was it somebody told me once? That I love the game more than the girl. Perhaps, but the girl certainly helps. Women can be troublesome, and I have to double up the charm, find out their weak points, their desires.

I knock once, slowly and with deliberation, and then I open the door. She looks at me, eyes wide and accusing, like she can't believe I really showed up.

If this is an act, she's putting her entire body into the role.

She is a spectacle, like a parade float that has run its course and now waits to be dismantled. I've never seen her so undone. Her clothes and hair and even her confidence lie scattered around the suite, shreds of dignity mixed with piles of couture and credenza. I could almost feel sorry for her, except I'm not quite sure how much of this is real. The mascara adds to the effect, creates an aura of perfect chaos around her. But I know Sabrina. I know what she wants me to see. Her feigned vulnerability is almost beautiful, and I allow myself to admire it as she grabs my arm and pulls me into the room.

"Christophe," she says, "he knows."

I hold back my smile. I let a mask of concern drift over my features. "What does he know?"

Sabrina shoots me a look. She is confused by my calm, wonders if I'm foolish or clever or both. It is almost enough to stop her monologue, but not quite.

"Everything," she cries. "He found the bank statements. He found the receipts."

"What statements?"

"Don't do this," she says. "Not now."

"Then tell me, *ma chérie*. What is going on?"

It comes tumbling out, her tragic and hilarious tale. "My ring! I told him there was a chip in the ring, that I'm having it fixed. He doesn't believe me. He's threatening to divorce me." The words spill out, each one getting away from her a little faster than the last. "I think he knows about us and his lawyers will destroy me and not only that, my career." Her voice breaks, not once, but several times. "You took the ring, didn't you?"

"I didn't."

I did.

Sabrina collapses onto the sofa. Her legs curl beneath her, like they won't support her anymore, like they're props and not real.

"Relax," I tell her. "Everything will be fine."

She narrows her eyes, distrustful and hopeful. "Fine—if I get the money back I've loaned you."

I shrug, looking around the room. "It's tied up. Already spent. And it wasn't a loan, it was an investment. You have a copy of the contract. Read over the terms."

Her mouth forms a small 'o' of fear and disbelief. The silence grows large enough to fill the suite. Then she shatters it with a dramatic sigh. "You have to fix this," she pleads. "Tell him it was business. Tell him it was anything but what it is." She grabs my arm with more strength than I would expect. I pretend to wince, just to let her think she's gotten to me.

"Tell him about our investment plan," she continues.

If she wants to hang on, she'll have to let go of me first. I free myself from her grip and head to the bar. The contents are exactly what I'd expect in a place like this—too many choices, none of them as exclusive as they pretend to be. I pour a glass of Scotch, needing to drown out her whining.

"He saw our messages," she says. "He knows I was meeting you."

"What messages?"

"Our texts. From last week. He knows you were in Vegas."

"It's not that serious," I say, sipping my drink. "It never is."

She bites her lip, unsure if she believes me, unsure if she should. "He thinks I gave you the ring," she says. Her voice drops, becomes almost a whisper. "He thinks I gave you the bracelet."

Right. The tennis bracelet I'd lifted the last time we'd been here.

I let her watch me as I weigh the options. I could end this now, step away from the whole mess and focus my attention on Lexi, on the new life I've begun. On the next round of targets. Or I could keep her in my pocket a little longer, get what I can before her insecurity explodes into a final, fabulous catastrophe. I have made enough from her meager investments to consider walking away. Enough, but not so much that I won't consider one last dividend. She needs me to help her, to fix her, to rescue her.

"Set up a meeting," I say.

"With who?"

"Calvin," I say. "I'll tell him all about Miracule. And your investment."

"What about the ring?" she sniffles. "What do I do?"

"You should really be more careful with your things." My patience is wearing thin. I look at my watch. "I've got to go. Things are moving forward with Miracule. And you'll see your money back soon—and a lot more of it."

"But—"

"Just set up a meeting with Calvin. I'll explain everything—how we're launching a brand together and that you are going to be the face of the company."

That last statement got her—hook, line, and sinker.

TWENTY-SIX

LEXI

Finally, the showroom is set up—well, as good as it's going to get. Kind of like putting lipstick on a pig—but, admittedly, a cute one. Fresh and fun, the space has come together like a minor miracle, complete with a healthy juice-bar vibe. Tricia and I are adjusting the banner again when a package arrives. I head to the door, let out a sigh, and sign a form.

"It's for Christophe," I say with a groan.

Tricia looks over her shoulder. "Open it."

"Illegal."

"I don't care. Are you getting cold feet?" she adds, her tone half-teasing. "Whoops. My bad. Too late for that."

"Enough with your sarcasm, Trixie."

"Do you still want to see where this goes? I do."

I turn to face her. "You're really pushing your limits."

She taps her fingernails on the counter. "Not yet. Open that box."

I eye the package like it might explode and take me down with it. It sits by the door, taunting me.

"Don't go limp on me, Lex. This is happening." She nods toward the racks, the furniture, the modern look that seems to pulse with possibilities. "You're happening. And we are opening that box."

"I'm not going limp." I hesitate, looking at the box again. I think about the threatening text messages I've received and the detective's visit regarding Vescari's murder. "You really think he's trouble?" I mumble, a huge part of me wanting him to be real, for him to be the perfect man. Then I wouldn't have set myself up for the idiot of the year award.

Tricia snorts. "Please, girl. Trouble with a capital T. That man is a weasel in Prada."

I almost smile. It's not the first time she's said as much, and I suspect it won't be the last. But I still don't know how to read him. I don't know how to read any of this.

She points to the box. "We'll tape it back up. I know how to do it perfectly."

"Are you a criminal?"

"No, I'm just really good at sealing things back up, seeing my report cards before my parents did."

The box is heavier than it looks, and the label on it makes my stomach sink. It's addressed to Christophe at the showroom's address.

"It's from your other husband," she says, reading the return address over my shoulder. "I didn't know you had one in China."

The sound of ripping cardboard fills the showroom as Tricia slices the package open and I kneel beside it like I'm about to propose. The flaps spring open with surprising force, and I pull back the thick layers of packing foam to reveal glass bottles in tight rows. My heart skips a beat, then races to catch up.

They must be worth a fortune. Or maybe they're not worth anything, a fortune of fool's gold sent just to impress me. I run my fingers over the tops of the glass bottles, taking them in, taking in how much I don't know about Christophe.

My thoughts swirl, even faster than before. I hold back a sigh. None of this makes any sense. He'd told me his products were manufactured in France.

These could be the first step in Christophe's plan or the first step in losing control of it all. I lift the box, carefully tip each bottle onto the black velvet display, watch the overhead lights dance through the glass like a circus of possibilities. Or is it an illusion, a trick?

I examine the vials and jars, mesmerized by their clarity, by their potential, by their threat. I exhale, almost defeated but not quite. It's like the light glimmering off the bottles. The kind that could blind me like the glittering chaos of Vegas, or guide me. If I'm not completely fooled by a name and a pretty face.

A thought strikes me. I'll have to let him know what I've found, how he's surprised me, how it's almost like the life I'm trying to build. I'll tell him that, and he'll tell me more than he means to.

"Tape this box back up," I say with force.

"Yes, ma'am," says Tricia, saluting.

Her hands move faster than I expect, and before I realize it, the last layer of tape is on.

He doesn't know who I am. Not yet. But he's going to find out.

Tricia has sauntered off to the coffee place next door to pick us up some much-needed caffeine fixes. Christophe is standing in the doorway before I see him. A shadow moving faster than I expect, a surprise I should have anticipated but didn't.

"The place looks... interesting," he says, surveying the showroom. It sounds like a compliment, but his words leave just enough doubt that I don't know how to take them.

Before I can respond, he crosses the space in a few measured strides.

"I take it you're ready for your big meeting with Trendline," he continues.

I gulp. "Ready as we'll ever be."

"Do you need any help?"

"No, thanks. We've got everything covered. Just a couple of

finishing touches," I say, pointing to the box. "That arrived for you today."

I glance at the knife by its side, my breath catching in my throat. His gaze is impossible to read, but I see enough to wonder if this is part of his plan.

"I may have mistakenly opened it," I say. "I was going to tell you."

"You just did." His voice is easy, like I haven't caught him off guard at all. He wants me to believe it, wants me to fall for his reassurances.

I give him a level look. The same one I've given myself, hoping it will help me believe that I know what I'm doing. "I thought you manufactured in France."

"I do," he says.

"This package is from China."

"Better prices for the design I want—the one you saw."

The pause between us is awkward. It lingers like his secrets until he stoops down and picks up the knife, slicing the box open. He holds up one of the bottles. "Beautiful, isn't it? The glass, the way it captures the light like a shell."

Tricia comes in, surprise and disbelief painting her features when she sees him. I can already hear her voice: Is this a surprise visit, or am I walking into something else? Like a trap?

"I'm taking Lexi out on the town. Join us for a drink, Trixie?" he asks.

"Thanks," she says, making it clear she means the opposite. "But I don't think so. And only Lexi calls me Trixie. My name is Tricia."

The look she gives him is the one I want to, but my eyes wouldn't hold the same power as her steely glare does. Not when I don't know if I'm agreeing with her assessment that he's a complete fake, or if I want to. Christophe sets the bottle down, this time with less care than before.

His expression changes, amused and wounded at once. "Pity," he says.

Tricia holds his gaze, an unspoken dare.

"I have to go," she tells me, ignoring him. "I'll see you tomorrow."

I want to thank her, want to run after her and tell her not to leave. But the words catch in my throat, just like my trust, just like my doubts.

The door swings closed, and I don't think I'm imagining the sound of laughter. It might be Trixie. Or it might be Christophe.

He gives me an apologetic shrug, but I can see he's not sorry. "Touchy," he says.

"What did you expect?"

"A little more faith," he replies.

"And a little less product sent to our showroom?"

A smug grin tugs at the corner of his mouth, and I know he thinks he's won this round. "You have the space. It's just one box." He eyes my outfit, the dust on my clothes. "I thought I told you I was taking you out tonight?"

I force a smile, tilt my head to the side. "Don't worry. I brought a change of clothes."

The cocktail lounge is everything I expect from Christophe. Intimate. Insistent. Filled with Hollywood players. He chooses a booth with expert calculation, tucking us into a corner before spinning a web of celebrity names. I listen, my face a portrait of amusement, a Mona Lisa smile. It hangs, until I fill the silence with an unconvinced laugh.

"You sure know a lot of people."

His smile falters for a fraction of a second, then resurfaces, more polished than before.

He leans back. "Who cares about me? The industry is starting to know your name, Lexi. They're talking about you..."

"Right up there with Givenchy and Chanel, I'm sure," I quip, taking a sip of my drink. I glance around, noticing the clientele. More Armani and less Nike than I'm used to. The subtle scent of ambition mingles with top-shelf bourbon. I don't recognize anyone. I doubt any of them eat or drink at my usual haunts.

Christophe picks up his glass, inspecting it like it's a rare gemstone. "You've already captured the market's attention," he insists. "These people, they want to know what's next."

"The market's attention, sure. But what about yours? You'll have to forgive me if I'm skeptical."

"Skepticism suits you," he says. "It keeps you sharp. But sometimes, we must embrace a little risk."

I laugh again, a genuine sound. "That's easy to say when you're born into a safety net."

He leans in, closing the space between us like a practiced seduction. "The right marriage, the right connections can be more valuable than a safety net, don't you think?"

The conversation in the bar hums around us like white noise. I catch snippets, luxury brands, indie film deals, murmurs of potential. He gives me a look that says he knows exactly how out of place I should feel, yet how much I want to belong. It's infuriating. It's tempting.

"Let me guess," I say. "You know everyone who is anyone."

"Knowing them is not enough. They need to know you," he corrects.

He spins a tale of an upcoming gala, the kind of event where exclusivity is the dress code. I'm sure it's one of those whispered-about gatherings where even the security guards wear designer. I wait for him to finish before shrugging with intentional nonchalance.

"Not exactly my scene," I say. "At the last exclusive event you took me to, somebody ended up dead. And we ended up getting married."

There it is, that barely perceptible hesitation, the shift in the light of his eyes as he adjusts his mental playbook. "Vescari was into some very bad things. And, while we're on the subject, I don't think our marriage is bad."

I lift a brow. "Somebody texted me about you. Told me that I didn't know who you really are. But they do."

"It happens with a family name like mine. Empty threats. I'd just ignore it." His eyes flicker to the side and then he grins. "I booked the tickets for our honeymoon. Paris and then the Maldives."

I'm stumped. "What if I can't get away?"

"We can change the dates." He clasps my hand. "I emailed you the itinerary. Did you get it?"

I shake my head and pull out my phone, letting out a gasp. Air France. First class. In three months. "Wow. This is a dream."

"I know." He winks. "Let's talk about yours. Let's talk about LexICON."

There he goes, changing the subject back to me.

The dance of words continues, a rhythmic tango with Christophe leading and me refusing to follow the steps. He tries a new tack, drawing a portrait of our overlapping worlds. LexICON's cutting-edge appeal. Montclair's storied legacy. The picture of synergy. His new brand: Miracule.

"Your brand is poised for global reach," he says, emphasizing global as if it's a sacred word. "Imagine the heights you could scale with the right partnership."

My interest is piqued despite myself, but I'm not ready to let him see that. "The problem with heights," I tell him, "is that it's a long way down if you fall."

He gives a knowing nod, the kind that confirms he's planned for my objections. "True visionaries embrace the risk," he counters, his eyes alight with something that looks suspiciously like triumph. "That's what sets them apart."

My eyes are steady, unwilling to betray my thoughts. I built LexICON by ignoring naysayers and taking chances, by making calculated moves that paid off. But this—whatever Christophe's selling—feels different. Less tangible, more precarious.

It's a neat line, the kind that would play well in a corporate video or a lifestyle magazine. He means it to be convincing, but I can't quite shake the feeling that there's a layer beneath it all. Something undisclosed.

"You paint a pretty picture," I concede, keeping my voice measured, even.

He lifts his glass in a subtle toast. "One we can create together."

As I clink my glass against his, my thoughts spiral in a dozen directions, considering what, exactly, aligning with Christophe might look like. Whether it's an opportunity, a trap, or some alchemical combination of both.

"Well," I say finally, letting the word hang just long enough to suggest the possibility of something, "you certainly give me a lot to think about."

He stands, offering a hand as if this were a negotiation. "And perhaps a gala to attend."

I take his hand but not his bait, standing my ground as well as on my feet. "You said it yourself. The industry knows my name. They'll find me when they need me."

It's then he notices my left hand. He blinks. "Why aren't you wearing your rings?"

Why? Because I'm not sure about this marriage. But instead of saying what's on my mind, I tilt my head to the side. "You do realize I was scrubbing floors today?"

My answer seems to placate him. He leans forward and grins. "When are you going to tell your parents about us?"

"When the timing is right," I say, straightening my posture. "And that's not now. Until it is, I'm uncomfortable wearing the rings. Do I have to remind you that we barely know each other?"

I see him flinch. I see him recalibrate his strategy.

"Then get to know me," he whispers. "I have an idea. Let's set up a dinner with Tricia and her husband..."

"Jeff."

"Jeff. Tomorrow night. Anywhere you want to go." He grins. "My treat."

As we leave, I give the lounge one last look, as if memorizing the faces of people who might, someday soon, wish they had his committed to memory. Then again, we're in LA—it's all smoke and mirrors and people only see what they want to see, namely their own reflection.

On the way to the car, Christophe has checked his twice.

TWENTY-SEVEN

CHRISTOPHE

Lexi has barely spoken since we left the lounge, her silence a gift. She reminds me of a sulking feral cat—one I will domesticate if I'm patient enough. I know she's brooding on the warning she's received, trying to be quiet about it, trying to be clever. I keep my hands relaxed on the wheel, give her the space she needs.

The distance between us might be growing, but I'm planning on closing it. Her stubbornness is an indulgence I'm willing to put up with, her withdrawal a game that I know how to win. She tries to be still, but the tension seeps out in small, revealing movements—the crossing of her arms, the impatient tap of her foot. If she thinks I can't see the unease behind her careful composure, she's mistaken. It's written across her in bold letters, easy to read and even easier to exploit. The uncertainty suits her almost as much as her ambitions, and I'm determined to make the most of both.

It is a comfortable silence, for me at least. I don't mind the tension. I don't mind the wait. She doesn't realize it, but we have more in common than she wants to admit. Each of us is caught up in the game, each of us determined to be the last one standing. I turn the corner, already planning my next move. My patience is being measured. Hers is being tested.

I will give her time, let her adapt to her new role. Give her just enough room that she feels independent, and just enough intrigue to keep her involved. Keep her committed.

I think of Sabrina's messages, frantic with exclamation points and a looming sense of doom. Lexi is too careful for that. Too pragmatic. Her hesitance only furthers my determination. If she weren't so difficult, she wouldn't be so much fun.

We pull up to her apartment, and she's already unbuckling her seatbelt before I've put the Maserati in park.

I follow her to the door. She moves through the apartment with the kind of care that tells me she's not entirely sure about this, about us. Her hesitation is the best evidence that my plan to close her is almost working. I just need to be a little more patient. Lexi stops in the hallway, a silhouette of uncertainty. I watch as she glances back, almost says something. I wait, a bit hopeful. Maybe she'll invite me into her bed and we can relive those wild Vegas nights, her curvy, muscular body on mine.

"Goodnight," she says flatly. "I'll see you tomorrow."

"Goodnight, Lexi."

She looks at me a moment longer, then disappears into her room.

I stand there, a lone figure in the living area, listening to the familiar sounds of hesitation and regret. Lexi thinks she can resist, but it won't be long before she's completely invested. I know this as well as I know how to crack a safe—not easy, and it takes time. I know what I'm doing.

I sink onto the couch, pour myself a Scotch, and watch her shadow pass under the door, watch as it flickers and finally dims. There's still plenty of work to do, but I've made more progress than she'll ever admit.

I head to my room, to the stack of cardboard and crates that Lexi's makeshift budget demands. I move them aside, make room for what I have planned. The phone is right where I'd hidden it. S. Not for Sabrina, but for Showtime. It's too easy, but this time I enjoy it more than I should.

I scroll through the messages, see her impatience, see her

urgency, see her increasing doubt. I consider how long I'll let her think it's all slipping away, how much it's worth to have her worry a little longer.

I listen to her voicemails, each one more frantic than the last. Her voice climbs higher, each plea more desperate, each exclamation more like a child who's about to lose her allowance. She knows I'll get back to her, knows she'll get what she needs. That's what keeps her going, keeps her in the game, keeps me interested. Not nearly as interested as Lexi, but enough.

More than enough.

> Please, Christophe. Please, Christophe. Please, Christophe. Confirm. Calvin wants to meet you tomorrow. 8 am. Beverly Hills Hotel. You promised you'd make things right!

Finally, I respond with measured precision, the kind that makes them trust me more than they should. Not just her but all of them. I press send, watch as the message sits in the queue for a fraction of a second before disappearing.

> Don't worry, Sabrina. I'll be there. You have absolutely nothing to worry about.

I imagine her in her room, wild and dramatic, seeing the text and catching her breath in relief. I hear Sabrina's voice in my head. *I'm trying to make things right. I'm trying. I'm trying.*

Yes, *chérie*, I think. You are.

She'll have what she wants in the morning, and so will I.

Lexi doesn't know what to make of me. That makes her even more compelling. I'm prepared to make the most of all of it. All of her.

Lexi comes into the living room as I'm putting papers into my briefcase. She gives me a look of equal parts suspicion and dread. The way a hostage looks at her captor. The way a lover looks at her conquest. "I'll be back later," I say, my tone as noncommittal as her glance.

She narrows her eyes. "Where are you going?"

I can't tell if she's feigning disinterest or building suspense, but I like it either way. "Beverly Hills Hotel," I reply. "I have some business."

The early morning light outlines her profile, an ambiguous sketch of intent. "At a hotel?"

"I'm meeting with Calvin Vale."

"Will Sabrina be joining you?" She spits the name out like it's venom.

"Why?" I ask. "Jealous?"

"Of what?" she says.

I give her a smile, watch as she tries to hold back her own.

"Getting new investments," I tell her. "Or renewing old ones. It has to be done."

She pretends not to hear me, pretends not to care. I leave before she decides to ask anything else, before she has the chance to turn this conversation around on me.

The ride is fast and smooth, a sleek reminder of why I left the confines of a cramped apartment with unfinished dreams. Lexi is a lot like that, a lot like unfinished business. The difference is she'll never find out what I've been working on. If I play Calvin correctly.

The hotel is not too far, not too close, and I use the drive to convince myself how well this will work out. I know it will, but convincing myself is half the fun.

The difference between Lexi and Sabrina is between small and big, between worry and certainty. There is a middle ground, and I intend to stake my claim. This won't take much. I've played more difficult hands. I'll let Calvin think he's holding the cards.

The Beverly Hills Hotel is ostentatious and proud, but the look and the price are just vintage enough that people pay without thinking. I arrive late enough that it appears deliberate, like I have something better to do with my time. Calvin is already waiting.

I spot him before he sees me, which gives me a good head start on this little adventure. He looks like a Hollywood producer in the worst sense. Self-important, self-satisfied, and very, very pissed off. His hair is graying, he has a fat paunch, and I think he thinks the lighting may be doing him some favors. It's not.

The coffee at his table is still steaming when I arrive, and so is he. I wonder if he's going to throw it in my face, but that's not his style. Not dramatic enough. He's too accustomed to having assistants do the dirty work for him. I brace myself for the performance.

He looks up from his cup and gives me a smile. "Christophe," he says, his voice clipped.

"Calvin."

"Sit. Let's get right to it," he says with a scowl. "There are two things going on."

I pretend to be surprised, pretend to care more than I do. I take a seat. "Two?"

"One," he says, leaning across the table in what he must think is an intimidating pose. "I know you're fucking my wife."

I raise an eyebrow. "Is that what she told you?"

"That's what I'm telling you."

Calvin watches me like I'm the last reel of a very important film. He's waiting for the big plot twist. It's not going to happen.

"Not at all," I reply. "I think you're jumping to conclusions. You think I'm that careless? I'm not fucking Sabrina."

He doesn't answer, but the expression on his face tells me exactly what he thinks. He's wrong, and he's not used to that. This is going to be even more fun than I imagined.

"And two?" I ask. "There was a second thing?"

"Yes," he says. "I'm going to kill you."

This time I let him see me laugh. "Over her? She's not worth it."

I almost enjoy the look of anger and doubt that crosses his face. Almost. It doesn't last long.

"I'll decide that," he says.

"Be my guest," I tell him. "But you should know I've recently married the love of my life, Alexis Marlowe."

His confusion turns to respect. This time I do enjoy it. I enjoy the shocked expression on his face very much.

"Then what is this about? Why is she giving you money?"

I lean back, calm and composed. "Sabrina is an investor in my company, Miracule," I explain. "One of many investors. I'm a Montclair."

He looks at me like I'm speaking a foreign language. In a way, I am.

Calvin narrows his eyes, tries to size me up. "Does your product come with more risk than reward?"

"No risk, but more reward than you can imagine," I say. "A whole new line. And we're getting the first round of samples in now."

His eyebrows rise. I have his attention.

"You have five minutes to convince me."

"I don't need that long."

"Go," he says, waving a hand.

I reach into my jacket, watch his eyes widen as I pull out a single vial. The serum glows as brightly, I hope, as my credibility. I set it on the table between us.

He stares at it, then stares at me. "You think this is enough to change my mind?"

"I know it is."

"Prove it," he says.

I push the bottle toward him. He hesitates, but only for a moment. I see the possibility fill his eyes, see the temptation become stronger than the doubt.

"What is this?" he asks.

"Think of it as a new franchise," I say. "Miracule. A skin serum. It's a fountain of youth. Turns back time."

"Nothing can turn back time," he mutters. But he's not dismissing my pitch, and he's not dismissing me.

He picks up the bottle, holds it to the light.

"Try it," I say. "The effects are immediate but work better over time."

"FDA approved?"

"Working on that. It should be a matter of a couple of weeks."

His skepticism fades, replaced by something much more lucrative. Something much more to my advantage. I watch him calculate, watch him do the math. I can almost hear the ching-ching of a cash register, see the dollar signs in his eyes, as he rubs the serum onto his arm.

The caffeine in my composition really works wonders, tightens everything up—at least for a couple of hours.

"And Sabrina has invested how much?"

"Seventy-five," I say. "But she'll make it back. She's going to be the face of Miracule."

He's already convincing himself, point made when he pulls out his checkbook. "Let's double her investment, shall we?" he growls. "But if we don't see a return on our investment, I'll kill you."

"Give me three months. And, please, put your checkbook away. If you're serious, I'll need the funds wired to my account."

He nods as I write down the bank transfer instructions. Got to love my online bank.

This has played out better than I'd anticipated.

TWENTY-EIGHT
DETECTIVE SAMSON

I've been on Christophe Montclair for forty hours. That's two days and change of his schedule, his cigarettes. He likes his martinis shaken not stirred, his suits the color of bruised grapes. The files say "French", but the accent slides around, depending on who's listening. To me, he's the same flavor of dirt as every other grifter I've hauled out of a country club in Brentwood.

When he jerks the Maserati into the driveway at Château Marmont I idle past and double back on foot. No point in crowding the entrance—he moves fast, but he's not paranoid. I follow him up the stairs, past a pair of influencers pawing each other on the banister, and watch him enter one of the garden bungalows with careless authority.

I let myself drift into the lobby for ten minutes. The desk clerk glances at me, the way people do when they're trying to place you but don't want to make a scene. I keep my sunglasses on, tip my head like I belong. It's never the cop who gets noticed; it's the guy who tries not to look like one.

Back outside, the bungalow's curtains are open a slit. Through the glass: a woman. Sabrina Vale. She's easy on the eyes in a way that's never really been my type—everything designed, nothing accidental, right down to the cut of her hair and the slope of her ankle above a slingback heel. Actress. Philanthropist. Current "angel investor" in Christophe's skincare startup, at least according to Alexis Marlowe.

Inside the bungalow, Christophe and Sabrina do the dance. First drinks. Then the hand on the elbow and the full-body lean-in when he tells her something that makes her laugh. From the shrubs I can't hear every word, but I get the shape of it: he flatters, he pivots, he plants some fear of missing out, and then—like magic—the subject of money. Sabrina's lips twist, amused but curious. She asks him "when she'll see a return on her investment." He says, "We're on the verge." His French accent is heavier now. Always the sign of a con artist in the throes of seduction: the words sound more foreign as the bullshit piles up.

She looks at him the way people look at museum art. Admiring, but also a little suspicious. I see the moment she decides she wants to be fooled.

Back at the car, I jot down my notes: Montclair, Sabrina, 15:12, physical contact; subject reveals ongoing affair, subject requests additional capital; tone: aggressive, familiar, predatory.

In the morning, I buy coffee from a girl with a sleeve of cheap tattoos and take my place across the street from Marlowe's apartment. Montclair's car is still there. At 7:17, Montclair jumps into his Maserati. This time I follow him to the Beverly Hills Hotel, shocked when I see him meeting with Calvin Vale.

Christophe handles any accusations thrown at him. He's calm, clinical, the way all sociopaths are when they're holding the winning card. I can almost see him dissecting Calvin with a glance, figuring out which insecurity to dig into next.

After forty-five minutes, Vale shakes his hand and leaves. Deal concluded. Montclair waits exactly ninety seconds before stepping onto the patio, lights a cigarette, and dials his phone. This time, I listen.

"Oui, chérie, c'est fait," he says, and then switches to English for the punchline: "Don't worry, he won't be a problem."

I scribble that down, underlining it twice. I'm certain he's speaking with Sabrina Vale.

This Montclair is definitely up to no good, conning the only people in this city with enough money to pay for the pleasure. And from where I'm standing, that's a kind of murder, too.

Sometimes, if you stare at the same lie long enough, it'll blink first. I'm certain Christophe Montclair is Vescari's killer.

TWENTY-NINE
LEXI

No rest for the weary. Once again, I'm back in the showroom. Tricia's phone keeps ringing and dinging until I'm not sure if the noise is real or if it's the sound of my own pulse. Just when I think it's too much, I hear Tricia above it all. She shouts in my direction. "How do you like being at the top of your game?"

"Oh, that's where I am? I thought I was on the floor trying to scrub the last spot. It's not working."

My phone vibrates on the counter, and I rush to grab it before it scurries into a bucket of floor cleaner. Calls to answer, orders to fill. I can't keep up with everything. I let the call go to voicemail.

"This is what we wanted, isn't it?" Tricia's reply brims with enthusiasm. "Looks like our investment in Style Sphere paid off!"

I want to tell her to slow down, that I can't keep up with everything. But I don't, because she's right. This is exactly what I'd wanted. I tighten the laces on my gym shoes, preparing to run into my dreams. Hopefully, I won't faceplant on the way.

Boxes are scattered across the showroom floor, a mess of product and ambition. Some are open and half-empty. Others are sealed and waiting to be shipped. Tricia waves an order sheet overhead like a winner's flag at a race. "Relax," she says. "We're going to be fine. A chain of boutiques with five stores in Chicago. LexICON will be national in no time."

I look at the showroom, try to take it all in. Considering what we started with, it's more than I hoped for. I try to imagine this enthusiasm lasting. And I'm trying not to imagine what happens when it doesn't.

"One little problem," she says, which startles me. "We need models for the Trendline meeting. We can't pitch and twirl at the same time."

My gaze shoots to the window. I point. "Go grab those two girls —the ones waiting in front of the nail salon. They're cute."

"Since when is entitlement cute?" she scoffs. "Call FIDM. Have them send a couple of models over—the ones on the roster for the show."

"Good idea," I say.

She grins. "I know."

Her certainty steadies me, even as fear creeps in. She has no doubt that we're on top of the world, and she won't let me think otherwise.

We sort through the orders, and it feels like we're at the top of something. Or like we're going to be, right before we fall. Tricia grabs a marker and makes a note. "Don't go soft on me," she says, waving a piece of paper over her head. "This is happening. And we need to celebrate. Every little victory."

And now I have my in.

"Christophe wants to take us all to dinner tonight. His treat."

She raises an eyebrow. I glare at her. She shrugs, unfazed. "Fine," she says. "We should go someplace nice. French? See if he's for real."

Knowing where this conversation is headed, I roll my eyes, but I'm secretly grateful she doesn't let me get away with anything.

The restaurant is crowded and authentic, everything from the narrow wine glasses to the hushed waiters wearing black. Jeff arrives with casual elegance, wearing jeans, a button down, and a wry smile that says he expects more than a meal from this encounter. He waves to us, slides into the booth next to Tricia, and nods politely.

"Lex," Jeff says, raising a brow. "So this is the new husband."

"*Enchanté*," says Christophe, shaking hands. "Christophe. Christophe Montclair."

"Pleased to meet you," says Jeff, giving me a sly wink. "So, Lex, you didn't tell me you married a savvy aristocrat."

Tricia laughs. "He wishes," she says, but her eyes tell me she thinks Jeff's sarcasm is on point, that Christophe's going to be a hard sell.

Christophe focuses on Jeff. "I heard you're into real estate."

"I'm a developer." Jeff grins and then winks. "Lots of concrete. Working on a huge project right now. A new shopping center in Century City." He pats my hand. "Lexi worked for me for a couple of years, while building up LexICON. She's not just another pretty face. Tough as nails, that woman is."

I sink into my seat as Christophe's eyebrows rise. He swallows and scans the room, then each of us in turn, his composure back. "How did you meet, Lexi?" he asks, focusing his attention on Tricia.

Tricia gives him a pointed look. "She's impulsive, remember?"

Jeff waits for me to fill in the gaps. I swallow and take a sip of my water. This isn't going exactly the way I'd planned, but I should have known better. Christophe is watching me closely, gauging my every reaction. His gaze is hard to avoid, hard to interpret.

"I met Tricia at a fashion show," I say. "Eight years ago, when I'd completed my studies at FIDM."

"I went backstage after I saw her designs," Tricia says. "I thought I was in love. Turns out, I was."

Christophe's smile tightens. "So, an investment?" he asks.

Jeff chuckles, shakes his head. "More like seed money. Tricia didn't like working in real estate and now she has her own thing."

"We took off from there," I say.

Christophe laughs, giving me a look that says more than any words. I'd bet he wants me to get rid of Tricia. And that will never happen.

"Looking into a hostile takeover?" Tricia asks, straightening her posture, obviously picking up on Christophe's modus operandi.

Christophe looks at me, unfazed. "Not very hostile," he replies, all confidence and charm. "More wine?"

Jeff and I lock eyes as Tricia signals to Christophe with a mischievous tilt of her head—she's already in on my doubts, and Jeff's smiling like he's cracked the code. The server arrives—young, hair rumpled, bearing that distinctively French *je ne sais quoi*.

Tricia leans forward, her grin wicked, and angles her voice to make sure only our table hears. "You're from France," she asks, and the server nods. "Christophe is French, too—straight from Paris, no less."

To my surprise, Christophe's eyes light up instead of narrowing, and Jeff clears his throat.

"*Ah, bon,*" the server says, cheeks lifting in genuine pleasure at the mention of Paris. He spills out something in rapid French—words I only catch in fragments: Paris, Montréal, Québécois, "le Plateau," maybe. Christophe replies just as fast, animated and smooth, as though he's swapped his business suit for a beret. I see Jeff's expression hardening; Christophe, meanwhile, sips his wine with the air of someone who's exactly where he belongs.

Christophe beams at us, eyes dancing. Jeff glances at me, a silent question: "Are you buying any of this?" The look in his eyes already says he's made up his mind about Christophe, and he thinks he's full of *merde*.

Tricia stands up and tugs my arm. "We'll be right back," she says, her voice low and urgent. I follow her past a row of dark-stained tables, past bottles in ice buckets sweating on the marble bar. We slip down the narrow hallway toward the ladies' room.

Once we're hidden by the door, she spins on me. "Told you so," she says. "He's not who he says he is."

"Because he speaks French?" I ask, incredulous.

"No—because I know some French. Christophe lived in Montréal."

"That's not—"

"Lexi," she hisses, her tone all urgency and sisterly exasperation, "when a waiter starts out-Frenching somebody who is supposed to be French aristocracy, I get nervous. You should be, too."

"Worried about what, Trixie?"

"Not knowing what the hell you've signed up for."

I draw in a breath and let it out slow. "Let's just see how this night goes."

"Right," she says, letting out an exasperated sigh. "Just like your marriage."

We head back out through the clatter of forks and laughter, past walls plastered with sepia-toned snapshots of French bistros. At our table, Jeff's wearing that smug smirk again. Christophe has already ordered another bottle of Saint-Émilion.

"Another one? We haven't even finished the first," Tricia says, sliding in next to Jeff.

"It's gone," Jeff replies, gesturing to the empty bottle, flashing a look at Christophe.

I sit beside Christophe, his hand resting casually on my leg. He's claiming the evening as his own, claiming me along with it.

"To old and new friends," he says. "*Santé.*"

Jeff raises his glass but remains unimpressed. "Quite a night," he says, looking at me. "And quite a guy."

He's testing me, but he's testing Christophe even more.

"It's only the beginning," Christophe replies, confident as ever.

"So, Montréal," says Jeff. "Did you live there?"

"Ah," says Christophe. "You speak French."

"*Un peu.*"

"I spent some time in Montréal."

"In prison?" says Tricia with a laugh.

I glare at her.

Christophe doesn't miss a beat. "Celebrating my freedom away from my French family."

Over dinner, I try to keep up as Christophe and Jeff subtly jockey for control. For my allegiance. For everything. The conversation spirals around me. I catch bits and pieces, enough to feel overwhelmed. Enough to feel lost. It's a night to remember, but not in the way I thought.

"A digestif?" asks Christophe.

Jeff's gaze shifts from Christophe to me, searching, probing. I'm thinking about washing the bad taste out of my mouth. This night is a disaster.

"Not for me," says Jeff, looking at his watch. "Early start tomorrow. I think we should call it a night."

Christophe waves the server over, making the universal sign for the check. I hold my breath, wait for the next line in this script of surprise, wait for Christophe to falter and show us who he really is. The bill sits on the table, a silent judge, a reminder of all that's been said and all that hasn't. The noise of the restaurant fills the space between us. We wait, and it's the waiting that stretches and twists and makes me unsure. Christophe reaches for the check with confident fingers. I can't watch, but I do, because I have to know.

Tricia's eyes meet mine, but I look away before I see what's written in them. She knows, or she thinks she does. They both do. I can't let anybody see how much this is getting to me, how much I need this to be right, how much I need Christophe to be authentic, not some fake poser. Jeff leans back, a knowing smile still playing at the edges of his lips. He doesn't even try to hide it. His posture is casual, amused. His gaze is not.

I hold my breath and watch Christophe's fingers close around the bill, watch as he reads it, watch as he pulls his wallet from the inside pocket of his jacket. He's so composed, so sure, and I feel so much the opposite.

The server floats past and Christophe stops him.

"*Un moment,*" Christophe says, barely glancing up. He holds his card up, like he's already won this hand.

The server nods, a tight smile on his lips. I watch him walk away. I watch him come back, whispering in Christophe's ear. I hear his hushed whisper: "Sorry, sir, but your credit card has been declined."

Jeff's laugh cuts through the noise, and I know he's impressed with the show. "Must be tough," he says, looking at Christophe. "Can't imagine what that's like."

I swallow, and it tastes like shame.

"It happens sometimes with a foreign bank account," Christophe says with a tight smile. He tucks the card back into his wallet.

"I've got this," says Jeff.

"*Non,* you haven't," Christophe replies, reaching into his jacket, more deliberate this time. Jeff's expression is curious, a mixture of disbelief and amusement. His hand tightens around his wine glass, and he leans forward, not wanting to miss a second.

Christophe pulls out the cash, a thick roll of bills. The kind of gesture I'd expect from him. The kind that confirms everything Jeff is thinking, the kind that confirms everything I don't want to even consider. He peels off several bills, each movement measured and calm.

The server's composure falters, a split second of genuine surprise. Not enough for anyone but me to notice.

"*Bien sûr, monsieur,*" he says, his words clipped but not as sharp as before. He takes the cash.

Christophe nods. His confidence never wavers, but my faith in him is definitely on the edge of a precipice.

"This was a treat," Jeff says, and I can't tell if he means the dinner or the entertainment.

Christophe stands, helping me from my seat. He tucks a bill into the server's hand, confident and poised as when this all began. We head to the door, but Tricia pulls me aside before the valet arrives with Christophe's car, her grip firm on my arm. "Lex, be careful," she whispers.

"I'll be fine," I say, and I'm not lying to her.

On the drive home, Tricia sends me a text.

> Huge red flag. When we went to the ladies' room, the douchebag asked J if he wanted to invest 100k in Miracule.

I squeeze my eyes closed, hoping this is a joke. But it isn't. As I tuck my phone into my purse, Christophe shoots me a side glance. "You don't need Tricia," he says. "She's bringing you down. Using you."

"No, she isn't."

"She is. And if I were you, I'd send her packing. LexICON is your company."

I slump into my seat, shaking my head. I'm beginning to understand exactly how Christophe operates. And he doesn't know he's met his match.

THIRTY

CHRISTOPHE

In the morning, I receive a text from the bookie I'd "borrowed" money from at the poker game.

> Better have my $ in 3 days or you'll be paying with blood.

I swallow. The small guest room I've been sleeping in, the world, seems to close in. A tangle of mistakes and ambition. It's all so close to falling apart. So close I can taste the regret, sharp and sudden in my throat. I sit with my phone, watching it like it might explode in my hand. Everything I've worked for, everything I've schemed for. It's coming back to get me.

I try to gather myself, try to remember how it came to this. To play you have to pay, and this time I may be in over my head. The past is catching up faster than I can run from it, and I have to be faster so I can outsmart it. I have no choice but to press Sabrina. I look at my phone, consider the odds. They are not in my favor. But they have been like this before, and I've pulled through. I'm betting I can again.

My fingers are steady enough to type, but just barely.

> When is Calvin planning on sending the wire?

I pause, hesitate, rethink my entire strategy. Then I press send. Sabrina is quick with her response.

He didn't send it?

My heart pounds. My pulse roars in my ears. Is this really how it all ends? How it comes crashing down? I am scrambling, trying to make sense of this.

SABRINA, I told you that Miracule was on the verge of success. Without Calvin's $, you can say goodbye to your investment.

There is a longer pause. But not long enough. I watch the phone with mounting panic, watch it as if my entire future depends on it. This time, it just might.

Fine. I'll talk to him. He better see a return or he'll kill you.

I read it once, then again, then again. I think I've read it wrong. Another death threat. I stare at the phone, blinking.

My carefully constructed façade, my years of strategy. They crack like ice beneath my feet. I think of Lexi. I think of how close I am to losing it all. This is a disaster. My disaster. I let out a shaky breath, try to steady my nerves. I need a new plan, a new angle. I need to close Lexi.

Thinking about my options, I leave the guest room and pace the living room. She's way more difficult than I thought she'd be.

As the walls of Lexi's apartment close in on me, I sit, my fingers tapping nervously on the coffee table, exposing the desperation beneath my calm exterior. They stop when I see her expression. Lexi watches me, her arms crossed like a fortress. I think of all the ways this could go, and none of them are good if I can't get her on my side. She doesn't trust me. She is right not to. I need to change that.

"What's wrong?"

"Everything." I lower my head, let out a sigh. "I owe some very bad people some money. They want their investment in Miracule back within three days."

"Give it back."

"I'm still trying to straighten out my banking situation. It should be clear in a week."

She shrugs. "Then tell them you need a week."

I'd googled the image earlier. Sent myself a text from a burner phone. I hold out my phone to an image of a guy whose face has been beaten into a bloody pulp. "They don't work that way."

She slumps down onto the couch next to me. Her jaw goes slack and her eyes go wide. "This is serious, Christophe. How did you get involved with people like that?"

"I'm going to blame that decision on Vegas," I begin. My voice is too smooth for how shaky I feel. "I need a favor. I wouldn't ask if it weren't important. My life is on the line."

She looks at me, skepticism all over her face. It is not the reaction I'd hoped for. But I expected it.

"Fifty thousand dollars," I say, gulping. "Just until the end of the month."

She narrows her eyes. They don't blink. She doesn't flinch. She doesn't buy my story for a second. Her voice cuts through the space between us. "Are you serious?"

"I know it sounds bad—"

"It is catastrophic, Christophe," she whispers. "I don't have that kind of money. And why should I help you? Your credit card was declined at the restaurant. Remember?"

"It's a problem with my American account," I reply. "I'm still getting it set up. You have to believe me."

"Do I?" She raises an eyebrow, leans back further, further. The suspicion in her eyes almost makes me laugh, but I can't.

I try to regroup, try to find the words that will make her believe me. The right words. Any words. She waits, her posture stiffening with every second I don't speak.

"It's a temporary issue," I say. "Once it's resolved—"

"Don't," she interrupts. "Don't do that."

Her tone is harsh, and I feel myself faltering. This is going the wrong way.

She gives me a hard look, the kind that leaves no room for doubt. Except the doubt she has about me. "Christophe, be honest," she continues. "Are you really a Montclair? Or are you just a run of the mill con artist?"

My breath catches. It's a moment, a second, a lifetime, before I speak again. I let the silence draw out like a confession.

"Is that what you think?" I ask.

"It is," she replies.

There is a subtle shift in the air. It's not in my favor. She sees more than I've let her see. More than she should. I need to fix this.

"Then let me prove you wrong," I say. "Let me show you I am who I say I am."

"How?" Her eyes challenge me. The tone in her voice challenges me more.

"I don't need a loan. I'll write you a check," I say. "From Montclair Industries."

"A check?" she questions.

"I told you I'm still setting up my American account," I say with a sigh. "The process is taking longer than I thought."

She doesn't say anything. She doesn't have to. Her body language does all the talking. Her silence speaks volumes. Lexi watches me, and I wonder how much she sees. More than I want. More than I like. More than I can let her. Her lips press together, and she tilts her head to the side.

"I thought you didn't want to use your family's money," she says.

She's good. Too good. I let out a groan, and it feels like an admission.

"Desperate times," I say, "call for desperate measures."

She doesn't laugh. She doesn't even smile. Her expression is unchanged. I see what I'm up against. "Is that a no?"

She unfolds her arms.

"What happens when the check bounces?" she asks, her voice a quiet accusation, a delicate threat.

"It won't bounce," I reply, more assurance in my words than in my thoughts.

"Let me see the check," she finally says.

She loves me, but she's testing me. From her, I wouldn't expect anything less. She's going to come through. I know it. Writing this check is a risk, but at least I can breathe again.

The bank is crowded, but the only thing more oppressive than the bodies pressing around me is the doubt pressing in. Lexi's. Mine. I don't know which is worse, and I don't know which will break me first. I wipe sweat from my brow, a last-minute effort to stay in control.

Lexi watches me like she knows what will happen next. I try to act calm, but it's impossible with her here. With her doubting me. The line moves forward, and so do we. The walls seem to close in, the same way everything has since I got that first text from the bookie. The second one was worse.

> Tick tock. We're going to rip your balls off and
> feed them to the pigs.

I've never felt this much pressure. Not from a bank, not from a girl, not from all sides.

I have to keep it together. We reach the counter, and I hand the check to the teller with practiced ease, but my hands shake more than I'd like. Lexi looks at me with the same leveled accusation as at her apartment. I feel the sting of that more than I thought I would.

"You won't get any money until the check clears," Lexi reminds me. Her voice is calm, but her words are sharp enough to cut.

"I know," I say, trying to sound confident, trying to sound like I've got it all figured out. Like I know what I'm doing. That is a lie, and I think we both know it.

The teller examines the check, looks at it as though it's a strange curiosity. Forty thousand euros. A small fortune. A gamble. He turns it over, glancing at me, glancing at Lexi. I feel the heat of his scrutiny, the heat of her disbelief.

The lights are bright, glaring. They show too much, make my panic too obvious. My brow is damp, my jaw is clenched. The teller squints at the check, then at me. I try to hold my composure, try to hold my ground. I'm slipping.

"Do you have ID?" he asks finally. His voice is clipped, professional, unimpressed.

I give him my best smile. "Of course," I say. "It's all in order."

Lexi peers over my shoulder as I hand my passport to him. The beads of sweat multiply on my forehead. Lexi watches it all unfold, watches me fumble and falter, watches me as I barely keep it together.

"It might take some time to clear," the teller says.

"How long?" Lexi asks, sounding like she already knows.

"Three to seven business days."

Three to seven days. I don't have three to seven days. I have one, maybe two, before the bookie loses it.

"That's fine," I say. It's not. It's a disaster. I hope I can convince the bookie to give me a couple more days. I'm sure he'd rather get his money back before inflicting physical harm.

The check is stamped and marked for deposit. Lexi studies me, and I know what she's thinking. She's not as wrong as I want her to be.

"It won't bounce," I say, trying one last time, trying to make her believe.

She nods, but not in agreement. "We'll see," she says.

That stupid gamble in Vegas might be the one that takes me out of the game.

THIRTY-ONE

LEXI

Tricia is holding down the fort today while I'm back at the apartment with Christophe. He grins at me, but it's not the confident smile I'm used to. It's different. Sad. Pathetic.

"Come here," he says, patting the seat beside him.

I sit but leave space between us.

He clears his throat. "It was not always like this," he says, his accent thick, his words careful. "I was the black sheep of the Montclair family. Everything I did, it was never enough."

I swallow. He's finally going to open up to me. "What happened?"

"I happened," he replies, a bitter smile twisting his lips. "Drinking. Fighting. Disappointing them."

My heart twinges at the unexpected truth in his confession. My finger traces the small scar under his eye. "Is that how you got this?"

He shakes his head and squeezes his eyes shut. "I had a bit of a temper when I was younger."

"And now?" I ask.

"I'm trying to rebuild my life." His shoulders slump. "Before I left, my mother gave me a couple of checks in case of emergency.

She told me I'd never amount to anything. I did not want you to know."

"Why?" I ask, my eyes meeting his.

"Because I want to be someone else for you," he replies, his voice cracking. "I don't want to be a disappointment."

"You're not," I say, surprising myself with how much I mean it.

"I don't want to pretend to be something I'm not," he says with a shrug. "Are you disappointed that I'm only connected to Montclair Industries by name?"

I am not expecting this question, and I'm tempted to tell him about my past, but I don't want to. Not now. Not ever. "What's in a name?"

His hand reaches for mine, but it stops. It waits. I reach for it. The touch is electric. I take a breath, take a chance, and pull him to his feet. His eyes search mine, and I lead him to the bedroom, my decision already made.

"Lexi," he says, and I pull him closer. "Are you sure?"

I hesitate, but only for a second. "I'm sure."

The night is a blur of doubt and excitement. It's more comfortable than it should be. I hear his breath, slow and steady. I feel my own, fast and uneven. I close my eyes, try to shut out the doubt, the thrill, the mix of both. Every instinct screams at me to retreat, to push him away. But my body betrays me, curves itself toward him, leaning into the comfort I've learned to fear.

My mind replays our conversation.

He is too good at this, and I know it. He'd been honest to a point, but, as I watch him sleep, his chest rising and falling, I'm wondering what else he hasn't told me, the truths he hasn't yet shared. If I let my guard down any lower, he might never let me raise it again. Still, if my doubts about him are my wake-up call, I just want to hit snooze, fall back asleep, and dream.

THIRTY-TWO
CHRISTOPHE

I stand at the stove in a plain white shirt, unbuttoned, dark jeans. Casual. Relaxed. It suits me. It suits Lexi's apartment and its polished surfaces, the quiet, the air, the morning light. I hum a soft French tune and watch the batter take shape. The scent of crêpes is warm and alive. They are perfectly formed.

My fingers are dusted with flour. But not much. The whisk beats with precision. I flip each crêpe and arrange them on plates as delicate as my plans, my moves. Berry compote. Fresh coffee. Foolish intimacy.

Lexi watches from the doorway, and I let her see me like this. Like I am. Like I am not. She crosses her arms, a mix of suspicion and something else. The doubt, the need, the hunger. Her eyes are bright with all of it, with more, with the sight of this unexpected version of me. I stop humming, just long enough to meet her gaze.

"Surprised?" I ask, and I see that she is, and I see that she loves it.

She doesn't say anything for a moment. Her laughter breaks the silence. "I am."

"I thought I'd cook breakfast for you," I say, "just like *ma mère* did when I was a *petit garçon*." The words, the French, the life. It spills out, this lie I've learned to love. I guide her to the table.

She watches, and I let her. The kitchen is intimate, and I am exposed. It should feel more dangerous than it does.

We sit. We eat. The morning is warm, like the false intimacy I'm giving her. She doesn't see it yet. But she will. The food is good, but the thrill is better.

So is the risk.

I let my accent out, let it draw her in, let it do what I shouldn't let it. She thinks she knows me now. I think so, too. The moment stretches, the past and future collide, the game is set, the play is real. Or fake as plastic shit.

She laughs again, a sound as fragile as her faith in me.

I watch her, watch her think she has this, think she has me, think she knows. The silence grows, and I let it. Until I break it with words. With stories. With a new kind of move, a new kind of hit, a new kind of life. I learned from the best and those lessons are paying off.

"We used to make these on special occasions," I tell her, my voice soft, intimate.

My words are smooth. My stories are made up.

Lexi leans in, close, eager. Her eyes are sharp with the thrill, her smile brighter than I expect. The risk of the past feels close. Too close. The risk of her feels closer. And I want her. More than she knows. More than I want to.

The past always looks different in the morning, casting the shadows. Empty plates. Half-drunk glasses. It looks like a goddamn risk. Lexi tucks her legs under her, laughs, watches me.

"Raised on a vineyard in Bordeaux," I tell her, my voice careful, loose, exact. It hangs in the air with the newness, the surprise, the thrill. I love the way she watches me, bright, keen, sure. I smile, letting the lies weave, letting the thrill build.

I keep talking, the smooth litany of an old life. "I think, at one point, my parents wanted me to take over the company—the Montclair Beauty Empire," I say, "but the world called. And I couldn't let it go to voicemail."

She laughs. I think she's fallen for my stories. I think I have, too.

"It was hard," I tell her. "Growing up in a family like mine. The galas, the women, the fancy suits, they came later." My voice is a smooth echo of who I might be if I let this happen.

She listens, and I watch her hanging on my every word.

"Enough about me. I want to know more about you."

Her eyes darken. "Not much to say."

"I'm sure you have stories about growing up a Marlowe."

She looks away. "Right now, my focus is on LexICON. It's everything."

I don't know why she's avoiding the subject, but I won't push her. Not yet. I brush a curl from her forehead. I kiss her, guiding her. It feels dangerous. It feels real.

THIRTY-THREE

LEXI

For the past two nights, the awkwardness between Christophe and me has evaporated. Turns out, he's just as obsessive-compulsive as I am. When he cooks, he arranges everything perfectly in the cabinets, and the pots and pans sparkle. He's funny and charming and, well, there's something sexy about a hot Frenchman who can cook. I like this side of Christophe, the one without all the pretense and the flash, and, although I still have my reservations, I'm thinking I could get used to this.

I'm still tempted to tell him about my past, but I don't want him to run. We're just getting to know one another. So, he thinks I'm a Marlowe? For now, I'm more curious about where this relationship is headed—if anywhere. And I'll tell him everything when I'm ready. Just not yet.

Today, as I inspect the sparkling stone on my ring finger, I brace myself for Tricia's reaction when I arrive at the showroom.

"Holy moly," she says, her eyes almost as big as the diamond as she stares at my hand, lips parted in shock.

"We're finding our groove."

"So, you're really giving this relationship a shot?" She sounds incredulous. "Even with Vescari's murder, and those texts you received about him?" Her eyes widen even further. She freezes and then slaps her hand over her mouth. "Sugar. I didn't mean to say that."

I didn't tell her about the texts.

Sudden pieces of a puzzle, previously scattered, click into place with a nauseating snap. The cryptic warnings, the pointed language—they had her signature all over them. I should have known. I fold my arms as my stare drills into her, waiting for an answer she seems afraid to give.

"It was you." My heart skips, and I take a step back. The words leave my mouth in disbelief. "I mean, I know you don't like him, but sending anonymous texts is really fucked up."

Tricia raises her chin and sighs, as if her deceit is my burden. "It was," she admits. "I'm just looking out for your best interests."

The nerve. The gall. She stands there, defiant, as if sending those messages was some noble act of friendship. I feel the temperature in the room rise. I can barely contain the heat of the anger clawing inside me.

Every word feels like an insult as she continues, unwavering. "You're not seeing things clearly with him."

Her confidence grates against my nerves. Tricia, knowing more than me. Tricia, knowing what's best. The tension is so thick you could cut it with a pair of the scissors we use for samples. This is not what I expected. Not from her, not like this. I feel like everything is coming apart at the seams. It might as well be.

My voice rises with my fury. "You have really crossed a line!"

Her look is as smug as it is concerned, and that makes it worse. "Someone has to look out for you," she fires back, folding her arms and her smugness around her. "You're not acting like the Lexi I know and love."

The heat of pure anger rushes to my face. I can't even respond.

"Have you forgotten everything we've gone through to get this business up and running?" Her eyes flash with a mix of accusation and care. The care pisses me off more.

"Of course not," I snap. I wish it were that easy. "But you had no right—"

"No right?" Her voice climbs with disbelief. "He's shifting your focus, and he could destroy everything. I mean, I can't believe he asked Jeff for money."

Her words hit like stones. My breath comes hard.

"He is who he says he is!" I shout, desperate to believe my own words, as if saying them loud enough will make them true. "And you—you're just making everything worse!"

Tricia narrows her eyes, steps closer. "He has you wrapped around his finger," she says. "I've been your friend for eight years. You've known this guy for five minutes." She glares at me, defiance written across her face. It's not a look I'm used to from her, and it's not one I like. Her betrayal. My doubt. They are pushing at me from every angle, and I think I'll explode if I don't clear my head. Her face shifts, from righteous to guilty, from guilty to caring.

I hate her for caring, especially after she says, "I've hired a private investigator to look into him."

Her words hang in the air. I grab my jacket and storm out of the showroom. I hear her calling after me, hear her shouting my name. I don't stop. I don't turn around. Not this time.

I run until I feel like I can't, then run more. It burns. It clears my mind just enough to fill it back up with everything I don't want to face. I don't stop. I need to push until it hurts even more, until I'm out of breath and out of anger. It's my only escape, the only thing that gets me through. I run harder, my feet pounding out a rhythm I don't know how to follow.

I think of her, the betrayal, the texts. But what if Tricia is right?

The thought makes me push even faster, even harder. Makes me burn with more than just exhaustion. My pace picks up, frantic and uneven. I won't let her, him, or anybody else get to me.

"Shut up," I hear myself say, but it sounds like a whisper, like a plea.

The park is small, dark, a haven from my own thoughts. I don't remember getting here. I sink onto a bench, my breath ragged and my legs trembling. I try to catch my breath. I try to catch my thoughts.

A family walks by, the mother eyeing me with something like concern, something like pity. She keeps moving, doesn't stop, doesn't ask if I'm okay.

I wipe sweat from my forehead. The noise of the city hums in the distance. It's almost enough to keep my mind off everything. Almost. I pull my phone from my pocket, its screen lighting up with a series of frantic texts from Tricia.

> I know you think I'm being paranoid, but I'm not.
>
> I only want what's best for you.
>
> He's a con artist. And he's conning you.
>
> I'm sorry the truth hurts.

She's not sorry. I want to throw my phone. I want to scream. I want to silence everything. I want it all to stop, even for a minute.

I swallow back my rage, swallow back the urge to text back. My finger hovers over Christophe's name. My head spins with every reason not to trust him, every reason not to trust myself. My pulse finally slows, and so does my racing mind. With a long breath, I stand. The ground feels more solid beneath my feet. I turn away from the park, turn away from my doubt. I'm not the kind of person who just gives up when the going gets tough. No, I'm going to dig my heels in and push forward, the same way I built my business.

THIRTY-FOUR
DETECTIVE SAMSON

I've been trailing Christophe Montclair and Sabrina Vale, yet I have nothing to move forward on with Vescari's murder. The two haven't even seen each other since Château Marmont. Nothing but the same LA bullshit—an affair, an angry husband, and a possible grifter. All Marlowe does is work hard in her showroom, scrubbing floors, setting up her merchandise. That girl has got more grit and stamina than me.

Everything connects Montclair to Vescari's murder, but I'm missing the last piece of the puzzle, especially without evidence. For now, I'm spinning my wheels, wasting my time, and I have to focus on the pile of "smiley face" robbery cases on my desk. And I'm frustrated as hell.

Something has got to give.

THIRTY-FIVE

CHRISTOPHE

While Lexi is at the showroom, my phones beep with a fury of relentless demands and warnings. The buzz of them rattles the nightstand, shakes them to the floor. I grab a couple before they fall, wondering if I'll do the same. I read the latest round of ultimatums. Sabrina—one phone. My bookie—another. Even Lexi, in her own way. All of them think they have me pinned. But I've been pinned before, and this isn't what it looks like. Not from where I'm standing. The messages pile up, stack themselves in threatening towers. I let them build. I let them sway. Then I knock them all down with a smirk.

I have what I need. Unlike Sabrina, the bookie will be getting his money back.

I toss the phones on the bed and pull out a small leather bag from the closet. I count the cash I have left, flipping through each bill. Six thousand, to be exact. Used to have at least fifty thousand at my disposal, and I can almost feel the panic of being cash poor, but I'm not there yet. I will be if I don't take care of this soon.

I brush off the thought, refusing to let doubt settle in my gut. My past, my future, my head—there is too much to unravel if I don't unwind first.

The club is crowded, loud, full of neon and desperate pleasure.

Like my life, but more predictable. I take it in, pretend it's enough. Pretend it's not a reminder. The lights flash, and I see my reflection in them. A smile creeps to my lips, something I can't quite convince myself of. The drinks here cost more than the dancers make, and I order the most expensive on the menu.

My table is in the back, away from the noise, away from the inevitable crash that I will see coming long before it hits. The bourbon arrives and I enjoy the moment, a brief peace before I make it all happen, make it all fall into place. But this time, it feels like I'm waiting on more than just the money.

The woman on stage looks a bit like Lexi. Dark hair, slender, muscular build. But this woman really is nothing like Lexi. The dancer wears her vanity like a costume, and Lexi doesn't need to try this hard. I finish the drink and feel a rush. Not of excitement. Of Lexi. I wonder what she's doing.

A server comes by my table, but I wave her off. Another woman, another drink. I should be more into this. But I'm not. I'm already restless. I'm already planning my next move. But now it feels different. This time, it feels like I might be losing before I've even begun.

I push the thought away, let it sink with everything else I don't want to admit. My eyes drift to the dancers, but my mind drifts back to Lexi. To what she said. What she didn't. The loudness of the room matches the confusion in my head. I try to drown it out, but it floats, it surfaces, it refuses to sink.

Why do I care so much?

A brunette walks by, sees my drink is empty, bends to ask if I want another. I don't. What I want isn't here. I toss a couple of hundreds on the table and leave before they notice.

The air outside is a relief, even if the tension isn't. I knew it would come to this, and I knew I'd be unprepared when it did.

When it really mattered.

I stand on the curb, already calculating my next step, my next strategy, my next everything. I need Lexi. I need her to come through like the rest wouldn't. She's my best chance, and I've come too far to lose her.

The days tick by, each one closer to disaster, each one closer to success. I watch Lexi, study her, learn her tells. I thought she would be a harder read, but she is too caught up to be careful. I see her chinks, her insecurities. They are exactly like mine.

She picks up her phone, looks at it as if it will surprise her. I see her fingers tap at the screen, see her shoulders slump. The balance hasn't changed. The funds are still pending. I knew it would take time, knew it would take patience.

The following day, she checks again. I let her, knowing she'll have her answer, knowing she'll have it soon. It takes everything I have to keep my own impatience from showing. To keep my own risk from becoming as desperate as hers. I'm getting nervous, too. It's not until the third day, the fourth try, the final confirmation, that she lets herself relax. That I let myself.

She looks at the bank app, and this time her disbelief turns to surprise. This time it's in her favor. In mine. She has the funds. The smile is broad, natural. The funds are available, and she knows what that means. She has me figured out, or she thinks she does. The most satisfying part is that I can pretend it was all for her.

The bank is crowded, filled with people who look like they have somewhere else to be. I fidget in line, fidget like I never do. Lexi stands with her arms crossed over her chest. My foot taps a rhythm I don't recognize, a rhythm I want to ignore.

We amble to the counter. The teller stares, unimpressed. It's the same look Lexi gave me when I asked for the loan, the same look I'm sure she'll give me when I make her the next offer, the big one, the one I hope she won't refuse.

I push the slip toward him, toward the skepticism. "She'd like to make a withdrawal," I say, making my accent thicker than usual, making my needs clear.

He glances at the form, at me, then at Lexi. His eyes narrow, like he can see the money laundering through my veins, like he can see right through my name, right through the charm.

"It's a large sum," he says, his voice flat, as though this doesn't happen every day, but I'm positive people in LA demand transactions like this all the time.

"It is," I reply, adding nothing more. What I'm doing with the money is none of his business.

His frown is deliberate. "Maybe a cashier's check?" he suggests.

"Cash," I insist.

The teller's fingers dance across the keyboard. His suspicion grates on my nerves, grinds my composure into fine powder. I try not to show it, try not to lose my cool. I hold my breath. I hold everything.

"Cash?" the teller asks again and I glower at him.

Lexi nods, and it feels like relief.

"Cash," she says.

It's like another engagement. Another promise. It's like her. The longer it takes, the more I crave it. Money isn't the only thing I want. Not anymore. I think I've fallen in love with her. The lovesick feeling sticks to my heart like glue. It follows me from the bank, straight to her apartment. I tell myself it's all going to plan, that Lexi is on my side. I need to believe it.

The cash is more reassuring than it should be. I want this to be easy, but I know it's not. I have to hold it together until the end, have to hold it together like I held my breath at the counter, held my ground with the teller, held my promises to Lexi.

The woman at Western Union looks like she's heard every sob story, seen every man like me. She takes the money, fills out the forms. She hands me the receipt, hands me the way out of the biggest risk I've taken in a long time.

"Will he get it?" I ask.

She shrugs, indifferent to the way my life hangs on this wire transfer.

"Should," she says.

I don't wait to see if she's right. I don't wait for anything. The words echo as I leave. The doubt fades. The panic fades. Everything fades except the satisfaction. I pocket the slip, and this time I know it's real.

My freedom. My safety. I can almost feel it. I'm back in the game. I call up Lexi. "Let's celebrate. My treat."

We are dining above Los Angeles in a tower of polished glass. The city spreads out below us, alive and blinking. The ceiling is draped in satin, a canopy of pretense and intrigue. The waitstaff glide, their expressions bland, not competing with the exquisite plates they carry.

Lexi looks at me with suspicion and a little awe. She sees her reflection in every window, every showbiz glance. They all meet me with air kisses and jealous eyes. Lexi's skepticism makes me love this even more. I see her interest grow, but she won't let me see it all at once.

Several tables down, a man waves. I return the gesture. I tell Lexi his name, drop it like a clue. "Producer," I say. It thrills her, I can tell by the way her cheeks flush, by the way she tries to act unaffected.

"This is quite the place," she says, sipping her champagne like she knows how much it costs.

"I'm glad you think so."

She narrows her eyes, like she's still deciding whether to believe me. I want to give her time.

"I could get used to this," she says.

"Good," I tell her, leaning in, closing the space between us. "You will."

The menu is obscene. It sparkles with delicacies and overpriced ambitions. Lexi is quieter than usual. "What if I told you I have an idea," I say, my voice low, enticing. "What if I told you we could expand this into something bigger than either of us imagined?"

"I'd say you don't know what I've imagined." She folds her arms across her chest. I can't decide if she's immune to my charms or on the defense.

"I do," I say. "I know exactly."

It takes her a moment to respond. I can tell she's working out how this fits.

"I don't like gambling," she says.

"Maybe you don't." I sip my drink. "But you've already taken a chance on me."

She leans back, the way she did when I asked her for a loan. I see the way she glances at the glittering view, then at me.

"Lexi," I say, making my next words sound more urgent and pleading than they should. "We can do this."

She considers my words, weighs them like I knew she would. Like I want her to. She's cautious, but also tempted. I can tell by the way she taps her fingers on the table, deliberating.

The food arrives, and so do more looks from the crowd. They want to know who she is. So do I.

"What exactly are you proposing?" she finally asks. "We're already married."

It's my opening, and I take it like a thief takes a pearl necklace. Without regret, without apology. I know what to say. I always do.

"Partnership," I say, letting the word hang between us. I see the intrigue flicker across her features, across her reluctance. "Montclair and LexICON."

"Sounds fancy." Her tone is indulgent but amused.

"It will be."

"On paper," she says, "or in real life?"

I lean back, savoring the uncertainty. "In both," I reply.

She shifts, adjusts her dress. "We're on the verge of something big," I tell her. "With your designs and my name, we'll be unstoppable."

She lifts her glass, sips. I want to tell her it's a risk worth taking. But I have to let her get there herself first.

"International," I continue. "Within months."

I see her interest grow, the way her eyes glint. "We're already doing well," she says, testing her conviction. "Maybe too well to add another partner."

She's smart, smarter than the others. That makes me want this more. Want her more.

"Get rid of Tricia and add a family name," I tell her, shrugging. "The one you just took. The Montclair name still opens doors."

She laughs, but not like she's finding it funny.

"I'm never getting rid of Tricia and I'm offended that you suggested it. Again."

"Lexi," I say, and the way she looks at me, the way she smiles, makes me reconsider my strategy. "Really think about it."

"I promise you that I won't," she replies, lifting an eyebrow, and the look in her eyes is more intense than I expect. She's pissed.

THIRTY-SIX
LEXI

My sour mood has lifted. Instead of rehashing everything, after much thought I've decided to forgive Tricia—easy to do when she keeps apologizing, her bottom lip puffed out. "I just don't want you to get hurt..."

I hold out a hand to stop her. "We're not talking about Christophe."

"I don't know anybody by that name," she says, smirking. "I'm just pumped for the Trendline meeting."

I know she comes from a place of good intentions. As for me, I can't give up on Christophe until I figure out what's going on with him—obstinacy is engrained in my system. It's ten in the morning and we have half an hour to make final preparations for the meeting. Four lanky models have been here since eight, their wardrobe changes in the ladies' room. Instead of paying the girls, we're giving them outfits of their choosing. A win-win!

Fashionably late, the buyers, Tiffany and Claire, saunter into the space, both dressed in what I'd call military chic, and, aside from their hair color, they could be twins. After introductions are made, we're settling in for the pitch when Christophe shows up with a tray of coffee and croissants. Tricia shoots me a pointed look.

"What a handsome delivery boy," says Tiffany.

Christophe laughs. "I'm not a delivery boy. I'm Christophe Montclair."

Claire blinks. "From the Montclair Beauty Empire?"

"The very one," he says with a wink.

The women are practically drooling. I get it. I do. "Are you staying for the pitch?"

"I'm afraid I can't," he says, and Tricia blows out a sigh of relief. "I just came by to wish Lexi luck..."

"She'll be luckier if you stay," says Claire.

"If you insist."

Tricia gives a low groan that says "kill me now."

As he takes his seat, Christophe introduces himself with a deft blend of humility and confidence, painting a picture of an astute investor and erudite Montclair heir. He makes it sound as if joining LexICON was his plan all along, a perfect merger of minds and resources. The Trendline team eats it up, their enthusiasm palpable. They are hanging onto his every word, nodding like students in the presence of a particularly charismatic professor.

I can practically see the smoke and fire coming out of Tricia's ears. I don't blame her. I've been sideswiped by this kamikaze visit and I'm fuming, too.

Christophe infiltrates. That's the only word for it. Less than two weeks since our infamous "I dos", and here he is sitting at the head of our makeshift conference table, surrounded by the trusted buyers of Trendline. His presence dominates the room, not by force, of course, but by invitation. His game is flawless, all polished wit and discreet ambition.

"LexICON is really on the cusp of something tremendous," he says, clapping his hands together.

"We are—" begins Tricia.

Tiffany shoots her a pointed look. "We'd like to hear more of Christophe's thoughts."

"Shut him down now," hisses Tricia, nudging me.

I whisper, "Not a good idea. The buyers love him."

She crosses her arms over her chest. "If I didn't like him before, I hate him now."

I know she does. I'm beginning to see why.

Christophe's gaze lands on me, pulling me back to the present with the precision of a sniper. His eyes lock onto mine, and there's a silent exchange that only I'm meant to catch. It's a reminder that he's aware of my unease, and maybe even counting on it. He smoothly shifts the conversation to include me, delivering the line with impeccable timing. "With Alexis's vision and my resources, there's nothing we can't accomplish."

It's both an endorsement and a challenge, and I meet it with a steadying breath. I can't afford to be seen as anything less than completely on board. Not now. Not when he's made such quick work of the initial siege. I nod, the gesture deliberate and controlled, signaling my reluctant alliance.

"Ladies," he says, standing up and looking at his watch. "It was lovely to meet you, but I have a previous engagement."

Tiffany leans over, handing him her card. "Call Trendline if you're working on anything."

He grins. "I am. But today's meeting is about LexICON."

After our models catwalk around the space, showing off our wares, the meeting winds down, leaving me with more questions than answers. Christophe's parting smile suggested that everything was going exactly as *he* planned.

Claire grins. "We love the line! And we'd like to have you on the show in six months. A ten p.m. slot."

"That's so late."

"Not in New York." Tiffany stands up. "We'll email the contract and order tomorrow."

"And the initial payment?" asks Tricia.

Tiffany's eyebrows lift. "Is sent after sales are made."

I smile, but inside I'm dying.

The buyers leave. And then it's just Tricia and me.

"Well," she says, frowning. "That didn't go as planned. You should really put that new husband of yours on a tight leash."

She has every right to be angry. I'm angry with him, too.

I should be strategizing, regrouping, plotting my next move. But all I can think about is how utterly out of my depth I am. And then Sabrina Vale barges into the showroom. A sculpted eyebrow arched in disbelief. "I didn't know you had a store."

"It isn't a store," says Tricia with a sneer. "It's our showroom and it's not open to the public."

"I'm not the public," she says. "Have you sent me my things?"

"We've been kind of busy," says Tricia.

"Did Christophe send you here?" I ask.

"No, I was getting my nails done next door. I saw the banner when I was walking to my car." Her eyes darken and she sifts through a display. "Pretty things," she says, lifting a jacket with an elegant flick of her wrist. "Well, as long as I'm here, I'll take the merch you promised me. It's kismet. You won't have to pay for shipping."

I watch Sabrina pile clothing on a table, my jaw dropped.

The bell above the door rings, a shrill punctuation. A delivery man enters the space, holding a large box. "For Christophe Mont-clair," he says, and I amble over to sign for the package.

I look at the shipping label. The world tilts, and so has my confidence in him.

Tricia smirks, too satisfied. "What do you think it is?"

"I'm not sure yet," I say, keeping my voice steady. "But I will be."

The package sits on the table. I look at it, look at Sabrina, and then Tricia. I feel my heart race. I feel the doubt race faster. It might explode, and I might let it.

I'm about to open it, but Sabrina is quicker. She growls, "I, for one, am not waiting."

She tears through the packing material like it's a rival's acting contract. Her fingers tremble as she digs into the cardboard, pulling at the contents, pulling at the truth. Each layer reveals more. Bottles. Cheap. Plastic. Packed in Styrofoam. Serums filled with Christophe's lies. The breath leaves my chest, and I can't seem to find it. My composure drains. My hope drains faster.

"Is this what you expected?" Tricia asks. She knows the answer.

Sabrina's hand, her fresh manicure now ruined, clutches one of the bottles. The desperation in her eyes fades, replaced by anger. "I knew it," she whispers and then raises her voice, smashing one of the serums on the ground. "Miracule is a scam. Did he tell you I invested in his company?"

I feel sick. "He did," I say, the words an echo of my disbelief.

Tricia picks up another bottle, examines it. She reads the labels, inspects the packaging. Her satisfaction turns to something else. "So this is what they call Miracule?" she asks, her voice incredulous.

"He told me it was manufactured in France," Sabrina says, but her anger is laced with an unexpected camaraderie. "And that it would be ready by this week."

Her vulnerability mirrors mine, a bitter and binding truth. "I think he's manufacturing them himself," Tricia replies, the last blow in her knowing assault. The last proof of her suspicions. The final nail in Christophe's coffin. My awakening.

My stomach sinks, and I cling to the edge of the table.

"Looks like the two of you are his new factory," continues Tricia.

The certainty in her voice crushes me, and I want to crush the words. I want to deny everything. But the evidence is right in front of me. It stares back at me with cheap labels and counterfeit intentions. The room spins. My mind spins. Everything Christophe told me spins until it crumbles.

"How long have you known?" demands Sabrina.

"She didn't," Tricia says, her smirk widening. "Not until now."

"He said I'd get my investment back," Sabrina says, her voice low. "He said it was almost ready." She turns to me, her eyes searching. "Did you invest in his company, too? What did he tell you?"

I can't breathe. "I didn't invest in Miracule. He told me that we had a future," I finally say. "We got married in Vegas."

Tricia laughs. It's not kind. I steady my hands on the table.

Sabrina's eyes go wide. She grabs my wrist, looks at my ring finger. "That's my diamond. Do you have my tennis bracelet, too?"

My eyes meet hers. "What?"

"I knew it. I knew it. He stole them from me." She slams her hands to her sides. "In addition to being scammed, I was having an affair with him." Her eyes go wide with worry. "Please don't tell my husband. I do love him in my own way."

My mind is spinning on information overload. I don't know what to say. "I thought—"

"Of course you did," Tricia says, her voice taunting. She loves this more than she should.

The accusations, the truths—they hit harder than I'd expected. I don't want to face reality, but I have to. The color drains from my face. I wiggle the ring off my finger, handing it over. Sabrina snatches it from my grip.

"Enough is enough. I'm going to call the police," says Tricia.

"No! Don't! We're both getting played," Sabrina says, her anger turning to something more vulnerable. "We can't let him. We have to play him. To do that we can't let him know we're on to him. Not yet. Not until I get the money back he's stolen from me."

"How much?" I ask.

"Seventy-five K."

Money. A shiver of dread shimmies down my spine. It's a gut instinct. I sink into a chair and pull out my phone, logging into my bank account. It's in the negative—forty thousand dollars. This is impossible. I blink rapidly. This can't be happening.

"Sabrina is right," I whimper. "I have to get my money back, too."

"You gave him money?" Tricia huffs.

"No," I say. "He wrote me a check. And, well, I have to get to the bank to find out what happened because my account is now burning in the negative."

It takes supreme effort to stand. You want to believe the best in people and when they prove you wrong it feels like you're being shot down by a firing squad, one bullet hitting right after the other. I should have known better. I should have predicated what was coming.

Sabrina takes my hand, placing the ring back in it. "It's a loaner until we figure out a way to take him down."

"I don't understand."

"You're the closest to him." She gives me a tight smile and places her hands on my shoulders, squeezing them. "Call me if you find out what his next move is." She nods toward Tricia. "She has my number."

Tricia gives me a long look, a look that says I told you so. But it's not cruel. It's not mean. It's what I need to see right now, even if I don't want to.

THIRTY-SEVEN

CHRISTOPHE

I slide into my Maserati, slamming the door shut like a defiant exclamation of triumph. My breath is steady, the air is light. The glass reflects the unexpected success of today. Of my life, this scheme, the way I've orchestrated it all. I glance at myself in the rearview mirror. I don't have one wrinkle—no number elevens, no crow's feet.

A montage of names and faces spins around in my head. Helena. Susan. Tatiana. Brigid. Florence. Sabrina. Lexi—my most impressive work. I take a moment to enjoy the latest feather in my cap, to enjoy myself.

The phone's ring shatters my indulgence, its timing unerring. Sabrina's name flashes on the screen. I answer, pretending it's a surprise.

"We need to talk." Her voice is sharp, urgent.

"Not unless Calvin is pulling through with his promise," I say, making my French accent more pronounced.

"I have your money."

"I thought he wasn't going to invest."

"He changed his mind," Sabrina replies.

I wonder how long it will last, but not too much. It doesn't matter, not when it all goes this well. I listen to the sound of her breath.

"Wire it to me," I say.

"No, we have some terms and I have the cash," Sabrina insists. "Come to the house."

She gives me the address, we hang up, and I feel the pulse of adrenaline hammering through my blood, the way my thoughts feel when they're this clear, this certain.

I am two steps ahead. "The best day of my life," I think. This time it feels as real as the steering wheel beneath my hands. I adjust my tie, adjust to the idea of winning. The way I win everybody over, the way I win it all. I revel in the tension, the chance of proving myself right.

And, this time, I am so very right.

I drive to the address she gave me, my heart humming. It is a lightness I have never known, a certainty that nothing will fall apart or break.

Beverly Hills unfolds like a map of fortune, a territory I'm going to claim. The neighborhood is sprawling, familiar. The street narrows, and I turn into the circular drive, iron gates opening before I press the call button. Manicured hedges, a fountain that sparkles like her jewelry.

The plan is ambitious. It takes nerve. It takes everything, and I can give it that. I walk to the entrance, each step more assured than the last. The door swings open before I can ring the doorbell, and my assurance is met with Sabrina's face.

"Come in, Christophe," she says, turning her back on me.

She leads me into the living room. My eyes latch onto the stack of bills on the coffee table. "Have a seat." She gestures toward the couch. "Would you like a drink?" she asks, heading to the bar. "I'm having one."

"*Non, merci,*" I say. "I'm good."

Ice clinks into a glass. Liquid is poured. "Suit yourself."

After slamming back a shot of vodka, Sabrina turns. The gun shaking in her hand does not match her style. She points it at my head. "You bastard!" she screams, her voice raw and terrifying. "You liar!"

I almost laugh. She thinks the gun will rattle me, thinks her anger is more than I can take. She doesn't know what I can take. Not yet. Not until it's too late.

"Sabrina, I thought we had an understanding," I say.

My calmness is convincing and she lowers the gun to her side.

"Your product is a scam," she says, almost crying. Almost. "And so are you."

The gun shakes. Her confidence shakes more. I watch her closely, like I watch all the things that could go wrong, all the things I want to avoid.

"Miracule is not a scam. You have to trust me."

Sabrina screams and then blurts out an angry laugh, "Trust you! Are you kidding me?"

I tune out the rest of her verbal assault.

Sabrina's fury is running out like my patience. I can't run. I can't dodge. I can't win. But I can grab the gun. And so I do, leaping off the couch, holding Sabrina's arm to her head. Then, I squeeze her hand on the trigger.

Calvin stops, frozen at the door. Before she falls, the gun rises. It feels familiar, an instinct I don't recognize. Two shots. Two lives.

Calvin falls. She falls. Blood pools beneath him, beneath her. The bodies sprawl in awkward contortions, like marionettes with their strings severed. The scene is quiet. A perfect, damning silence. It's overwhelming. It's thrilling.

I force myself to move, force my mind to work. The urgency takes over. I take over. I begin to orchestrate what I couldn't before. A crime of passion. A loss of control. The wild desperation of betrayal. Not mine. Theirs.

I breathe, and my pulse is steady. My thoughts, too. I nudge her hand closer to Calvin's body. They will say it was a fight. They will say it was tragic. They'll say it's a murder-suicide. How poetic.

Calvin's eyes stare blankly, accusingly. I adjust them. I adjust everything. I'll have to get my story straight, the one about my affair with Sabrina and how Calvin found out, how he'd confronted me. And how I'd left.

I am above it, above the scene, above them all.

Before leaving, I wipe down the doorknobs, anything I might have touched. The cash sits on the coffee table, begging, "Take me," and so I do, thumbing through it quickly as I hop into my car. Disappointment sets in. At a quick glance, there's only five thousand. Ten-dollar bills stacked in between hundreds. It looked like a lot more. I think about surveying the rest of the house, but I don't. The less time I spend here the better.

I jump into the Maserati, start up the engine. The gates to their home open upon my approach and then, after leaving the neighborhood, I press down on the accelerator, thinking of my future with Lexi.

THIRTY-EIGHT

LEXI

The bank teller's words pulse in my ears. I have to repeat myself. "But the check cleared," I say, my voice quivering.

"I'm sorry, Ms. Marlowe, but the funds cleared before we found out there was a stop-payment placed on it." He shrugs. "Sometimes it happens with foreign checks. There's nothing we can do."

I feel like I'm going to faint. "My account is in the negative. What do I do?"

"Put the money back into your account."

The lights are bright, harsh. The room is full. People push around me, and I push through them, desperate to breathe, desperate to think. The doors swing wide open, the street is cold; I stumble to the parking lot, woozy.

I sink into the driver's seat of my Jeep, let my breath catch up with the rest of me. I can't drive. I can't move. All I can do is shake. The phone chirps with desperate insistence, the screen a taunt, a dare. I answer. Silence. Then a woman's voice. "Alexis Marlowe?" Her tone brims with disdain, thick and foreign, more threats than consonants. "Tell Christophe he's a dead man."

Before whoever this is hangs up, I blurt out angrily, "You can't kill a man twice."

She lets out a breath. "You killed him?"

The words hang until I say, "Not yet. But I'm going to after I get my money back."

I really shouldn't have said that.

"He stole from you, too?"

My posture straightens. "Who is this?"

"Florence Montclair," she finally says. "He is alive?"

"For now," I say, wondering about the pictures Christophe had shown me on his Instagram. They hadn't been photoshopped. "I thought he was your son."

The shiver of a long, drawn-out silence.

She lowers her voice into a growl. "That diabolical bastard is not my son. He was my lover, a dangerous fling that almost made me swear off men for the rest of my life. After he asked for my hand in marriage, he tried to kill me. Thallium poisoning." She takes a dramatic pause, exhales a deep breath. "The good news is that one of my staff members found me just in time, rushed me to the hospital, and I survived."

The air is sharp, suffocating. I grip my phone so tight I think it might break. My breath comes harder, faster. My spite. Her anger. They are meeting.

"There's an antidote?" I ask, wanting to know just in case Christophe attempts to poison me.

"It's called Prussian Blue, and I won't get into how it works on a call." She lets out another breath. "*Bon*. The man you know as Christophe Montclair's true identity is Christophe Bouchard," she continues, letting the syllables of his last name sting. "You have learned that he is not who he says he is, yes?"

I clench the phone, clench my teeth, clench everything. "I know that now."

"The checks he stole from me, we've canceled all of them," she says. "When he left, he also stole one million euros and a formula for a proprietary skincare serum. Then he ran. But, thanks to the check, we know where he is now. That's how I found you. And you?" Florence asks after another long pause. "Does he know who you are?"

I swallow, rubbing my eyes with confusion. "I'm not sure what you mean."

"But you do; I know everything about your past from the age of thirteen onwards. My family is very well connected," she adds by means of explanation before I can ask her anything. "You do realize with whom you are speaking."

I swallow. Hard. Tricia is right. No matter how fast you run, the past—the truth—always catches up to you. I've read all the stories about Florence—how she took over Montclair Industries when she was only twenty-two, and how powerful she is.

"He's not as clever as he thinks he is," she continues when I don't say anything. "In addition to the check, I have a google alert on the Montclair name. We have photos of him with Franco Vescari in Santa Monica and in Vegas from Getty images, confirming he's using my family name." She clears her throat. "Alexis, let Christophe think you are Phillip Marlowe's grand-daughter and that you're madly in love with him. Talk about future plans and nothing will happen to you. It's the only way you'll get your money back, unless you'd like me to loan it to you."

I let my anger simmer, let it burn. "No, he needs to pay."

"I understand," she says. "I'm actually on my jet headed for Los Angeles right now and I'll explain my plans in person. Until I arrive, don't do anything rash and keep me informed. I'll text you my contact information. I'll be in touch."

The line goes dead. I sit there, trembling. I sit there until I can't. Finally, I turn the key and the ignition catches. The truth about Christophe's duplicity rattles around in my brain. I let my fear turn to certainty, let my certainty turn to determination.

I think of Christophe. I think of his face when I tell him I know who he is and what he's done. The car speeds, my thoughts speed, and the distance closes until my apartment complex looms. So does Christophe. He's parked on the street, getting out of his stupid Maserati. His shadow darkens the street like the bruise I'm ready to inflict. My anger grips the wheel. My determination slams the gas. He is closer. Too close. The car surges, and he leaps back.

"You could have killed me!" he shouts, eyes wide.

"Oh, I want to," I say, spittle flying out of my mouth.

He blinks with confusion, then terror. The feeling is sweet. But not as sweet as his desperation will be. Forget about not doing anything rash. I'm angrier than I've ever been in my entire life. All I can see is red. Red. Red. And the look on his face. I rev the engine, inching the Jeep forward.

"Lexi, stop!" He holds up both of his hands defensively, as if he could stop my car. "If this is about the shipment I can explain. I—"

I cut him off. And it feels damn good. I can't take any more of his lies. "I don't give a flying fuck about your fake French snail products and the ingredients you're ordering from China." I glare at him. "But I do care about something. Your check didn't clear. My bank account is in the negative."

His face goes blank. "I don't understand."

"What's there to understand? I want my money back," I hiss. "Now."

Christophe stands in a stunned stupor as I park. I jump out and walk quickly toward the front door. He trails behind me, head hanging low like a scolded child.

"We took out the money. I really don't understand," he says again.

"What's there to understand?" I demand, tired of repeating myself. "The check didn't clear because there was a stop-payment on it. You took the money. And I need it back in my account." I turn to face him. "Can I be any clearer?"

He tries to look innocent, his bottom lip pouting, his eyes wide. "I don't have it."

My breath catches, but my resolve grows, bigger than his excuses, bigger than his lies. "What do you mean, you don't have it?"

"I spent half on products, paid the threat off. I was serious about that," he admits, looking as guilty as I want him to. As guilty as he is. "But I still have ten thousand left. I can give you that."

The hope in his voice is more than pathetic. I want to laugh, but I don't. I let him hear the anger instead, let him hear the threat.

"I want all of it back," I say.

I sound strong. Stronger than he thought I'd be. He flinches, looking at me like I'm holding an invisible gun to his head. Maybe I am. Maybe it feels good to hold it, even if he doesn't see it yet.

"I'll come up with a plan," he promises.

My next words are bullets. "You better. I mean, you know who my family is, the connections we have. And I don't want to ask them for money. You know that. This is your mess. You clean it up."

The threat hits like it was meant to and he winces.

"Christophe," I say, drawing out his name the way he often draws out mine, watching him squirm.

The expression on his face reveals more than he's willing to admit. Panic. Fear. All the things he thinks I won't see. But I do, and I love it. I'm so tempted to out him, call him Christophe Bouchard, but I've done enough already, and I don't want to mess up Florence's plan, whatever it is.

"Lexi, I love you," he says. "We're in this together. We're married."

His words don't reach me, falling blankly on my ears. I can tell he doesn't know what to make of this, of me, of the whole situation he thought he controlled. "I can't even look at you," I say, heading to my room.

"I'll fix this."

"You better."

I watch him simper, watch him wonder about this side of Lexi he's never met. I slam the door to my room closed and let out the breath I've been holding in.

THIRTY-NINE

CHRISTOPHE

While Lexi is stewing in her room, I pull out my M phone—for money, for Maxine, and also for mother—something she's clearly terrible at, hence the moniker of Monster.

> That favor you owe me? I'm calling it in. And I'll need a lot of it. Sending wiring instructions.

Her phone is always glued to her hand and Maxine replies instantly.

MONSTER

> I'm not wiring you $$$. Don't want a paper trail.

Fuck! My hands grip my hair.

> I'm serious.

> Need $? Come and get it yourself. I'd like to try your new product. Bring it.

> Leaving tonight. I'll text you the details when I have them.

> Can't wait.

Thankfully, I still have twenty thousand dollars in one of my online accounts. A cushion in case anything goes haywire, which it definitely has. I book my ticket using the name Ryan Daniels, the passport and driver's license bought on the black market, splurging. My funds will be refilled soon. After booking the redeye, I tap on Lexi's door.

"Do you have my money?" she yells.

"No."

"Then go away."

"I'll have it soon," I say, opening the door. She glowers at me. "I'm leaving tonight for Miami. I'll be back in a few days... with your money."

Her eyes narrow into tinier slits. "What's in Miami?"

"A solution."

"Good," she says, waving me off with an impatient flick of her wrist.

As I expected, there are no problems checking in, the staff member batting her fake eyelashes. I make my way to the gate, passing through the security checkpoint with the same ease. The plush first-class cabin is empty except for a businessman on his phone and me. The reading lights are dimmed, the polished tray table unfolds before me, and a crystal tumbler of bourbon makes its way into my hand. I swirl the amber liquid and savor the warmth, letting out a breath. The plane rolls away from the terminal and takes off. The vast city of Los Angeles blinks beneath me like a sparkling necklace of fortune that never quite fits.

How did this game get so exhausting? I down the drink and listen to the ice settle, to the quiet clink of challenges I've made for myself. My fingers drum against the armrest. The flight is longer than I recall.

I remember how Lexi reacted when I'd surprised her at the showroom. It's a small thrill to have her play this hard. A challenge. But she might become less of what I want, or need, or more than I can even handle. I laugh to myself, knowing I can't resist. I'd tried to call her before boarding, tried to let her know this is not as easy as I let her think it is. But I couldn't reach her. That's when I'd texted Maxine from my M phone, let her know to expect me by noon. She'd replied:

I'll have a car pick you up.

Unlike Maxine, Lexi's demands are more precise, and that makes them more dangerous. I close my eyes, imagining her in the showroom packing up the boxes of my ingredients and taking a picture to send to the Feds if I don't get the money back to her. I wonder if a threat is already in my inbox, waiting to ambush me the moment I land. I wonder if Lexi is the biggest risk of all.

I'm willing to take it.

The ice in my glass clinks, and I try to imagine a scenario where this doesn't end with both of us shattered. It might be the best, but it also might be the worst.

I take a breath and another drink, let the cabin's plush solitude work its magic. Lexi doesn't know me as well as she thinks she does, but she's getting there. She might surprise me, but not as much as I will surprise her. I'll leave my phone unanswered. Let her wonder, let her get used to it.

I set the glass back on the polished table, press my fingertips to my temple to stave off the headache brewing, and steel myself for the real work ahead: Alexis Marlowe is going to be a far greater challenge than I'd ever anticipated.

The scent of gardenias drifts through the open windows, mixing with the acidic bite of new wealth. This is Maxine's Palm Beach mansion, her Florida fortress of nouveau dreams, thanks to husband number two or three. I forget which one, and I don't care. I hang my tailored blazer on a bronze rack, smooth my hair in a gilded mirror, and listen for her. If I can get through this trip without interruption, it will be the first time. But I doubt it. She's almost as impatient as I am, and not as afraid to show it.

This is the world of leisure and white fabric, of blue diamonds and distrustful families. Not much different from Los Angeles. I think of her wealth, how it moves around her like air. But it's not air that fills the villa, it's perfume and envy.

I know Maxine's limits. If I didn't, I wouldn't be here, I wouldn't take the chance. I wander down the marble gallery lined with portraits of all her dead husbands, running a hand along the glossy banister.

Husband one: my father, Pierre Bouchard, drowned in a swimming pool (with a little help).

Husband two: Harold Winston, drank himself to death (poisoned).

Husband three: Gordon Sharp, boating accident (an explosion! boom!).

Husband four: Gregory Summers, fell down the marble stairs (he was pushed).

They don't call Maxine the black widow for nothing—and she has me to thank for that. I seriously don't have a clue as to why these men were attracted to my mother. Perhaps she's really good in bed, but I don't want to think about that. The thought disgusts me and I remind myself why I'm here: I am demanding my payday, the one promised to me after the last husband met his fate.

Ever since I was a kid, Mom and I have had an agreement. She takes care of me; I take care of them. *Voilà!* The good life.

The hallway is shorter than I recall, but it always feels this way after Vegas. Luxurious but empty. A gaudy confidence. If Lexi could see it, she'd want to redesign it, but not as much as she probably wants to redesign me.

As I saunter down the hall, I think about how the past few weeks with Lexi have been thrilling and exhausting, how she will be more difficult than the others, but not so much that I can't keep her off balance. It will take the right timing and the right moves, but those are the two things I'm best at. I make my way to the living room. Maxine greets me with a cool, "Hello, darling."

"Hello, Mother."

"I told you not to call me that. It ages me and, well, people can never know you're my son."

"Why? Aren't you proud of me?" I ask and she blinks.

"I believe you have something for me. The fountain of youth? The formula you stole from the Montclairs?"

"I do."

Unzipping my custom-leather briefcase, I retrieve a velvet pouch that holds the amber bottle of Miracule I bottled last night. When Maxine sees what's inside, when she knows what it's worth, her surprise will be luminous.

While Maxine eyes my hands, I see Lexi setting up her scheme with Tricia. See her doubt, her uncertainty. It worries me more than I care to admit. She might be further ahead than I think. She might know more about me than she lets on, more than any of them. When I consider that I feel a strange satisfaction, like I've lost control, but not quite.

Tricia needs to go next. She's the one poisoning my worth, my plan.

I present Maxine the sleek black box of Miracule on a silver tray, watch her uncork the vial, and feel a rush as she smears the serum across her cheeks, exclaiming, "Darling, this packaging is divine, the texture—I feel ten years younger already!" Her enthusiasm matches her jewelry and my expectations. It thrills me.

"I'm glad you approve."

"Cut the crap, Christophe," she growls. "You need money and it's not for this shit I just put on my face."

She knows me too well. She's the one who trained me—to con and to kill.

FORTY

LEXI

After a sleepless night, I imagine Christophe's polished charm hard at work in Miami while I sit cross-legged on the floor of the guest bedroom, unraveling the secrets of his meticulously organized life. His clothes hang with such clinical precision that I almost feel the need to sterilize my hands before touching them. A phone charger wrapped with surgical accuracy. Leather shoes stuffed with wooden blocks. For the sake of my sanity, I've nearly convinced myself that he is, in fact, the man he claims to be. But I know he's not.

Christophe's absence is a calculated freedom, a brief intermission before the next act of his not so dazzling performance. I've got to get my hands on the wedding certificate so I can burn it. I make a mental note to contact the chapel in Vegas, see if I can find out which one has a drag queen performing the nuptials with Elvis as a witness.

My hands move with determined precision through his wardrobe, exploring each pocket with a finger-sweeping thoroughness. The navy silk jacket—Gucci—is spotless, immaculate. How he makes each designer label sound like a term of endearment. I know his brands like I know the words to a song I pretend not to like. The black Saint Laurent holds nothing but a lingering scent of his expensive cologne, a whisper of his presence.

I want to throw up.

Instead, I throw each jacket onto the bed with increasing frustration, watching the discarded suits pile up like abandoned pretenses. My hands are shaking, just a little, by the time I finish with the last one.

"This is how you play it?" I say to the empty room. "Leave nothing to chance, or to me?" I can almost hear him answer, see the practiced smile softening his mouth, as he slips a ring he's stolen onto my finger. "But, *ma chérie*, I keep no secrets from you."

The thought feels absurd as soon as it crosses my mind. I'm almost ready to laugh it off until the comment from Florence creeps into the edges of my mind.

Don't do anything rash.

Too late for that.

My eyes focus on a suitcase tucked into the corner of the closet. I scramble toward it and unzip it. Everything inside is Christophe in miniature—compulsively ordered and frighteningly intact. Shoes in drawstring bags, exactly paired. Sweaters folded with architectural precision. Toiletries in a monogrammed leather kit, holding dominion over the zipped interior. I open the kit and poke around. Nothing but razor blades and aftershave and my reflection, staring back at me from the shine on his gold-plated nail clippers.

Maybe, I start to wonder, it really is this simple. Maybe he's exactly like me—the former me. My laugh is bitter as I picture Christophe holding court with marks in Miami, pouring wine and flashing the same killer smile he used to close me.

A man like Christophe doesn't need anything up his sleeve; he just has to wait until people talk themselves into buying whatever he's selling. I'm putting things back when my fingers catch on the zipper at the edge of the suitcase lining. I pull it, slowly, half expecting the whole bag to dissolve like a mirage. Instead, the bottom peels away, revealing a hidden compartment so shallow I almost don't see them.

My breath catches for a moment.

Objects rest inside, inscrutable in their ordinariness. But they are far from ordinary. A small black notebook, three burner phones, and a couple of passports. I flick through the latter quickly. Christophe Bouchard—Canadian, born in Montréal. Liam Moore —American, born in New York. Only one of these passports is real; the other ones, including the one he's probably traveling with under the name Christophe Montclair, are fake.

The burner phones fit too comfortably in my hand. He probably has more of them. I'm tempted to turn one on, but afraid that if I do, somebody will track me. I try to picture him holding it, conducting some covert double life with the same nonchalance he showed when he slipped that monstrosity of a ring onto my finger. What a perfect way to keep himself hidden, not only from the world, but from me.

The first page of the notebook is filled with Christophe's impeccable handwriting, a series of names, some crossed out and replaced by others. Phone numbers, financial figures, currency signs, country codes. I flip the page and see more of the same, an international roll call that screams secret deals and hidden agendas.

The paper under my fingers is thick, expensive. The ink in his penmanship is bold and unforgiving. JB—MARRAKESH— EUROS. HS—MILAN—EUROS. The list runs on and on. I scan the pages for initials I recognize.

FM—PARIS—EUROS $$$$$$$-X̶?̶
FV—LOS ANGELES—$$$-X̶
SV—LOS ANGELES—DOLLARS $$-X̶X̶

Florence Montclair. Franco Vescari. Sabrina Vale.
I find mine:

AM—LOS ANGELES—$$$$$-X?

And then I discover the initials:

TH—LOS ANGELES—X

Christophe's notebook lies open on my lap. Is he keeping track of his other marks, or am I his last, best score? The page blurs and comes back into focus as the sound of my phone splits the stillness of the room. Tricia's initials bloom on the screen. I stare at the caller ID, the letters of her name looking bolder and sharper than they should. I press answer, feel my pulse flicker, let the room settle around me.

"Lex, you there?"

I glance at the notebook, at my name on the list, at Tricia's initials.

"What's up?" I ask, managing to sound almost normal.

"You won't believe what I just saw on the news," she starts, breathless. Always urgent, always in the know. "Sabrina Vale and her husband, Calvin, are dead. They're calling it a murder-suicide."

Her words land in my gut like a sucker punch. I can't breathe. Can't think. I hold the phone away, let Trixie's news roll through me in sharp waves. My phone feels hot in my hand, all my questions alive, pulsing. Did he kill Sabrina and Calvin? I try to get a grip, try to make sense of this. TH? Tricia Hoffman? He'd told me to get rid of Tricia. This has to be Christophe's hit list.

It all connects too well, too perfectly. I want to laugh. I want to scream. I want to...

Kill him.

Tricia exhales into the phone. It sounds like traffic, like my life unraveling one thread at a time. "Lex?"

"I'll see you in an hour," I say and end the call.

I close my eyes and picture his face. Cool. Composed. I can confront him. I can take what I know, shove it in his hands, make him admit that he's a con artist and a murderer. I can watch him talk his way out of the accusation with pretty words. He'll play his role, and I'll play mine.

I look up. My reflection stares back from the blank, bare window. I've got another option: I can go full Lexi. If he wants to believe I'm the kind of woman who just trusts, who just loves, who just walks away, he's wrong. This woman doesn't lose. Not to him. Not to anyone. Like Christophe has said, she's tenacious.

FORTY-ONE
CHRISTOPHE

The living room feels as curated as Maxine's lack of charm. Each piece of furniture, every awkward antique, seems selected to match her talent for accusation, especially the head of the deer staring me down above the fireplace mantel. Everything screams money, except her lips, which form a tight and bitter line. Her silence demands. It is the same way with her company, with her questions.

"I have a new mark," I tell her, making my voice light, flippant. Like her. "Bigger than before."

I see her doubt, the way it curls at the corner of her smile. I don't like the way she watches me, like I'm her favorite television show and she already knows the ending.

"Bigger than Florence Montclair?" she asks, her Botoxed forehead trying for mock surprise. "I thought she'd be the last big con." Her eyes narrow with interest, and she swirls the lime in her martini glass, giving it a disapproving glance before taking a sip. "But you had to mess that one up, didn't you?"

My smile falters, but not for long. "A minor setback."

"A major one," she insists.

"I'll recover," I say, hoping I believe it as much as she doesn't.

"Why didn't she marry you?"

"Does it matter? Like I said, I have a much more lucrative mark."

Her eyes are all gloss, all demand. "And? Who is it?"

"Alexis Marlowe," I say, updating her on recent events, saving the best part for last.

"A Marlowe is the bigtime, Christophe. You can't charm your way into her life."

I sit across from her, letting my face go blank. "I did. We got married in Vegas."

She looks at me as if she's measuring my worth by the glass, and I hate her lack of faith in me. "Under what name?"

"My real one. Christophe Bouchard."

"My dear," she says, "that could backfire on both of us. And if you don't succeed this time, I will have to stop believing in you."

I laugh. "You'll never stop believing in me."

"Oh?" She leans in, breathes in the desperation she knows I feel. "I trusted you to take on Florence Montclair. And you lost her before the big pay day." Her lips curl, cruel and amused. "That's why you're in Palm Beach, isn't it? France got too hot for you. And California is burning."

"Not yet," I say, although her words sting. "Not as much as you think."

"Then why do you need money?"

I raise my glass, take a sip, pretend my reason is a celebration rather than a defense. "I'm only asking for what is owed to me."

"And Alexis Marlowe," she says, drawing out her name. "Are you going to be just as careless with her as the others?"

My eyes go wide. "I don't know what you're talking about."

Maxine's fingers clench on her glass, delicate and deliberate. "Florence thought you were such a prize." She narrows her eyes, cuts with them. "And now the only prize is disappointment."

I look away, but not for long. It shows weakness, and I can't. I refuse to be undone, to be outdone. My chin lifts, my composure returns. Maxine can smell doubt, but I let her smell resolve. I have just enough left.

I know what's next. She leans in, memory leaning in with her.

"Florence thought she was better than me. The grand dame," Maxine says, and the sound of it leaves her withering mouth as she pours more of the gin, more of the regret. "She snubbed me, told people I was a worthless, gold-digging whore. White trash. A public affair. Everyone there." Her lips twist into a cracked and crooked expression. "The humiliation was enormous."

The same old sob story lands between us like a body, heavy and lifeless and dead. I hear it every time, and I am tired of the sound. She does not remember the charity, but she remembers the gala. She remembers every painful detail, but most of all she remembers that she was hurt.

I listen, wait, and do not breathe. I am, I have been, and I will always be like her. She knows it, and she will never let me forget. For years, I'd been snubbed by high society, too—except for the bored wives who wanted a fling with the pool boy.

"Never again," she says. Her breath comes quick, her insults quicker. "You have always been ambitious," she says, her voice still a blade. "But not careful. Florence could have been dead by now, and we could have lived like royalty. We could have shown them all. But you are soft, just like your little conquests."

I watch, detached and aloof, waiting for her to get on with it, to get over it, to get over herself. I want to say something, to break the terrible sound of her disappointment. But I know she won't listen. She never does.

Maxine narrows her eyes, like a hawk. Like the predator she is, like me. She turns away, but not before she sees the hope, the lie, the truth in my eyes. Not before she sees too much. Compliant. It's how she wants me to be.

"Thanks to you, I may be the wealthiest widow in Palm Beach," she says, "but I am not a fool." I feel each word, the hard edges as they hit. Maxine rises, a fluid movement for someone so old and so bitter. I watch her cross the room with dreadful grace, watch the wall safe swing open. "This is the last time," she tells me.

It echoes, hard and metallic, as she tosses the words and the money at my feet. The bills scatter on the floor. "Hush money."

I watch it fall. It lands just like she wants it to, with shame, with disdain, with what is left of my dignity. My pride remains intact, if only just. She knows this. It is why she plays it this way. She wants me to crawl on the floor like a dog.

"Two hundred thousand dollars," she says. Her words come out cold, dismissive. "You should be grateful, and you better put it to good use."

She points to the cash, makes an effort to raise an eyebrow. I give her a long, considered look. I need to play this right.

I give her my best smile. "Thank you," I say. "I knew you'd pull through."

"I want a return on this investment." She grins and gives a hoot, a wicked laugh. "We'll see if I can count on you, Christophe *Montclair*."

She uses my new identity like a threat and walks away, leaving me to scramble on the floor, gathering the bills.

Dealing with Maxine is the longest stretch of torture I've ever faced. But this time it's different, because if winning Lexi over wasn't such a challenge, I would never have put myself in this position.

FORTY-TWO

LEXI

After a sleepless night, I wake up to a text from Florence.

> I'm in Los Angeles. And I'm taking you to dinner tonight. 7 p.m. Phillip won't be joining us, but you'll meet him today. He's already on the ground and we have a plan. I'll send a car to pick you up. Where?

I rub my eyes, trying to make sense of everything. I'm not liking the position I'm in, but, if I'm being honest with myself, it's far better than yesterday. I text Florence back.

> The showroom in Brentwood.

> I have the address.

Of course she does. She's like the all-seeing eye.

The piddly amount of money Christophe has given me sits on my nightstand in a messy stack. Before heading to the showroom, I race to the bank. I handle the stack of bills like it's counterfeit—unreal, unreliable—and hand it over to the teller. Ten thousand dollars. My hands shake. Blood money, I'm sure of it. The amount feels like a grain of sand compared to the desert of red stretching across my financial statements. It's still numbingly inadequate, a band-aid on a bloody hemorrhage.

Aside from Florence, I wonder about the other victims he's left in his wake, or if he's ever had to hold his breath while his balance plummeted like mine. The numbers flash on the screen, confirming what I already know: despite the deposit, I'm still desperately in the negative. It's a reminder of what's at stake—of why I have to pull this off. I bury the resentment, grit my teeth, and head to the showroom, where it's only a matter of time before Tricia starts in on me again.

"Where have you been? You were supposed to be here an hour ago."

I could lie and tell her I got stuck in traffic—the typical LA excuse. But I don't.

"I'm dealing with a lot right now."

"Right. Christophe." Tricia paces, her voice more frantic with every step. "He's not just a con artist, he could be a killer! Vescari! Sabrina and Calvin Vale! Odd, his investors are dropping off like flies," she exclaims. "What if you're next?"

I sink into a chair, my knuckles tight against the table. "I'm not letting him get away with it," I say, updating her on the communication I've had with Florence. I don't tell her much, just enough to make her back off.

Her expression is everything I expect: outraged, disbelieving. She stops in front of me, hands on her hips, foot tapping. "He's a criminal, Lex. He's dangerous!" she insists, her voice as fierce as her loyalty. "And by the way, my PI came through, and his real name is Christophe Bouchard." She shakes her head. "And he used his real identity when you married him."

She slams a copy of the marriage license on the table.

I want to tell her that I already know, but I hold back, even when I feel my control slipping. "He's going to pay me back," I say. "And then I'm getting rid of him."

My words sound weak, but, for now, they're all I have.

"And you believe that?" she shoots back.

I let out a breath, try to sound more certain. "I have to."

Her eyes narrow, skeptical and caring. "Before you know it, he'll disappear. He'll take the money and run."

Her disbelief cuts through me, sharper than I want to admit. She folds her arms, giving me that look that says she knows better, that says she's always known. But he won't run now, mostly because he thinks I'm somebody I'm not. A Marlowe. He wants a bigtime pay day.

"He's coming back with it," I tell her. "I'm sure of it."

"You think he actually cares about you?"

I try to match her, try to let her know I'm on top of this. "He doesn't," I say, repeating Florence's words. "He's not as clever as he thinks he is."

She waits, expecting me to expand on this. Instead, I hold her gaze, hoping she doesn't see how close I am to breaking.

She leans closer, voice softening. "He's going to ruin you."

"Not if I ruin him first," I say.

"I don't know who you are right now," she huffs.

She watches me, a mix of anger and concern. It's the concern that almost undoes me. It's the anger that pushes me to keep this up, to prove I can play this better than he thinks I can. Better than she thinks I can.

"Yes, you do," I finally say. "You know I'm driven, and you know I'd never let anybody cross me. Not like this."

"You need to call the police."

I straighten my posture. "And I will. Once I get my money back."

Tricia stops her pacing long enough to give me a hard look. I feel it, deep and doubting. "Let me loan you the money," she offers.

I shake my head, trying to stay firm, trying to stay in control. "And what? Be indebted to you for the rest of my life? No, thank you."

Her expression shifts, softer, and it's harder to fight. But I have to do this on my terms.

"What if you and Florence are wrong?" she asks, resuming her pacing.

"We won't be," I say, hoping I sound more confident than I feel.

I can see her doubt, see the worry etched on her face. I hate putting her in this position. Her hands lock onto her hair.

"Just trust me," I say. "Please."

"Trust you?" Her laugh is short, not unkind. "You don't even trust yourself. If you did, you wouldn't be in this situation." She sighs. "Lex, I'm worried," she says, and her voice wavers just enough to make me waver, too.

"Don't be," I reply, wishing it didn't sound so pathetic.

She waits for me to say more. When I don't, she throws her hands in the air, exasperated and helpless. It makes me want to scream, makes me want to give in. But I can't, so I don't. She gives me one last glance, the kind that's meant to make me crack, meant to make me doubt. But I don't, not yet.

"I have to get a shipment out," she finally says.

I watch her walk away. "I have everything under control," I whisper, telling her, telling myself, telling the doubt that still circles in my head like buzzards looking for a fresh kill.

The printer stutters, the sound an invasion in the tight space between us. I look at it, at Tricia. "Trendline?" I ask, already sure we won't like what we'll see.

Tricia reads as the pages spew out. Her expression falls, just like my stomach, just like the hope I had. "It's terrible," she says, laying the papers on the desk. The numbers confirm it. A bad order, no advance, and us stuck in the middle. We crowd over the desk, calculators and desperation scattered around us.

Tricia shakes her head, but not as if she's surprised. She never is—that is, until Christophe popped up in our world. "They really think we can pull this off for so little?"

"They think they're doing us a favor," I reply. "But, nope, they're not."

I punch the numbers into the calculator, hoping they'll change, hoping they'll lie. But they don't. They're as honest as I need them to be. I hand her the results, and the cold digits stare back at us.

"We'll barely breakeven if we're lucky," Tricia says, frowning. "I thought this could have been our big break. But"—she shakes her head—"it could break us."

She flips through the pages again, more furious with each one, more fed up with the way they look. Finally, she slaps them facedown and then leans back, rubbing her eyes. I watch her, watch the way she moves. I don't think I've ever seen her look this tired. I pick up the contract. "We can't sign this. Maybe we can negotiate a better deal?"

"My thoughts exactly. They want us to knock off twenty percent of our wholesale cost? Absolutely insane," she replies.

My gaze drifts to the window, hoping to escape. I catch the movement in the parking lot, catch the convoy as it pulls in. SUVs, big and dark, gliding into position. Men spill from the cars, dressed in suits that match the color of my impending doom. They move with purpose, with precision.

Aside from his serums, what if Christophe has left something incriminating here? My heart races. "Police?"

Tricia follows my stare, then looks back to me. "Not if they're dressed in Prada suits."

"They might be here for him," I reply, feeling the tension rise with every step they take.

The men approach the showroom, an intimidating force that makes my pulse quicken. The bell above the door chimes, and I brace for the worst.

The leader enters first, a man with gray hair and a stern expression. He scans the room with the authority of someone who knows he has it. "I'm looking for Alexis Marlowe," he says, his voice as commanding as his presence.

I swallow, stand up, and hope I don't regret it. "That would be me."

Tricia watches, her eyes wide with a mix of curiosity and fear. I try to act unfazed, like I have this figured out.

The man studies me, his expression softening. He laughs, the sound booming and unexpected. "Well, what do you know? You're the granddaughter I've never met."

It takes a moment for his words to sink in, a moment for the shock to register. I can't believe Florence Montclair really pulled through. The king of retail is here and he's here to help. I hope. "Mr. Marlowe?"

"Call me Phillip. Florence Montclair is a dear friend," he says, pausing. "So good, she even convinced me not to sue you for attaching yourself and your brand to the Marlowe name."

I swallow. "That's not my fault. Everybody just assumed—"

"And you let them ride with that assumption," he says, meeting my gaze. "But that's not why I'm here. I've come to talk about Christophe."

"Christophe Bouchard? The con artist with a rap sheet a mile long? The one you married?" Tricia asks, but I don't respond. I'm still reeling from Phillip's presence. I stare at the man who's supposed to help me fix this situation. It's overwhelming. It's thrilling. It's too much and not enough at the same time.

"The less she knows, the better," says Phillip, gesturing in Tricia's direction.

"She's my best friend and business partner. She's in this with me. We can trust her..."

"Could you stop talking about me in the third person?" Tricia waves. "I'm right here."

Phillip gives a soft chuckle. "Full name?"

"Tricia Hoffman," she says.

He looks toward one of his men. "Mark, run a background check."

In stunned silence, Tricia and I openly gawk as Mark sits in one of the booths and pulls out a laptop, taps a couple of keys. Phillip returns his focus to me. "We already have our due diligence on you. Quite the story about your mother's incarceration and the death of your adoptive parents."

Tricia's jaw goes slack. "How does he know all this?"

I lower my head, avoiding her gaze. "I'll tell you everything later."

Thankfully, she doesn't have time to pump me for information.

"She's clear," says Mark. "Married to a real-estate developer. Construction. Jeffery Hoffman. Built this strip mall. Working on the new shopping center in Century City. Not one speck of dirt."

"Cement. Could come in handy." Phillip smiles and rubs his hands together. "We have a plan to get rid of him. A good one."

His confidence is steady, like he knows exactly what he's doing. Like he's done this before. He knows how to play this. Maybe even better than Christophe. He knows the game, the stakes, the way it looks when you win. And he's willing to let me sit at his table.

Tricia finds her voice, though it's shaky. "A plan to get rid of Christophe?" she wheezes, catching on, catching up, catching her breath.

"After he returns with my money?" I ask, the only question I can think of, the only thing I can say.

Phillip laughs again, the sound more than reassuring. "Exactly," he says. "I'm going to meet him as your grandfather. Ultimately, he's after my fortune, thinks you're its heir and that you're set up for life. He tried to play Florence the same way, wanted to marry her."

Tricia clears her throat. "Lexi married him in Vegas."

"Big mistake." Phillip eyes me. "Tell him I want to meet the newest member of my family. Set up a dinner and we'll take things from there."

"He's in Miami."

"Text him." He winks. "He'll be sure to come back."

I pull out my phone, swallowing. It's only just occurred to

me that he might just have taken off with my money. Then again, his stupid car is still parked on the street. He'd definitely come back for that. I'm thinking about selling it for fifty thousand.

Tricia leans over my shoulder as I tap my phone.

> My grandfather, Phillip, is here. He'd like to take us out to dinner to celebrate our marriage and LexICON. When do you return to LA? Sorry about how we left things. Miss you.

Tricia blurts out a laugh. "You miss him?"

I snap my head up. "Too much?"

"Just right," says Phillip. "He's a narcissist. He'll fall for it."

"No, it may clue him in." I clear my throat. "Before he left, I might have tried to run him over with my car."

Phillip lets out a hearty laugh. "Too bad you didn't kill him."

I shrug. "I wouldn't have gotten my money back."

"I like you," says Phillip.

While we wait for Christophe's response, Phillip walks around the showroom, his hands running through the racks of clothes. He points to the deli display, to the sports bras and colorful, rolled-up T-shirts. "Nice merchandise. Great quality. I love the set-up. Who do you sell to?"

"Fred Segal and Alice and Olivia are our biggest accounts," says Tricia. "We made a lot of sales at Style Sphere. And we met with Trendline the other day." She taps the papers in front of her. "Before you arrived, we were going over the terms..."

Phillip picks up the contract and thumbs through it. "Do not sign this piece of shit. I'll give you a better deal with Marlowe's and we'll run with this set-up."

Tricia is shaking like a small dog. "You have over one thousand stores..."

"One thousand, five hundred and forty-six to be exact. We'll start with two hundred—see how it goes." He eyes the deli display and shoots me a wink. "Your line will sell like hotcakes." He pulls out his phone, taps a couple of keys. "The head of buying will be here next week with our merchandising team."

I am beyond stumped. "I don't know what to say."

"Say nothing." He winks. "Apparently, we're family now and we're in this together."

My phone buzzes and Tricia lets out a sound—something in between a yelp and a squeal. I eye the caller ID. I cringe. I hold up my phone. "It's him."

> I'll be back tomorrow afternoon. With the money. Tu me manques, aussi. Can't wait to meet your grandfather. I'll make a reservation at Musso's at eight. My treat.

Phillip takes my phone, eyes the message, and then looks at me. "Text him back. Say you'll pick him up. I'll have one of my drivers with you. You'll sneak out the back into the alley."

"Why?"

"Because there are two undercover officers in unmarked vehicles watching your place—one at the showroom, just passed him." He pauses. "We did a drive by. And when you're at the airport, do not get out of the car."

He hands me my phone and I do as I'm told.

> I'll pick you up. My grandpa hired me a driver. Send me your flight details. We'll be waiting out front.

Christophe responds immediately, flight number and a smiley face. My eyes lock on Phillip.

"Ready?" he asks, a mischievous smile playing on his lips.

"Ready for what?" I ask, not ready for anything, yet at the same time ready for everything.

"All of it," he says. "He's just a fisherman. I'm a hunter. I understand you're having dinner with Florence. I'll see you tomorrow night."

Phillip and his men move toward the door, leaving as quickly as they arrived. I stare, trying to process this, trying to make sense of it. Tricia stares, too, the same disbelief etched on her face.

When they're gone, Tricia sucks in a breath and turns to me. "What the hell just happened?" she asks, as if I have the answer.

"I don't know," I admit.

"But you're going with it, aren't you?"

"Yeah," I say. "Whatever it is, I am."

She laughs, a genuine laugh, a relief of a laugh. "This is so insane," she says.

I don't argue. It really is.

FORTY-THREE
CHRISTOPHE

I don't need Maxine anymore. I have exactly what I've come for.

I feel her death in my breath. Sharp. Quick. A calculated blade. I don't slow down, don't let the panic sink in. Maxine's final drama. The climax. The fade to black. I dry my hands and check my phone. It's dry, too. Like her old bones. Like the fear she should have felt. The text from Lexi tells me I have her exactly where I want her. My face lights up, a bright reminder that I am still here. I settle in Maxine's plush armchair, savor the text, and wait for more.

The sun rises high, almost perfect. Like my plan. Like me. I see her body, imagine the story they will tell. She slipped, they will say. But she didn't slip. She didn't slip at all. She drowned drunk in her bathtub. With a little assistance. My absence is loud, my anticipation louder. It's a comfort. It's the relief of knowing how far ahead I am, how ready I am to leave. I am calm. I am sure. I am almost gone.

Then the ring of the doorbell, sharp and quick like a bullet. I let it ring, the last of the risk, the last of my lingering nerves.

The silence comes thick with reassurance. I breathe it in, let it fill the space she once did. It smells like expensive failure, like all the times she let her guard down. It smells like Maxine. The door is open, just like I left it. Her body floats, more dramatic than she was in life. I return to the living room and start to gather what I came for. My movements are deliberate. My patience, endless. Her trust. Her cash. Her antique pearls. Her millions. I take them all, stuffing the remains of her wealth into my bag.

The walls watch me, the Monet keeping secrets it can't tell. The safe is still open, more satisfying than her final gasp. The jewelry spills out in an intoxicating shimmer. The money, too. I think of Maxine and what she thought she had. It's mine now. It always was.

Time is on my side, and so is her wealth. Seeing that I'm her only heir, I'll inherit the rest, including this monstrosity of a house.

I should have done this sooner. Bad on me.

My movements are smooth, just like the family jewels. I count, and I count on her stupidity, on her greed. One hundred thousand. The number is precise, like the cut of the diamonds I take. Two hundred. Three. The cash is better. More fluid. Just like me. It's what I needed. What I came for.

I savor my own efficiency, my own lack of remorse. This is what Maxine should have expected, what she should have known. She is my mother and my mentor, after all. I close the safe, the mystery of her death solved. The truth is as brilliant as the bracelet I pocket.

Her last husband's clothes hang in the closet, untouched. I swap my damp shirt for a fresh one, more concerned about my reflection than her life.

They'll call it tragic. But not for me. I'm finally free of her. Monster.

The prints are easy; I wipe them away just like my plans when they go wrong. They don't go wrong. Not this time.

I look for anything I've missed, but I haven't. My own certainty is my best accessory.

I leave through the front, leave it all behind. A dramatic end to an even more dramatic affair. My hands are steady, steadier than the life I took. The neighbors see a man too polished for crime, too composed for suspicion. I give them a nod. They nod back.

Money isn't the only thing I want. Not anymore.

The world shrinks. Thirty thousand feet below. I have never been more above it all. My seat is soft. My drink smoother than a thousand lies. The passengers sleep, oblivious to the fortune in the bag I'd checked in, the fortune I have. I think of Lexi. I think of the stakes, and the bourbon tastes like ambition. The flight attendant smiles, unaware that I've taken so much more than her free drink. She flirts, and I flirt back, knowing it will lead to nothing. I think of how to tell her this, but I don't. It's better.

She wants to know my name. I tell her Ryan Daniels. She writes her name, Sandra, and her phone number down, handing it over to me, her handwriting an exotic swirl. She is curious, asks what brings me to LA. I want to tell her a new life, a new risk, a new fortune. But I say business instead. Her look is coy, and I give her one back. I give her what I can. Not everything. I'm saving that for someone else. Someone like Lexi.

She brings another drink, and my American accent is as thick as the stacks of money in my bag. My thoughts drift. The clouds drift. The drink is smooth. My plan is smoother. I am as detached as I need to be.

This is how it should be. I knew it when I took Lexi to the restaurant, when I took Maxine to the bath, when I took the cash. It's the luxury of not having to look back, of letting go without regret, without remorse. I look at the reflection in the glass. I am still here. I am still in the game. The future excites me. I raise my glass and, in my head, I toast Maxine.

You will not be missed, but thanks for the lessons, Monster.

FORTY-FOUR
CHRISTOPHE

Then

Maxine leads me through her mansion, thanks to husband number two. The doors are wide, but not as wide as this new world of mine. A mentor. A home. A way in. I have learned to want. I have learned to take. Now I learn to wait. It is the hardest thing of all.

"Patience, Christophe," she says.

I'm trying, I am.

I follow her slowly, when I want to run.

The rooms are lavish, lavish like I've never seen, lavish like I've always wanted. A library bigger than the basement I shared with the crew. Art that hangs from the walls like jewels. Sofas that beg me to remember how I got here.

Her patience is endless, and I need it, need it as much as the papers she hands me. More documents. New names. More of everything. It is beautiful, and at fourteen years old I am new again.

Maxine calls it fluid. I call it mine.

She leads me out of the main home to the pool house. "This is where you will stay." She sighs. "Just so you know, my husband was pretty upset that I've brought you here."

My upper lip lifts. "I'm your son. Where else would I go?"

"I was hoping you'd stay in that juvenile detention center for a while longer—until you were a legal adult." Her posture straightens. "But we can't always get what we want. Understand?"

I don't. She's the one who had me kill my own father and then told me to get involved with the jewelry crew. She's the reason I am the way I am. That's what I tell myself.

She pinches my cheek. "Here's the way things are going to work around here. You'll go to school. You'll work. You'll live here. You won't bring friends home. You won't call me Mother. You won't mention my new husband's name. And you'll do exactly what I tell you to do. Think of it as a training program."

"For what?"

"Your life," she says, shooting me a grin. "The good news is you can leave Montréal in the past. Thanks to my marriage, I'm working on your American citizenship. And, after that, you'll get rid of the man I'm now married to just like you did with your father."

"You don't love him?"

"People believe what they want to believe and we're building a better life for both of us," she says, and I believe it.

I believe her.

The training is like nothing I have done before. It is harder. It is better. It is more. She teaches me, and I soak it up, drink it in, fill myself with everything I never knew, never had, never wanted more than this.

French wines. German cars. Swiss watches. I learn the details, the history, the elegance, the lie. I learn to speak French without the Canadian accent. I am exactly who I want to be.

She gives me time. I take it. I take everything. The life I will have, the life she wants me to have, the life I already have. Her advice, my bible. My savior. My new goddamn life.

"Identity is fluid, darling," she says. "And you're going to create a new you."

It is new, and it is old. I see it the way I saw the jewels, the fakes, the crew, the other boys, the thin mattresses and thin sheets and thin lies I used to live. Now I live here. I live in the world. I live like I always knew I would.

Maxine shows me how it is done. I do not know why I am surprised. I have seen her plans, seen the way they work, seen her at the peak of her cold brilliance. It was bound to happen. A new kind of art, a new kind of heist, a new kind of death. Her husbands, too old to matter. I am good at this. I should be. I'm being taught by a master manipulator.

It is methodical. It is brutal. She is a good teacher, and I am an excellent student.

Identity is fluid, darling.

So is a good con. So is murder.

I watch her the way I watch everything. The poisons, the meds, the precision of her planning. I am impressed, but she thinks it is more. I let her. I learn. Another job, another hit, another way to show her I am up to it.

I know what I am doing, she tells me, but I already know. It is harder than I want it to be, easier than I think. Easier with each step. Each lesson. Each time I get it right.

The first husband. The second. The third.

The thrill of the kill is mine. A perfect, practiced art.

The third is easy. Easy as the first, as the second, as I knew it would be. She thinks it's hers, thinks it's her plan, her scheme, her way of being smarter than they are. Smarter than I am. The husband. The old man. The new game. The mistake he makes is not mine, is not hers.

Maxine has a new plan for me—find my own marks. See how much I can take, get away with.

FORTY-FIVE
DETECTIVE SAMSON

Sabrina and Calvin Vale's deaths have piqued my interest, especially with the Vescari investigation, and the first person I want to talk to is Alexis Marlowe. She'll be honest with me. Or she won't. She might be the world's best liar. I walk into her showroom without knocking. She's sitting on the floor, folding shirts, and looks up. "Detective Samson," she says. "I wasn't expecting you."

"I'm sure you know why I'm here."

She rolls her shoulders and then stands up, her breath catching. "I saw the news."

"You mentioned her before, said she'd invested in Montclair's company. But how well did you know Sabrina Vale?"

"I didn't really. She's nice, a little intense, and I told you she offered to be the brand ambassador for LexICON."

"We understand you might have been one of the last people to see her alive." He points toward the window, to the left. "We have her schedule and the ladies at the nail salon saw her come into the space after her appointment."

Tricia walks out from the kitchen/stock room, eyes wide. "Yeah, she wanted to pick up the merchandise we'd promised to send her."

"So you know her, too?"

"Like Lexi said, not really. Actresses help promote the brand. We—"

"And you are?"

"Tricia Hoffman, Lexi's business partner."

I pull out a pad of paper and pen, jotting her name down.

"We have footage of a silver Maserati leaving the property around the time of death," I continue. "The plates match the car parked in front of your apartment complex."

"Christophe's car?" Tricia asks. "The fancy-ass one? The Maserati?"

"That's the one, but it's registered to a Christophe Bouchard from Palm Beach."

Her friend, Tricia, blurts out, "Lexi's husband's real name is Christophe Bouchard," and Alexis scowls at her. "He's a con artist. And I think he's a killer." Tricia snorts. "Lexi is impulsive and obviously made a very bad decision when she married him."

My eyes narrow. I face Alexis. Her head hangs low. "I just found out," she mumbles. "I have bad taste in men, apparently."

The pieces are clicking together. "How many aliases does he have?"

"I don't know."

"We found these at the scene," I say, my face blank. I throw a crisp, marked bill on the table. "Ms. Marlowe, you made a deposit at your bank this morning. Same serial numbers. Where did you get the money? Did Mrs. Vale pay you for her clothes?"

I wait for her reaction, watch her throat constrict. "No, Christophe gave the money to me before he took off."

"Where to?"

"Miami."

"Are you aware he was at the Vale residence yesterday? And he is a suspect in a double homicide?" I clear my throat. "We also have reason to believe he murdered Franco Vescari."

She's trying to steady herself, find balance, but the ground is shaky. She's having an internal earthquake. "No," she says, her voice small. "No, I didn't know. Like I said, he left for Miami yesterday."

"You think he's in Miami?" Tricia grips her arm and Alexis winces. "He's probably conning another mark just like he's conned you."

I suck in a breath, my gaze whipping to Alexis. "He conned you?"

"Not my proudest moment." She lowers her head again, shaking it. "He wrote me a bad check and took off. He's supposed to come back with the rest of the money he owes me, but I doubt he will."

She sounds convincing. Almost. I write everything down. Check bank. Check flights. Check everything. Twice.

"If you hear from him," I finally say, "you'll let me know."

She doesn't say yes. She doesn't say no. She doesn't say anything. And I understand. She's another one of his victims.

Her friend Tricia looks like she's going to faint. From what I can tell, she's not Christophe's biggest fan.

FORTY-SIX

LEXI

I sit down, the weight of it all crashing into me. Into us. Tricia looks at me, a mix of horror and wonder.

"You married a con artist," she whispers. "And he's actually killed people."

"Allegedly," I tell her. It's the only word I can think of.

Tricia laughs. It's bitter. Not the laugh I expect. "Not allegedly enough."

The doubts swarm, but not like before.

"This is serious. I'm scared for you," she replies with a gasp. "Jesus, Lexi, what's going on inside of that head of yours?"

I don't answer, because I don't know.

"Are you really going to risk it?" Tricia asks. Her concern almost convinces me to change my mind.

"Yes," I tell her.

She shakes her head, more resigned than angry. "I thought I was crazy for marrying Jeff when I was so young, fresh out of college, never dated anybody else," she says, raising her voice a level or two. "But you, Lex? You are certifiable. Do you actually believe he's going to come back with your money?"

"I do," I reply, nodding my head with vigor. "And, I promise, swear on my life, after I get the funds back into my account, I'll loop in the cops."

"You're not thinking clearly." She glowers at me. "And, as for your life, you're playing around with it."

"You can't stop me," I huff.

She lets out a sigh, and it sounds like defeat. "Looks like I can't stop anything," she says. I see her facial expressions twist and change, the one that wants to help, the one that wants to let me do this, the one that can't decide.

Tricia stomps away, hands raised in resignation, the front door slamming behind her.

I realize she's angry with me, and she's coming from a place of concern. But I know what I need to do. And I'm not scared of Christophe. He's not going to get away with anything. Not this time.

The early evening traffic hums as I wait inside the showroom, staring out the window. A black Mercedes sedan pulls up, the door opening, a tailored Chanel skirt suit, a long leg, a commanding air—Florence.

She gives me a nod. "Alexis, thank you for agreeing to see me."

"How was your flight?"

"Perfect." She lifts her sunglasses to the top of her head. "There's nothing quite like flying private."

I nod like I agree. The wind stirs, as uncertain as my plans. As unpredictable as Christophe's. Florence's arrival unsettles me, just like it should. She looks around the showroom, her eyes taking stock, measuring, more impressed than she lets on.

"Phillip was right about you." She nods with approval. "You're onto something, my dear." She purses her lips. "Shall we go? I made a reservation at Nobu in Malibu. I hope you like sushi."

I stand there, feeling like the wind has been knocked out of me. "I do. Just let me grab my purse."

After locking up, I follow her to a car. Two men sit up front.

The sedan glides through evening traffic, as fast as my heart. Florence looks toward the ocean. I imagine her, cool and elegant, seated among her entourage, a lifetime of defiance, of building her company. For now, we're just sticking to awkward small talk, mostly about LexICON. But I know she has a plan. And I know it matches mine.

The air changes. The air feels alive. The coastline unfurls in front of us. It is fast. The way I have to be. I gaze at Florence, the fierce look in her eyes. I probably have the same intensity lighting mine.

The low hum of Nobu's dining room buzzes around us as we settle at a corner table on the outside terrace, away from prying eyes and ears. The ocean crashes, rhythmic and certain. I open my tote, placing small bottles between us, their contents marked in red ink.

She picks up a bottle, examining it. "He stole the formula from me. But they don't make Montclair's in China." She laughs and then her eyes narrow. "Prison isn't good enough for him."

My breath holds, but my panic doesn't. I meet her gaze. "I agree."

"Have you heard the rumors about my family's ties to Marseilles?"

"I have," I say, wondering where this conversation is headed.

"They are very much true."

Florence is direct, like the danger, like her laughter. "He was supposed to be a fling," she says. "But that wasn't enough for him. I believe I told you that he wanted to marry me."

Her words hang over me like a cloud for a moment.

"How did you meet him?"

"At a gala in Palm Beach. I thought he was a beautiful disaster, but charm and beauty only last for so long." She gives a soft laugh. "My husband had recently passed, and Christophe became a temporary addiction. A toy boy, if you will. I never had plans to marry him." She pauses. "And you? How did you end up marrying him?"

"Vegas."

Her head tilts to the side and she pulls out a piece of paper from her purse. "Yes, I have a copy of your marriage certificate."

She hands it to me, and I look at the names again. Alexis Elizabeth Marlowe. Christophe Edmond Bouchard. I swallow. "He used his real name," I mumble. "Which means the marriage is real."

"Because he thinks you're a Marlowe. And California is a fifty percent state." She clears her throat. "I should have done my due diligence on him before I took a risk. His mother, Maxine Bouchard, from Montréal, is a former stripper, white trash, now known as the Black Widow of Palm Beach."

I take a large sip of my sake. I'll never forget that name. Ever. "Maxine. She's the reason my mother is in prison. My mother stole from her. She sent some thug over to our place..."

"Yes, I made the connection and I'm sorry about that." Florence clasps my hand. "Do you speak with your mother?"

I lower my head, shaking it. "She refuses to see me, even sends back my letters."

"She's protecting you."

I want to tell her the truth, that my mother shouldn't be in prison. But by the way Florence is eyeing me, she already knows this. Confirmed when she says, "I read the transcripts from the trial. She should have gotten off on self-defense."

"But she didn't."

"Sadly, no. As for Christophe, I'm wagering he killed Maxine's husbands. All four of them." She smiles. It's tight. It's brilliant. "He's not that smart, but he's smarter than most. He always insists on more and that's how we can trap him. You're his more."

She lifts her sake cup and sets it back down. Her lips never touch the rim.

The ocean's crash is a steady backdrop, a steady reminder. I take a deep breath. I have to. Her words fill my ears and our sake grows cold. I do, too.

Florence laughs again, more bitter than before. "He thought I'd let him get away with it," she says. "He thought he was ahead." Her tone shifts, drops lower, hardens. "The little bastard defied me. He stole. He lied." She pauses. "He tried to kill me. Eventually, he'll try to kill you, but only after he gets what he wants. We have to strike first."

Florence watches me, as certain as the waves, as sharp as his lies. I watch her expression darken, and it's like looking into a mirror. The ocean is loud with its rage. So are we. I need to know how this ends. I need to know that it doesn't end until he's dead. I'll do anything to protect the people I love, my mother, Tricia. And I'll do anything to protect myself. I have a life worth living.

Florence looks at me as if she knows what I want, knows what I am, knows who I am and what I'm capable of. I hold her gaze and I feel the unspoken words, I feel them hard.

"The audacity of using the Montclair name—a brilliant move on his part." Her eyes light up and she takes a sip of her sake. "Until now. We have him right where we want him."

Florence glances at the ocean, her focus tight. "I was thinking of having my men take him back to Marseilles in my plane, bound and gagged. Tortured. And I think you'd like the same thing," Florence whispers. "Dead. Not in prison."

Our plans collide, a rush of confession. A pact. The ocean crashes, and her voice is a tide that swells with danger. I listen, hold my breath until I speak again. "It's what I want, too," I say, as steady as the waves.

Florence leans forward, and I feel the heat of her conviction, the heat of her voice. "Is it?" she asks.

"Yes," I say, my gaze fierce. "Very much."

"Then you know what we have to do," she says, her voice soft, her intent clear, her look a fucking beacon of hope. "You're like me. You have a killer instinct."

I watch her eyes, and it scares me, the way they look, the way they burn with fire, with vengeance, the way mine are burning as well.

"We'll come up with a plan after we eat," she says, waving a server over.

I stare at the ocean, and then back at Florence.

I'm thinking about how much I admire her confidence. How I want to be just like her. I think of Tricia's initials on Christophe's hit list and how I'd do anything to protect her. I think of all his victims, wondering how his brain has been wired, how Maxine has programmed him. How Maxine, his mother, took my mother away from me.

My mind flashes with imagined segments of Christophe's past as Florence shares more about him over our meal. It's almost like watching a movie—a horror film, the kind where you're screaming at the screen, telling the woman to run away.

FORTY-SEVEN
CHRISTOPHE

Then

In the glass-walled solarium, everything feels like luxury and threat. Maxine's presence is larger than the mansion. Larger than Palm Beach. I sit across from her, but her grip on me is tighter than the diamond bracelet around her wrist. Although it dazzles, it is nothing compared to her words. "You're ready to strike out on your own," she says, and I know I am. I've just taken care of husband number four. Gregory Summers slipped down the marble stairway, splitting his head open—after I pushed him. The police are calling it a tragic accident.

"Go on, darling," she continues, sliding the profiles across the table. "Make me proud."

Her smile is crisp. So is the white suit she wears, an armor I am learning to perfect. She waits for me to speak, to react. My fingers trace the files. The wealthy widows. The vulnerable. The desperate. I run my hand across their names, their photos, and see my future.

Maxine's lips twist into a wicked grin. "I'm funding your adventures, but I expect to see returns."

I play it cool, but my excitement burns as hot as her glance, the one that tells me I am ready for more. I tuck the folder under my arm, feeling the thrill, the rush, the way it lights me up and binds me to her.

Days later, I know I've found my calling. I'm a fisherman, reel them in and then throw them back into the water.

The private jet touches down in Nice, and I can't believe how the thrill of hunting down marks feels. The Mediterranean sparkles. The city sparkles. It is all within reach. The name. The fortune. The new me. I hear her voice, the precision of it, the drive. Her presence pushes me and I'm going to make her proud.

The heat of the June night follows me like I knew it would, like the crowd does, like the scent of Maxine's ambition. I dress for it, evening wear and confidence, playing the part she taught me. The part I own. From Nice I take a private car to Monaco. A casino at midnight. My world at midnight. The first mark is clear, and so is the thrill.

Don't fall in love with the woman. Fall in love with the money.

I see her. The Russian heiress. Alone at a baccarat table, dripping with wealth, with prospects, with more than she can keep. She plays, and I am at her side. My hands steady. My breath calm. My need sharp. Hers is, too. She wants me. A roll of the dice, and her hand runs down my thigh.

I am no longer Christophe. I am Count de Beaumont with the papers to prove it.

The woman believes me. She will believe what I want. The money comes faster than I think. The win is quicker than I'd planned for. I am unstoppable.

Marrakesh is warm. The desert air clings, and the city overwhelms. I am better than this. Better than Maxine ever expected. The rush, the high, the thrill of the con. It feeds me like the sun. The transformation is swift, brilliant, everything I dreamed.

Jean-Luc Fournier, a Franco-Algerian art dealer, is my next role to reel in the second mark four months later. I look the part, feel the part, am the part. It's so easy. It's so much fun.

The studio loft is small but effective. It works the way I work the city. With skill. With precision. With elegance. I arrange a series of crude sketches around the walls. The drawings hang loose, abstract.

It's easy here. Easy in a way that fuels me. I keep my cover simple, but my ambition is grand. I am an artist. I am a dealer. I am hers, and I am my own. A collector will invest in the gallery I pretend to open. A collector will invest in me. She will fuel my dreams.

The Parisian is easy to find and easier to charm. The color, the vibrancy, the music, the perfect opportunity. I slip into her life like it's my own, and I am ready to take it. Her name is Leona, a fortune to be had.

My enthusiasm soars.

I am whoever I want or need to be.

Each success fills me. Each mark. Each lie. I feel the rush. I feel the brilliance of it, the newness of it, the more it always gives. Marrakesh, Monaco, the names, the marks, the money. This life is thrilling. I love it. I need more of it.

Four years later, I'm back in Palm Beach with more money than I've ever dreamed of. I'm ready for Maxine's next play.

Maxine's fingernails tap the table with a manicured impatience. My mind spins faster than my escape from Rome, faster than Maxine's plane, faster than my last con. "Florence Montclair," she says, the name a challenge and a thrill.

I know all about her.

"Florence ruined me," Maxine continues, her voice full of demand and old anger. She holds my focus. "You can either become the heir they lost," she says, her gray eyes colder than the diamonds at her throat. "Or you ensnare her, marry her, and take her for everything." She grins. "She lost her husband six months ago. And she's here in Palm Beach. You'll meet her at the gala."

The file on Florence is thick. Her history. Her business. Her fortune. Her life. If Maxine thinks we can steal it, I know we can. "I thought I was supposed to stay away from those parties, to keep a low profile when I'm in town."

"There are always exceptions." She taps the file. "She is one of them."

"Is it that simple?" I ask.

"Nothing worthwhile is simple, darling," she replies. "But you make it look easy. You are Christophe. You are above it all."

I arrive in Bordeaux on a chilly February night. The plane was faster than I thought, my ambition faster. I have never moved this fast, and I like it.

"*Bienvenue*," the chauffeur says as he takes my bags. His voice is practiced. Respectful. Exactly what it should be.

I step into the grand hall, and it is everything I want. Gilt and gleaming and ready for me. I take it all in. The grandeur. The staff. The look on Florence's face as she sees me, the surprise, the excitement. I cross the room, her gaze fixed on me like I knew it would be. We, of course, will be speaking in my French, my Québécois accent long gone.

"You look stunning," I say, my words deliberate to disarm her. "I haven't stopped thinking about you since we met at the gala."

"You came all this way for me?" Florence says with a flirty laugh.

"I did. And you were the one who sent the plane to pick me up."

We sit, candlelit, in the formal dining room. I hold the wineglass like it's mine, like this life is mine. The light is warm, perfect. Florence holds her own, more than I thought, but not for long. She watches me. She wonders.

I tell her more. My history. The connection she didn't expect, the one I have always wanted, the lies rolling off my tongue like honey. I tell her more than I'd planned, and it makes me feel the thrill. The challenge. "It's wonderful to know I'm not alone," Florence says. "I'm so happy to speak with somebody who isn't asking me why I'm not crying over the death of my husband. I don't like focusing on tragedy."

"Neither do I."

We toast, meeting eyes as one does in France. "To the future."

Florence takes me to see the grounds. They are hers and soon will be mine. We walk, and she talks, and I listen. I listen the way I was taught. I listen for the cracks, the way I'll settle in them.

The Montclair grounds are endless. I think of the marks, the new names, the ease. I think of the Parisian woman and how much quicker that was. I think of my breath, my pulse, my ambition, and I think I will make it.

When she's not working, for the next few months Florence shows me everything, everything she thinks I want, including her bed. We travel to Nice and to Cannes, to Saint-Tropez and from Paris to Marrakesh, flying on her jet, the expanse and luxury almost enough. But not quite. It never is. Florence needs more convincing. She's not completely mine yet, but she will be. "It's like we have known each other forever," I say.

"I feel the same way," she says, "but I'm twice your age. And my daughters would be furious with me."

Maybe she's worried I'd fall for one of her girls, both gorgeous, or maybe she's afraid one of them would fall in love with me. I haven't met one person in her family—not Amandine or Sophie, both of her girls around the same age as me. Like Maxine, she's been keeping me a secret. Maybe that's why we've been traveling so much.

"Age is only a number," I lie, although for a woman in her sixties she looks incredible. Her body is fit. Her skin is divine, glowing, as it should be considering she runs a beauty empire. And her hair is always perfectly coiffed.

She's nothing like Maxine and this makes me want her more than I should.

She's giving me money, "an allowance" she calls it, for putting up with her. She's buying me clothes. But I want more. The anticipation makes me impatient.

One month later, we're back in Bordeaux. I tell her I have to leave, that because I'm American my three-month visa is up. I wait for the words to settle, the moment she asks me to stay. She doesn't. She just shrugs and says, "*Alors*, we've had our fun."

Fun? My jaw goes slack. I feel like a toy boy, a gigolo.

"I'm in love with you, Florence," I say, leaning forward to grab one of her hands. "Marry me."

Florence pulls back her hand and lifts her wine glass. Her movements are precise. My breath holds. My nerve holds. My ambition holds. She smiles, and the expression is hard. Harder than it was when I first arrived. She says nothing.

"I'm exactly what you need," I say. "You can't do this alone."

The words settle, thick, like the red wine we are drinking, made on the château's vineyard.

"No," she says. "I do not want to marry you, Christophe. You were only a distraction, albeit a very nice one. Like I said, we had our fun. Nothing more, nothing less. And I've done everything on my own so far. I'll be sad to see you go."

Three months in. I should have known better, read her better. But I've come prepared. I'm always prepared. I'm not leaving here empty-handed. No, I've worked too hard on this.

Her eyes focus on something in the distance. While she's not looking, I slip the poison—one part thallium, two parts propofol—into her wine, then I watch her eyes flicker and fade, listen to her murmur, "What did you do?" until her body slumps over, her head resting on the table. Her crystal glass crashes onto the stone terrace, shattering, red wine seeping into the cracks like blood.

My mind races. My body doesn't. I know where she keeps the secret formula Montclair Industries is working on. Thanks to a keen sense of hearing, I also know the combination to the safe, the one she keeps a million dollars in for emergencies.

ACT THREE

"Beauty is more than skin deep."

~ Charlize Theron

FORTY-EIGHT

LEXI

Tricia is in the kitchen—now our stock room—doing inventory when Detective Samson stops by the showroom. He doesn't wait for a greeting, just dives right in with his question. "Have you heard from him yet?"

"I haven't," I lie, hoping he doesn't see right through me.

"We've checked all flights coming to LA from Miami. He's not scheduled to fly back on any of them."

I have the perfect distraction.

"Maybe he's using another alias," I mutter.

Samson looks startled. "Another one?"

I should tell him about the passports, the burner phones, and the ledger I'd discovered, but I've given them to Florence for safe-keeping.

"Florence Montclair contacted me and we had dinner last night. She wanted to warn me, tell me how he'd conned her. She told me her story." I lower my gaze, focusing on my feet. "She thinks he's using another identity."

"Whatever name he's using, he's a very dangerous man." He sucks in a breath. "You won't get your money back. He's probably scoping out his next mark."

I know he's more than serious and concerned, his gaze never

leaving mine. I fidget, pulling an invisible thread on my top. He notices. I shove my hands into my pockets.

"I have a strong feeling there's something else you're not telling me. Do you know his whereabouts? Are you protecting him?"

My eyebrows pinch together. So do my teeth. "I assure you I'm not."

"And why is Florence Montclair in Los Angeles?"

This time I can tell the truth. "She found out Christophe's location when she stopped payment on the check. She had my name, my bank account information. Then she found me."

"Why?"

"To warn me." I swallow. "He didn't get what he wanted from her, so he tried to kill her. Poison. Clearly, she didn't die."

Samson scratches his chin. "I'm going to need her contact information."

I write it down, hand it over.

I watch him leave, heading toward the coffee shop next door. Tricia stomps up to me, her anger ricocheting off the walls. She glowers at me. "I heard everything, but I wanted to stay out of it. You lied to a detective. What the hell is wrong with you?"

"Nothing," I say, meeting her eyes. "You have to trust me."

"Trust you? I do," she scoffs, "but I don't trust him. He's a killer. Who's next? What if he comes after me?" Her hands shoot to her belly. "My baby."

I really didn't expect to be sideswiped like this. The timing—everything is so off. And I really do care for her, more than anybody in the entire world. She's the only person who truly believes I'm a good person. She's the only person I'd never take advantage of. She's my only friend.

"You're pregnant? Why didn't you tell me?"

Her shoulders slouch. "Because you're not supposed to share the news until you're out of the woods. And I'm out of the woods. Fourteen weeks." Her gaze meets mine, softer this time. "Morning sickness has been mild, and I've been pretending to drink, or ordering something that looks like champagne: ginger ale."

I suck in a breath. "I'm thrilled for you and Jeff, really."

"We're going to be raising the baby Catholic and Jewish." She lifts up her chin. "On that, I was going to ask you to be the baby's godmother. But that won't happen if you're dead."

"He's not going to kill me," I say, huffing. "I'm a Marlowe. You heard Phillip."

Tricia's laughter comes hard, brittle. "Oh my God, Lexi. Do you even hear yourself?" Her stare pierces, insistent and searching. "This guy, this plan—he's got you exactly where he wants you and that place isn't good."

I have to steady myself against her disbelief, against the dread I can't let myself feel. "Christophe is finished. He just doesn't know it yet."

Tricia folds her arms, and I see it in her eyes, the doubt, the worry, the panic. "And if you're wrong?" she asks. "Damn it, Lexi. The moment he gets back, if he does, call Detective Samson."

I breathe in the doubt, the fear, the plan. "I'm not wrong. My plan will work. I get my money back and then I'll release the dogs."

"You know he's got a target on your head," Tricia says. "And you're doing what? Sitting right in front of the fucking bullseye?" She shakes her head, more disgust than anger. "You threatened to run him over." She shakes her head with dismay. "Why didn't you tell the detective?"

I wish I hadn't told her about the "incident." I don't answer her, just clamp my lips together.

Tricia frowns, concern deepening the lines of her mouth. "He's a snake, Lex. A real deadly one."

I look at her, hold her gaze. "I've got it under control," I say, and it sounds true, sounds like I believe it. But I know Tricia doesn't.

"Why can't you listen?" she asks, and it almost cracks me. "For once. Why can't you be smart? Just this once?"

I laugh, the sound shaky. "I am smart. Smarter than him."

"Did you hear the detective? He said he's dangerous. Do you think he was joking around?" Tricia throws her hands up, the gesture wild, frantic.

"You're crazy," she continues. "Crazy if you think you're that far ahead of him."

Her certainty hits, and it hurts more than I thought it would.

"I have to stick with the plan," I say. "I know there's a huge risk, but it's the only way."

He wants to kill you. And it won't happen on my *watch.*

I keep my thoughts to myself.

"Hope you survive this shit storm," she says, a tear sliding down her cheek. "Call me when you get your head out of your ass. Until then I don't want to hear from you. You're acting reckless. And I'm out. I'm not messing around with my life while you mess up yours."

Her words cut, and she storms out. I watch her go. The glass door slams behind her, and I am left in the shimmering emptiness of my plan. Then again, Tricia doesn't know my whole story, what I'm capable of.

To keep my mind from spinning, I turn on the TV, a ticker flashing across the screen.

BREAKING NEWS: THIS JUST IN. TWO MORE MURDERS IN VEGAS.

I go rigid as a female reporter with cropped hair recounts the story. "Police have discovered the bodies of two organized-crime gang members from Montréal, Remy Gagnon and Gilles Cloutier, at the abandoned site of one of Las Vegas's most historical hotels and casinos—The Moulin Rouge, currently a deserted lot with plans for development.

"According to local authorities, the throats of the victims had been slashed, the bodies doused with gasoline and set on fire. However, there was enough DNA left behind to identify both men, connecting the two to the recent smiley face robberies in Los Angeles County, particularly Beverly Hills."

Her words swim in my ears and I'm about to turn the television off when Detective Samson's face comes into focus. "We have reason to believe that the murders of Franco Vescari, Sabrina and

Calvin Vale, Remy Gagnon, and Gilles Cloutier are connected, and we're asking for anybody with information to come forward."

"Do you have any persons of interest?" the reporter asks.

Samson doesn't answer at first, just looks squarely at the camera, his eyes boring into mine. "We don't. Not at the moment, but we do have a couple of leads, and I highly suggest they stay in town."

I turn off the television, knowing he'll be knocking on my door at any second, but my mother taught me well and I'll be prepared.

FORTY-NINE
LEXI

Then

My mother always knew what to say.

"Hold the button down," she'd say. "Like you mean it. I'm training you for your life."

I watched her work, her fingers quick, precise, as they guided the fabric through the old sewing machine. Our tiny apartment in West Palm Beach was crowded with sequined bodices and feathered headdresses, bright dresses for the upper crust of society with way more money than sense. They paid her next to nothing for her creations, so she made more with other work, the kind that started after dark.

"Give it a good yank," she'd say, and I pulled the fabric tight. "And never let them rip the carpet out from under your feet."

Her fingers moved like magic, and I tried to keep up. Our days were long, our nights longer. I watched the dresses pile up, brilliant colors in a dim space. She kept the fabric rolling, just like she kept us alive. Her laughter was easy and sweet, the sound of a woman who knew how to work a stitch and a story.

The sewing machine was old, rattling and groaning like it would give out at any second, but she knew how to coax life from it. Just like she did with everything else. She let me try my hand at the machine, and I took to it as fast as she did. She taught me stitches, watched on with a proud smile as I caught on quick. She said I had a knack. I felt it, felt the rhythm, basked in her praise. She thought I'd follow her, a natural fit in the lines she'd drawn, which were oftentimes colored outside of the law.

By night, her voice changed, the soft music of it turning edgy. That's when I learned how quickly things could shift. I watched her trade one identity for another like a chameleon. She transformed before my eyes, her face turning from gentle to sharp as she readied for the nighttime hustle.

At night, she taught me more than stitching. She showed me the art of the con, the game behind the hustle. My small face and big eyes got us more money than her dresses ever did. I'd watch her change, like a performer on stage, her gentleness turning sly. "You need to look pale," she'd say. "Like you just got out of the hospital." I did as I was told, pretending to cough and wheeze, the picture of childhood illness.

"A sick kid brings in the cash," she'd laugh.

It was thrilling, fooling the grown-ups, seeing them fall for my little act. I knew I was good at it. Knew I could be as quick as she was. But there was a pinch of something else, something I didn't have a name for. I think it might have been pride. I watched her switch from sewing machine to street hustle, her hands just as quick and nimble with both. I watched, wanting to be like her, not knowing how.

"You make your own luck," she told me. "If you want something, take it." She said it like gospel, and I wanted to believe. She was right; she always was. "This isn't enough," she'd say, sweeping her arm around the cramped apartment. "We need more. We need what they have. They don't deserve it."

Sometimes she'd bring me to a client's mansion for a fitting. "Think of it as a candy store," she'd whisper. "Take anything that fits into your pockets."

She'd let me sleep curled up next to the fabric rolls, whispering that I was smart, that I had what it took. I believed her. The dresses glimmered like jewels in the shadows, a bright promise in a dark room. She didn't feel bad about tricking them, and neither did I. "You're like me," she'd say, and I'd nod. Maybe I was. Maybe that's all I needed to be.

Sometimes you have to make your own luck in this world, baby girl.

And then, one night, our luck ran out, and the shit hit the fan.

The chair creaked as I shifted. The waiting area was cold. My heart pounded, the memory of the gunshot ringing loud. I wrapped my arms around my knees, pulled them close to my chest, wished I was anywhere but at a police station. Each minute felt longer, every second colder. I remembered the bald man with the tattooed sleeve of snakes grabbing her throat, the fury in his eyes as his voice rose. "You stole from Maxine. You're going to pay. And so is your daughter."

I had to save her, save me. I knew where my mother kept the gun, the drawer in the nightstand. He didn't see me when I snuck up behind him. I closed my eyes for a brief moment, opened them, and saw the moment before the shot, saw my finger on the trigger, the deafening sound as the bullet tore through the room. I watched the man stagger backward, shock on his face, his grip on my mother loosening. I watched him fall. Watched the blood spread on the floor like a secret I couldn't keep. Mom picked up the gun and shot him again.

"Tell them I did it," she had whispered, and her words would never leave me. Her words would haunt me forever.

I watched the police cuff her, watched her cry out as they pulled her from the apartment.

"It's going to be okay," they told me, but I didn't believe them. I couldn't.

Nothing was okay.

"Tell them I did it."

Her voice wouldn't leave me, just like she couldn't. It echoed in my head.

The minutes stretched, long and empty, the chill sinking deeper. I wanted to scream, to cry, to do anything but sit there. But I couldn't move, couldn't let the confusion go. It held me, wrapped around me like the cold, a tight and unforgiving embrace. They said it would be okay, said it like I could believe it. But I didn't know how. Didn't know how to believe, or to understand. I just knew I was alone and that they'd lied.

The emergency placement home felt more like a jail. Cold and sterile, with locks on the windows and bars on my future. My fingers remembered what my mom had taught me, but I couldn't keep up. Not there. There were no sewing machines. Not in the bleak bedrooms or the crowded tables where everyone watched what I ate. Each foster home was more dismal than the last, until, one day, child services found me a forever home—like I was a stray dog or cat. The Marlowes adopted me. I was their charity case, their new accessory, their temporary gift to themselves. And they treated me like shit.

I was eighteen when I lit the match.

The orange glow of the flames reflected in my terror-stricken eyes as they engulfed the Marlowes' home. The crackling of the fire grew louder, dancing and swirling, turning walls and furniture to ash, and casting a haunting glow across the sky. The thick scent of smoke and burning wood filled the air, choking my lungs, making it hard to breathe—a smell that would never fully leave my memory.

When the firefighters found me passed out in the basement, my mouth was dry and bitter, the taste of regret and guilt lingering on my tongue.

Part of me wanted to die that night, too. Until I pushed the guilt of what I'd done out of my head, realizing I was now in control of my life. The investigators ruled out arson, blaming the fire on a faulty gas valve in the kitchen. The only heir to their modest fortune, I could move to another state. I could have a fresh start. I could go to school, become the person I wanted to be.

But there was always a constant reminder of where I came from.

That's why I named my business LexICON.

Not icon. And, clearly, a true play on words.

Lex I Con.

FIFTY

DETECTIVE SAMSON

The bodies are piling up and the cases are all connected. Gut instinct tells me that Alexis Marlowe is protecting her husband. Perhaps he doesn't know about her past. I wouldn't peg Marlowe as a killer, but it's the quiet ones that surprise you. That and her mother's history.

I read over my files, what I know about Christophe, born Bouchard and using false identities, scamming the rich left and right. At the age of thirteen sent to juvenile detention with Remy Gagnon and Gilles Cloutier. Moved to Palm Beach to live with his mother, Maxine. All four of her husbands dead, dying under mysterious circumstances. Lived under the radar, stayed out of sight like a ghost. Forensics has enough evidence to attach Bouchard to the Vales' double murder, but nothing concrete to connect him to anything else.

Turns out, the smiley-face robberies case is closed. "Samson," said Banks when he called. "We have their car—spray-paint cans in the trunk, tons of cash, and the jewelry they stole." He paused. "You're welcome. See you soon."

"Soon," I repeated, scratching my head. "And thanks. I owe you one."

Banks laughed. "More than one. I'm making your career."

We have photos of Alexis in Vegas with Vescari, Gagnon, and Cloutier, the eye in the sky. We only have surveillance of Christophe with Vescari. I'm going to stay on her like white on rice. Although I don't have a motive, I'm going to pay her another visit.

I'm about to knock on her door when she opens it, like she's expecting me. She ushers me into the living room. "Detective Samson, have a seat. I haven't heard from him yet, if that's why you're here. And, yes, I saw the news." She gives me a slight smile. "Coffee? Just made a fresh pot. And I have this amazing hazelnut cream."

She's disarming me. I want to say no. I don't. I sit. "Sounds great."

I watch her reach for a cup, pour the coffee, and add in the cream. Her hands don't shake as she hands over the mug. "I met them in Vegas. Gagnon and Cloutier," she says.

"I know," I say, pulling out the photo, placing it on the coffee table.

I take a sip of coffee. Damn, it's good. I want to ask her what blend she uses. I don't.

She glances at the photo and shudders. "Creepy men."

"Had you met them before?"

"No," she says, shaking her head. "But I think they were following him, maybe me."

"Why?"

She huffs. "I was supposed to be the big pay day. They think I'm a real Marlowe."

I jot down a note. "And why did you marry him?"

She hangs her head. "He's very charming. And I thought..."

"He was actually a Montclair."

"I know that sounds bad." She nods. "It was a princess fantasy. You probably know how I grew up."

I do.

I tell her about Christophe's past, watching every single reaction. Her fingers move to her temples. After a moment of silence, she says, "Well, that explains a lot." She bites down on her bottom lip. "You must think I'm the dumbest girl on the planet. I not only married a liar, a con artist. I married a complete sociopath." She pauses, eyes wide, meeting mine. "You really think he killed his own father?"

"I do. And a lot more people, including the Vales."

"Honestly, I didn't like Sabrina at first, but when I found out he'd been scamming her too, we established an unspoken connection." She sucks in a breath. "I never met her husband."

Damn it. She's telling the truth.

But truth doesn't mean innocent.

I lean back, set my mug down, let the silence do the heavy lifting. People hate silence. They fill it with whatever's rattling around in their heads.

"You're awfully calm," I finally say.

Her brows tick upward. "Should I scream? Cry? Tear my hair out?"

"Might make you look less composed."

"Or more guilty." She crosses her legs, one ankle bouncing lightly. "I know the game, detective. Women who cry get labeled manipulative. Women who don't cry get labeled heartless. Pick your poison."

"You don't strike me as poisoned," I say. "You strike me as rehearsed."

That earns me a sharp laugh. "If I were rehearsed, I'd have a better script."

"Maybe." I watch her hands—still, except for the mug handle turning slow circles. "What else haven't you told me?"

Her eyes cut to mine, steady. "You think I'm hiding something?"

"I know you are."

A pause. Then a tilt of her head, almost playful. "You're supposed to catch me in a lie. Not just declare I'm lying."

"You're dodging."

She sighs, leans forward, elbows on her knees. "Fine. Christophe doesn't just charm women. He collects them. Friends, accomplices, admirers. They think he's brilliant. I thought he was brilliant. That's the con. He makes you feel like you're the only one in on the secret. Then you find out everyone's got the same invitation to the show."

"And you stayed."

Her jaw sets. "Because walking away from him is harder than walking into him. You don't understand."

"Try me."

"You ever been in love with someone who makes you feel both untouchable and disposable in the same breath?"

"No."

"Then you won't get it."

I let that hang. She's baiting me to argue. I don't. Instead, I press on. "Where was he the night of the Vales' murder?"

She flinches—small, but there. "I don't know."

"That's not an answer."

"It's the only answer I have."

Her hand goes to her throat, thumb brushing her collarbone. Nervous tic or calculated vulnerability—hard to say.

"You expect me to believe," I say, "that you have no clue where your husband was while two people were butchered?"

She meets my stare. Doesn't blink. "Yes. Because that's the truth."

I study her. Her voice steady. Her eyes glassy but dry.

"Tell me about Sabrina," I pivot. "This 'connection' you had."

"Once she realized he was playing both of us, there was this unspoken truce. She hated him. I hated him. Misery makes strange friends."

"She confide in you?"

"Bits and pieces. Enough to know she wanted out." Alexis swallows. "And enough to know he wouldn't let her go easily."

The words hang heavy. I watch her lips press together, as if she regrets saying them.

"You think he killed them?" I ask.

She doesn't answer right away. Her hand tightens around the

mug. Finally: "I think Christophe kills whatever doesn't serve him anymore."

There it is. Not just fear. Resentment.

I lean in. Lower my voice. "Then why are you still here, Alexis?"

She stares at me, unblinking. A flash of something in her eyes—defiance, maybe. "Because leaving him is more dangerous than staying, don't you think? And I have you on my side. I told you. I'll alert you if he returns."

"And if he doesn't?"

"I'll figure something out."

I don't write that down. I don't need to. It's burned into memory.

FIFTY-ONE

LEXI

True to her word, Tricia is staying away from me and hasn't come into the showroom. I'll call her, apologizing profusely, when this nightmare is over. Our business, our friendship, is real; I'd never con her. She's the only person who has ever truly believed in me. There is no giving Christophe the benefit of the doubt, especially after I call Air France. He'd sent me a bogus reservation number for the honeymoon trip. The tickets aren't real. And I'm a real idiot.

That's what I get for trying to take shortcuts.

I'm handling orders and contacting our manufacturers when I receive a text.

Out back

It's time for me to get to the airport. I lock the front door, grab my bag, and head to the back. A black sedan waits for me in the alley. I get in. The driver just nods, doesn't say anything.

Christophe strolls out of the terminal like a Prada-wearing grim reaper on fucking holiday. The driver steps out of the car, waving him over. He takes Christophe's bag, placing it in the trunk as Christophe joins me in the back seat.

I feel his breath on my neck. "Whose car is this?"

I shrug. "I told you. My grandfather hired me a driver. Isn't that cool?"

He blinks. "I can't wait to meet him."

I force another smile. "He can't wait to meet you."

He leans back, relaxed. Too relaxed. "Everything is going to be perfect. You'll see."

"Yes," I say. I keep my eyes fixed on the back of the driver's head, not on him. "I will."

"I missed you, *mon amour*," he says, and my stomach turns.

"I missed you, too."

His confidence is as crisp as the bills in the thick envelope he hands me. I count the cash. It's all there and then some. Fifty thousand dollars and more nerve than I expected.

"I told you everything would work out," he says. "You can trust me."

My eyes go wide—wide enough to make Christophe look twice. "I do," I say, trying my best not to cringe, trying not to give myself away.

He sits close, like nothing has happened. His hand runs down my side. He tries pulling me in for a kiss. I want to throw the envelope, throw it in his face. But I can't. I have to play it cool, play this out.

His cologne lingers, mingles with the air, mingles with something metallic I can't place.

"We should celebrate," he says.

"We are. And I have a surprise for you," I say and his eyes light up.

He thinks he's got this. But he doesn't know how far I'll go. He's not ahead, not this time. But he definitely thinks he is.

FIFTY-TWO

CHRISTOPHE

I adjust the cuffs, smooth the suit, perfect the illusion. The money, the love, the life. All of it within my reach. The air is mine, and I breathe it, breathe the thrill, breathe the truth that isn't. She's mine. The deal is mine. It settles like my cologne, rich and heavy, exactly where it should be.

The fabric of my suit is exquisite. European. Imported. The texture is smooth, a perfect blend of luxury and lies. I like it. My pulse is steady, as steady as the plan, the precision, the way I win.

I am still Christophe, but I am not. I am the ghost of him, the ghost that won't let go, the ghost that whispers and mocks and drives me. It is never enough. It is always more. I have never looked back, not at Maxine, not at the others, not at the bodies I left or the trail that follows. Lexi will follow, too. And she will love it, love the life I give her, the life I give myself, the life they all gave me.

I think of my pitch, the way I will secure Phillip's money, the way he will believe. I practice the words, practice the charm, practice the face I've worn for so long. This time it is bigger, the stakes higher, the risks the same. This time it is good for me. The best.

The money. The power. My name.

I love the way I didn't see this coming.

It is all in my reach, in my hands. My mother didn't break me. She'd made me. I close my eyes, see my life, my success, my way out. It is more than I want, more than I hoped for.

This time it's for me.

And this time I'll get the girl, too.

FIFTY-THREE

LEXI

The car rumbles over gravel. We arrive at the construction site and Christophe's eyebrows pinch together. He's confused. I would be, too. My lips quirk into a grin. "I said no to the Trendline deal, but I said yes to my grandfather." I hop out of the car and point. "You are looking at LexICON's future."

My footsteps are loud on the gravel. Christophe follows me. There are no workers, no questions, no one to see this except him and me. I stop when I have him exactly where I want him. Standing on the brink. Standing on borrowed time. His form is dark against the wet concrete, sharp against the possibility. He checks his watch. Checks his confidence. Checks what he shouldn't. His smile is too sure, and my approach is too fast. I don't wait. I shove him hard, catching him off-guard.

Christophe stumbles backward, his arms flailing. He fights to regain his balance, but the slick surface is a traitor. His jacket catches on a rebar spike, halting his fall. He looks shocked, as if disbelief can save him. But it can't. I push him, harder this time with a shovel. The spike tears through, and his gasp is sharp with agony.

He reaches for me, but I am out of his grasp. His movements are frantic. The newly poured concrete swallows him whole. I watch, and I push again. I push until his struggles weaken, until the mixture is heavy on him, heavy like his final moments.

I watch until I don't have to, until I'm sure. My breath is ragged, and his death is imminent. After his body is consumed, I smooth out the cement with the shovel. Then, I walk away, faster and faster, leaving him, leaving the site. The driver waits for me. He eyes me in the rearview mirror, nods, and starts the ignition. "Florence has taken care of everything else."

I swallow, sink into my seat, and, before I change my clothes, I text Florence.

> Looking forward to dinner. Lots to celebrate.

The steakhouse is a study in elegance, a tapestry of calm covering my disorder. Conversations hum like secrets, and my breath hums with them. Phillip and Florence are waiting at the corner table. Florence's pearls glisten under the soft light. Phillip's suit is dark and somber. My seat is empty. I take it, and I take the wine Phillip pours. It's rich and intoxicating, the way my story will be. They are expectant, but I am more so. The pause is short but long enough to rattle. "Where's Christophe?" he asks.

My voice is even, but my hands are not. "He won't be joining us," I say, lifting my shoulders into a shrug.

Phillip raises an eyebrow. "Was there trouble?" he asks, his voice steady.

Of course, he knows.

"Nothing I couldn't handle," I say. "It's done."

Florence reaches across the table to clasp my hand, her gesture tender. "Until I received your text, I was very worried," she says.

"I'm so glad this is over," Phillip says, his tone firm, paternal. "And you came out of this unscathed." He lets out a breath, clasps Florence's free hand. "I'm thinking we should celebrate."

Florence lifts her chin and holds up her wine glass. "But let's leave the past in the past. I think we should toast the future."

Our eyes meet. Our glasses clink. To the future. To survival. To payback. To revenge. We don't say these words out loud.

I'm watching the news in the morning, not really paying attention, a rerun of the night's restless dreams reminding me of things I don't want to remember, but then something catches my eye.

Breaking news this just in: Socialite Maxine Summers found dead in her Palm Beach estate. Foul play is suspected.

Maxine. Her name sends a rush of adrenaline through me, though I don't know if it's fear or disbelief or something else entirely. I picture her sprawled on the floor of her white marble foyer, upset that she didn't manage to look graceful even in death. I see Christophe standing over her, a little smile tugging at his lips as he walks away. Christophe truly deserved to die.

So did Maxine.

My mom used to tell me how Palm Beach would kill you if you let it, how its social circles could be as cutthroat as any battlefield. Maxine was a black widow in more ways than one, and now even she's caught in a web she won't get out of.

I blink and the screen jumps to bright commercials. Christophe's past really has caught up with him. I'm hoping mine won't catch up with me, too. The past is fast.

A sharp knock startles me. I feel it in my teeth, my bones. I flinch. The noise is harsh and I stand on shaky legs. I walk to the door, slower than my heart, and the knock comes once more, too loud for comfort. I brace myself and open the door.

Detective Samson and a uniformed officer. "Ms. Marlowe," Samson says, his voice a gruff intrusion, "Have you heard from your husband?"

The men step into the apartment before I can breathe, before I can stop them.

FIFTY-FOUR
DETECTIVE SAMSON

"I hope you're not harboring a criminal," I say, my eyes locking onto hers. "Are you?"

My pen is poised over a notepad.

She stumbles backward. A tear slides down her cheek. "I—I don't know where he is," she says. "I told you he just took off. He said he'd pay me and then he didn't come back."

Her voice is weak. It's desperate. "We have a warrant to search your place."

She doesn't ask to see it, just says, "Have at it."

I nod toward Deputy Garcia and Deputy O'Neil, wave a hand. My lips curve into a wicked grin. "We know he arrived in LA yesterday, confirmed by an airline hostess and security footage."

"I haven't seen him," she says. "I wouldn't know if he'd come back here as I was having dinner with Florence Montclair and Phillip Marlowe."

An alibi? And my guys didn't see her leave. Interesting. "Why?"

"They were concerned about me, wanted to help."

I scratch my chin. "How can you explain your bank account no longer being in the negative? Are you protecting him? Part of the plan?"

"Florence," she says. "Florence Montclair wired me the funds."

"I did," says a woman behind me, standing on the threshold.

I turn to face the most elegant woman I've ever seen in my life. It takes a second for me to get my bearings. I'm shellshocked as she continues talking.

"I'm investing in Lexi's company, LexICON, which is brilliant. And I'm also investing in her." She pauses. "Christophe Bouchard also conned me, tried to kill me. I sympathize with her stress, what she was going through, and I like to see my investments pay off."

Deputy Garcia comes back into the room. "He's definitely gone, cleared everything out, except some crap. But I found this."

He holds up a phone with an S carved into it. I take it from him, turning it on. My eyes lock onto an email, confirming a flight to Brazil, the name Ryan Daniels, the flight arriving yesterday.

I scroll through the texts. There must be a thousand from Sabrina Vale—none of them good.

"What's going on?" asks Alexis, eyes wide.

"He's skipped town." I slap my forehead. "We're going to get a warrant to search your storage unit and the showroom."

"You don't need one," she says. "I'll take you there."

"And the Maserati?"

She turns around and throws me the keys.

FIFTY-FIVE
LEXI

Three hours later, Samson finally makes a move to leave. His hand stays on the doorknob for a moment. "If you hear from him, call. Otherwise, you'll be arrested for obstructing justice and harboring a criminal."

"I will," I say, biting down on my bottom lip. "I promise."

"You better." He pulls the door open and walks out. His boots hit the stairs hard, one after another, until the sound fades.

As soon as I'm sure he's gone, I grab the phone and call Tricia.

She answers on the first ring. "Is your head out of your ass? If it isn't, I don't want to talk to you."

"He's gone," I say. "There's nothing to worry about. Not anymore."

"Gone?"

"Gone," I repeat. "He never came back. For now, Florence is covering his debt for me and she's also giving a bridge loan to LexI-CON. No interest."

Tricia doesn't speak for a few seconds, but I can hear her breathing, processing.

"Thank God," she says at last. "This nightmare is over."

"It is," I tell her.

But my hands are still shaking. The apartment is quiet, too quiet. I keep the phone in my hand even after the call ends, watching the door in case someone might walk through it, even though I know it won't be *him*.

FIFTY-SIX
FLORENCE

I see so much of myself in Lexi. The killer instinct. I knew she'd pull our diabolical plan off. Like I did. With my late husband, Guy Allard. He, like Christophe, wasn't a true Montclair. I am. I'd used my maiden name only, not his, as one can do in France.

The thought fills me with confidence, with determination, with certainty. There will be no more doubts. There will be no more con men. There will be no more failure. A smile plays across my lips. I know Guy had married me for my family name, the dynasty my grandfather created.

I know Lexi has worked tirelessly for her company. I know because I've done the same myself. Anything it takes... and taking no prisoners.

My husband Guy was a junior partner from one of the luxury conglomerates. He thought he was safe. He never knew what happened, not until it was too late, not until I won the war. My plan to get rid of him was perfect, the same goes for Christophe.

I wanted Guy to suffer, to know, to understand how ruthless I could be. He thought he'd run away with *my* company and the cash and the glory of a con well played. But I played harder, smarter. Guy didn't know what hit him, didn't know I'd been poisoning him slowly until it was too late. I remember watching his face go slack, his movements lethargic, his control slipping. His death.

Like Guy, Christophe thought he could con me, too—the same kind of men, with their pretty lies and charming fraud. He didn't know I'd canceled the checks he'd stolen from me. And that's when I found Lexi.

The parallels are not lost on me. I was as right about Christophe as I was about Guy. Christophe never stood a chance. He thought he did. Thought I'd marry him. Thought he could win.

The words, the family, the power, the business.

All mine.

And now the two people who'd tried to scam me, con me out of my life, are gone.

I wonder if Lexi will keep up, if she'll remain standing strong. It's a rhetorical question I'm asking myself. I know she will. Lexi is just like me. I am like her. And I am a force to be reckoned with. Christophe's things are on my plane. I'll burn his clothes, burn him out of my memory. I'll give Lexi the jewels and the cash when the timing is right. I don't need the money.

And I'll help her create her legacy, just like I've created mine.

FIFTY-SEVEN

LEXI

Plotting a murder over an eight-course sashimi menu—tuna toro so fatty it felt like butter on the tongue, cuts of silvery mackerel shimmering, razor-sharp slices of hamachi that melted in my mouth—wasn't something I'd ever pictured myself doing. Yet there we were, Florence and me, the low hum of the sea drifting through the air.

The soy was a dark, viscous ribbon in its porcelain dish; the wasabi burned my nostrils with every inhale. Chopsticks poised, we sipped chilled rice wine between bites. With every taste, I felt the thrill of every plan unfurling in my mind, as if those tiny morsels were kindling for the pyre I was about to light. The pink flesh of scallop, the pale streaks in amberjack—it all shimmered with promise, each course a discrete step in our conspiracy.

Course by course, my pulse undulated with equal parts hunger and anticipation. Florence sat opposite me, her silver hair coiled in a sleek knot, her smile slow and merciless. Her eyes reflected the candlelight and the jagged edges of our plan. I remembered in that moment how she told me she'd killed before. She spoke of her husband's slow, calculated poisoning—sips of tea laced with aconite over weeks until he croaked at the breakfast table, his last words a garbled question that died in his throat. She had served the most severe justice from behind the façade of the perfect spouse. I nodded, and between those nods, I could taste Christophe's fear.

Florence had known about my past the second I'd walked in, had made connections I'd tried to keep buried. She'd recognized in me the same sharp instinct, the same cold calculation. We traded stories between bites of uni—soft as memory, bittersweet. By the time the smoked toro arrived, my lips still smeared with soy and the ghost of wasabi tickling my senses, we both knew it could only end with blood. His blood.

That night, over the last slice of octopus, we sealed our pact with a quiet game of rock-paper-scissors. My paper beat her rock, and I took the "honor" of dealing with Christophe face to face. While I dealt with Christophe, one of her men slipped into my apartment, clearing out his closet. I hadn't locked the sliding doors out back. He'd left behind proof, carefully chosen clues for Detective Samson.

Once the physical traces were arranged, she promised me the jewels—emeralds the size of olives, sapphires blue as a tropical lagoon—and the filthy money he'd siphoned from Maxine. She doesn't need the money.

In the interim, she'd invest in me, in LexICON, money she never intended to reclaim. We clinked glasses, two predators in silk. She saw herself in me, and I saw the better part of me reflected in her—a ruthless ambition, unblinking and exact.

But the past never fully leaves you; it lingers in the creases of your eyes, in the faintest beat of your heart when you think you're safe. It surprises you when you've convinced yourself you've won. Now I carry those echoes everywhere: the click of a gun's safety, the scrape of metal on cement, the hot sting of tears I never let fall.

FIFTY-EIGHT
DETECTIVE SAMSON

Everything works out for a reason, I suppose. I know I'll never get the full truth from Alexis. I know she's colored outside of the lines of the law. But when I think about my own daughter, Grace, just a few years younger than she is, what I'd do to protect her if she ever met a guy like Christophe, I know what she's done is right, good for the world.

On that, I'll keep my suspicions to myself.

Alexis deserves to be happy. And I'm not going to take that away from her. The system broke her and she deserves a new life.

EPILOGUE

LEXI

One Year Later

The flagship LexICON store within the Marlowe store buzzes with opening-day excitement. They say our sales will break records. They say it will change everything. They say it, and I believe. I stand in the center, eyes on me, my past around the corner, failure not an option. The concrete floor holds me up, my heart holds me down, more than I think.

"We did it, Lexi," Tricia says, and her confidence almost makes it true.

Her gaze travels across the store, where sleek mannequins model my designs, and the display for the merchandise is just like our showroom, but cleaner. Customers hover, eager and unsuspecting, their interest genuine. As genuine as Tricia thinks it is. "Seriously," she says, her grin matching the sparkle in her eyes. "Wow. Just wow."

I've had my doubts about everything. I still do. If she only knew where we were standing, what's buried underneath us, right beneath our feet. Her eyes sweep over me. "Is something wrong?"

I look at her baby boy, my godson Ethan, his face bright with excitement. The doubts shrink, but not enough. I smile and let it linger. "Everything is right."

"Enjoy this," she says. "You've earned it. Did you see the line outside? It's insane. We are killing it."

I cringe.

"We?" Jeff teases, raising his champagne flute, the bubbles like a celebration I'm too numb to feel. "Don't tell me you plan on stealing Lexi's thunder."

They both look at me, a shared triumph that almost convinces me, almost sweeps me up, almost makes me forget about him.

"I'm just saying." Tricia winks. "And you should smile more."

"Believe me, I'm trying."

Phillip hovers nearby, keeping one eye on the crowd, one eye on me. He wears his new suit like a polished shell, like an investment. His gaze meets mine, a mix of expectation and pride. He wants this as much as I do. He thinks we have this.

I watch as customers browse, feeling the fabrics, their faces lit with the soft glow of LED lights and consumer desire. I watch them, but my mind keeps flashing back to the hard angles of the construction site. I close my eyes, inhale the faint scent of sea salt and steel, and open them again, only hearing the echo of my mother's words in my head, fierce and unwavering: "Tell them I did it." And beneath that echo, deeper lessons resonate through every vein.

How to run.

How to survive.

How to win.

I'm not sure I like the person I've become. But that's on me. Unlike Christophe, I have the opportunity to change. I'm happy that Christophe will never hurt another woman or man again. He'll never scam. He'll never kill again. I protected Tricia. I protected myself. I protected my mother. That's what I tell myself so I can sleep at night.

The people around me see what they want to see. They see confidence, success, excitement. But all I see is the concrete. I turn, scanning the faces, the energy, the mix of emotions as palpable as my own, the rush of it all hitting me harder than I expect.

Detective Samson makes his approach with a younger woman. "Ms. Marlowe," he says, nodding his head. "Nice turn out."

I force a tight smile. "It really is."

"This is my daughter, Grace. She's a big fan of yours."

Grace's blue eyes go wide. "More than big. Huge. I'm about to graduate from FIDM."

My eyes flick to Samson, back to her. She reminds me a lot of me. "And your plans?"

She drops her gaze. "I'm re-inventing denim, kind of like what you did with athleisure. I was hoping, uh, maybe you'd come see the final show." She pauses. "I mean, if that's not weird. You know, because of everything."

I smile and clasp her hand. "Send me the invite and we'll move on from there. Your pops has all my info."

"Thank you so, so much." Grace squeezes my hand. "I'm really looking for a mentor. Dad told me that yours was your mom."

"She was." She *is*.

"Mine would have been, but she's no longer with us," says Grace with a sigh.

"Cancer. Five years ago." Samson clears his throat, changing the subject with one quick breath. "Thought I'd let you know. There was a sighting in Rio. We're on to him."

"That's g-great," I stutter. "What a relief."

I wonder if he can see the story behind my eyes. I wonder if he knows the real one.

He lets out a chuckle as a server passes, takes a glass of champagne. "I'm off duty tonight. Congratulations." He pauses. "By the way, the Maserati will be released to you. And you're inheriting Maxine Summers' home in Palm Beach."

I shake my head to clear it. "Huh?"

"Technically, you were his wife." He winks and then shakes his head. "If I were you, I'd sell both. Bad karma."

Gobsmacked, I watch him down the glass of champagne and

saunter out of the store, shopping bag in hand, his daughter's in the other.

The sound of glasses clinking, of registers buzzing, fills the room.

My mind is as sharp as my fear, my guilt. But not as sharp as Florence's eyes, the dark blue of them sparkling with both judgment and approval. She advances toward me, a storm of control, and my heart skips a beat.

I try to catch my breath, to catch the tail end of the confidence she shows. She has more than enough assurance for both of us. She moves closer, the crowd parting in her wake.

"Prison wasn't good enough for him," Florence whispers. "You have nothing to fear, from the authorities or anyone else."

My heart is a wild, dangerous thing, but her certainty, her cool confidence, makes me steady, makes me almost like her. She smiles. "Your mother was released from prison the other day. I had my jet pick her up. She's coming here."

The music, the voices, they blur around me, everything fading. I sway, surprised by the news, by how much I want to see her.

"Thank you," I say, blinking back tears.

"There is no need to."

Florence waits, her eyes steady on mine, and I realize everything has changed. The game is different now. She smiles. It's a small smile. A triumphant smile.

"Here's to you and to LexICON's imminent success," she says, the words feeling like freedom.

I touch my flute to hers, the past sealed away. I have everything I've wanted and more. She wraps an arm around me, leans in. "Loyalty is what you sell when everything else runs out. For this, we have each other."

I tilt my head, confused.

She whispers, "I know Christophe killed a lot of people, including the Vales, but you killed Vescari."

"I-I..."

My shoulders go rigid. She's called me out and I can't lie or con my way out of this one.

"I understand," she continues. "You didn't want him taking your chance away from you when you thought Christophe was an actual Montclair."

I feel like I'm paralyzed. I can't move, can't breathe. Nobody knows what I did to Vescari, how he'd followed me to the ladies' room that night, how he'd threatened me, telling me to stay away from Christophe, how he'd destroy my company, how he'd found out who I truly was. Let's face it, the man wasn't in the best shape. He'd made a move to poke my clavicle and things escalated from there. I ripped his arm behind his back, grabbed his tie, and watched as he sank to the floor, gasping for his last breath. I wiped everything down with a washcloth, touched up my lipstick, and locked the door behind me.

Glamour. Glitter. Chaos. Nobody noticed until it was too late. Christophe was my alibi.

Florence places a hand on my shoulder. "Don't worry, your secret is safe with me. You did the world a favor. Vescari was a disgusting pedophile, which I'm sure you knew." She kisses me on the cheek. "You're an honorary Montclair now. I've done far worse things. You know my secrets. I know yours." She pauses, smiles. "And you're invited to my wedding."

I'm flabbergasted. All I can do is stutter. "To w-who?"

Somebody taps my shoulder, and I whip around to face Phillip standing next to a striking, younger version of himself. "To me," he says, and then indicates his younger self. "Alexis, this is my grandson, Edward. I wanted the two of you to meet."

I stumble backward, trying to loop all the connections into a single thread. Phillip's car. The meeting with Florence, meeting him. They already knew I'd volunteer to take Christophe out.

"He's already trying to arrange our marriage. Told me you had a killer instinct." Edward's laugh cuts through my thoughts. "You wouldn't have to change your last name. We could have a double wedding."

Still shocked, my eyes survey Edward in his preppy suit. He is the polar opposite of Christophe, definitely not a bad boy, a con artist, or a killer. I'm really glad I never got around to changing my name, although I'd thought I'd be a Montclair, not a Bouchard. But I don't want somebody else's last name, regardless of whether it's the same as mine, or whether it comes with more power and opens doors. I want everything Maxine took from me when she'd sent that man after my mom. I'm over relationships for a while, maybe forever.

My breath hitches, my attention moves toward the front doors, to the crowd circling my products. I scan the perimeter, looking over Edward's shoulder, and a VIP has just walked in, looking like an older version of me, but painfully uncomfortable. Her eyes meet mine and she shoots me a tentative wave.

"Excuse me, Edward, it was lovely meeting you, but I have to excuse myself."

"So soon?"

"Yep," I say, turning on my heel. "My mom is here, and we have a lot to catch up on. I haven't seen her in seventeen years."

"Can I ask for—" he begins.

I don't hear the rest of his sentence because I'm racing toward my mom. I throw my arms around her, tears streaming down her face, tears streaming down mine. The last time I cried was when the police had taken her away when she'd been protecting me from what I'd done.

"I'm so proud of you." She sucks in a breath. "You did all of this on your own. You've made it." Her hand clasps mine, gripping it tightly. "You're a fighter and you fought for your dreams. I always knew you could do it and I didn't want the past to get in the way." She pauses, her head hanging low. "That's the reason I pushed you away. I'm sorry."

"Mom, never apologize. You went to—"

"Prison wasn't that bad," she says with a slight smile. "But I don't want to talk about that experience. Not now. Not ever." She draws me into a tight hug. "I want to focus on the future."

"So do I."

It's time to rebrand ourselves, and although it won't be easy making up for lost time, the money from Christophe and Maxine will certainly help. I'm thinking of surprising her with a trip to Paris, then we'll take off for the Maldives. Christophe was right; I deserve to treat myself.

A LETTER FROM THE AUTHOR

Thank you so much for reading *The Perfect Catch*. If you'd like to keep up to date with all my Storm Publishing releases, you can sign up here:

www.stormpublishing.co/samantha-verant

And if you'd like to hear about all my upcoming releases and bonus content, including the occasional French recipe, please feel free to sign up for my author newsletter.

http://eepurl.com/UH8cP

If you enjoyed this book and could spare a few moments to leave a review, that would be hugely appreciated. Even a short review can make all the difference in encouraging a reader to discover my books for the first time. Thank you so much! Merci beaucoup!

This book was inspired by two events from my own life. One: When I was twenty-three, I dated a guy who wrote me bad checks. He did pay me back. I didn't kill him. I believe he's still in prison. Two: When I was in my thirties, I launched a handbag line, Samantha Kim/Samantha Mack, and really got to know the ins and outs of the fashion world, including going to a trade show in Vegas and hocking my bags on a televised show. Both of these events came together to create this story, one I've taken extreme creative liberties with.

With that said, I love hearing from readers and I hope you'll get in touch!

All my best wishes,
Samantha Vérant

https://www.samanthaverant.com

instagram.com/samantha_verant
facebook.com/AuthorSamanthaVerant
tiktok.com/@authorsamanthaverant
bookbub.com/profile/samantha-verant

ACKNOWLEDGMENTS

Once again, a huge merci goes to my fabulous editor, Kate Smith, who has patiently guided me through my fourth thriller... and multiple (fictional) killings.

Hearty thanks goes out to our trailblazer founder, Oliver 'Storm' Rhodes, editorial operations director Alexandra Begley; copyeditor Laurence Cole; proofreader Amanda Raybould; page designer Maheen Mehmood; brilliant cover designer James Macey; supremely talented voiceover artist Laurel Lefkow; and the magical marketing and promotion duo comprised of Elke Desanghere and Anna McKerrow. I'm thrilled and proud to be part of the Storm Publishing family.

To Sally Royer-Derr (fellow Storm authoress and Libra), thank you for beta reading this story. Your advice was on point and helped me out big time. As usual, thank you to the 2020 Debut author group for their continued support and encouragement.

Thank you! Thank you!

Finally, thank you to the readers I've connected with and those I've yet to connect with—thank you for joining me on this wild publishing journey. Happy reading! Cheers!